A
Typical Family
Summer

LIZ DAVIES

CHAPTER 1

Annabelle Litton checked her hand luggage for what seemed to be the hundredth time.

Passports? Check. Wallet? Check. Tickets on the phone? Check. Tickets printed out just in case? Check. Keys? Um…

Where were her keys? Frantically, she patted her pockets before realising she had them in her hand.

'Stop fussing,' her neighbour, Pauline, told her. 'You've got everything.'

Annabelle sighed. 'I know, but I can't help it.'

Pauline smiled indulgently, her grey eyes crinkling at the corners. 'Are you ready?'

'I suppose, although I've got a horrid feeling I've forgotten something.'

'Whatever it is, you can either get it at the airport or buy it on the other side. I believe England does have shops, you know.'

'You're right. They do. Ooh, I'm so excited, I don't know whether I'm coming or going! Jake, Izzie!' she yelled. 'Grab your stuff, we need to make a move.'

'You lucky thing! I'd love to visit the UK and see Buck House and the Tower of London, and have a ride on a double-decker bus.'

'We'll probably nip up to London as it's not far from Brighton, and go to the Natural History Museum and Madame Tussauds,' Annabelle said. 'The kids mightn't get another chance for ages, as I don't know when I'll get to the UK next.'

This was Annabelle's first trip back home in over ten years. Ever since the children were born, her parents usually flew out to Australia to visit her. It had seemed such a hassle travelling all that way with two small children, so it was easier for them to come to her.

Then, just when Jake and Izzie were old enough for Annabelle to contemplate taking them on such a long journey, Troy had dropped the bombshell that he was leaving her for another woman.

After that, money had become too tight to consider going anywhere for a while.

At least Troy had gone to live with his fancy woman (as her mother referred to Sallie), allowing Annabelle and the children to remain in the family home, so she hadn't had to worry about finding somewhere else to live. She did eventually end up having to pay the mortgage herself though, despite Troy's assurances that he'd contribute towards it. For the most part, he couldn't manage to pay child support, so she'd been a fool to expect him to pay his share of the mortgage.

He'd walked out on her two years ago, when Jake was seven and Izzie four, and life had been tough. Now though, she was back on an even keel, emotionally and financially. Going through the divorce hadn't been easy but she'd come out the other side a stronger person.

And now, after a great deal of scrimping and saving, she and the kids were off to see her parents in the UK for three weeks.

She was so excited that she hadn't slept for two nights straight!

'Can I take my surfboard?' Jake asked, appearing in the hall, dragging his backpack by the straps along the floor.

'Don't do that, you'll break it', Annabelle said automatically. 'No, you can't take your surfboard. For one thing, it won't fit in your case—'

'I can carry it,' Jake interrupted, his face hopeful.

'—and for another,' Annabelle continued, 'you won't get the opportunity to surf. Let's leave it in the garage, eh?'

'I need the bathroom,' Izzie said from behind her brother.

'Hurry up, then.' Annabelle rolled her eyes and said to Pauline, 'Getting these two ready and out of the door on time is like herding cats.'

'Let's get this lot into the car,' Pauline said, eyeing the two large cases and Jake's backpack which he'd dumped on the floor. Izzie was still wearing hers.

'I swear to God we've packed enough for six months, not three weeks. Although,' Annabelle conceded, 'that's my fault because I remember only too well how Britain can have four seasons in one day, so I've packed loads of hoodies and sweatshirts, as well as our usual summer gear.' She yanked the handle up on the nearest suitcase and dragged it down the drive towards Pauline's car.

After a final check around the house to make sure everything was switched off and the doors were locked, it was time to leave.

'Thanks again,' Annabelle said to her neighbour, as she ensured the kids were strapped in the back. 'It's so kind of you to take us to the airport.'

'You've done the same for me numerous times,' Pauline reminded her. 'I'll pick you up, too – just give me a quick call when you land, and I'll be there in fifteen minutes. Anything special you need me to do while you're away?'

'Can you water the plant in the kitchen, please? And collect the mail and leave it on the table in the… Speak of the devil, here's the postie now.' Annabelle was about to let him pop it in the letterbox but changed her mind and held her hand out for the letter he was holding. 'I'll take it, thanks,' she said to him, and got in the car. She was expecting an updated contract from work, so the official-looking envelope was probably that. She would read it through carefully later – after all, she'd have plenty of time on the plane.

She might be looking forward to being in Brighton and seeing her parents, but she wasn't looking forward to the journey one little bit.

***

'Are we nearly there yet?' Izzie was taking a turn to sit in the window seat – not that there was much to see out of it. The plane was currently over the South China Sea, and beneath it was an endless blue vista.

'Not yet, sweetie. Why don't you have a nap? It'll make the time go quicker,' Annabelle suggested. Jake was already a dead weight on her other side, his head resting on her arm, and she shifted position as carefully as she could so as not to wake him.

'There's a fleece in my bag,' she added. 'Fold it up and you can rest your head on it. Careful,' she warned, seeing the letter that the postie had handed to her before they'd left almost fall out as Izzie rooted around in the bag which Annabelle had stuffed underneath the seat in front. 'Can you pass me that letter, please?' she asked. She may as well read it now – it might take her mind off the endless hours ahead of her.

Izzie scrunched herself up in her seat, making Annabelle quite envious of her daughter's rubber limbs and bendy spine, then closed her eyes. Hopefully, both children would have a nice long sleep before they'd need to be entertained once more. She didn't regret not taking the children to the UK when they were younger, she decided, easing the flap of the letter open, and she felt rather sorry for the parents of a toddler three rows down who'd been letting everyone know his displeasure at not being allowed to run up and down the plane. Primary-aged kids were hard enough to keep amused and she could only imagine—

What?

Annabelle scanned the letter, her eyes refusing to believe what she was reading even as her blood froze in her veins and her whole body felt numb and cold.

It must be wrong. The letter was meant for someone else, surely. It happened sometimes – the postie would pop the wrong mail into the wrong letterbox. With her heart thudding uncomfortably and her mouth dry, Annabelle checked the name on the top and the address.

Oh, God… She felt sick when she realised that the letter was indeed meant for her.

Annabelle closed her eyes for a moment and took a deep breath. Telling herself that she must have misread it, she slowly opened them and gave it another go, this time reading every word slowly and carefully.

The letter's message hadn't changed on the second reading.

It still informed her that her house was being repossessed.

The bastard! The lowdown, dirty, sodding...

How could Troy do such a thing!

Annabelle read the letter for a third time, trying to take it in, and didn't know whether to laugh or cry. You couldn't write this stuff, she thought, hysteria bubbling close to the surface and threatening to spill over.

Troy, it seemed, had taken out a loan against the house – *her* house, the one she and his children lived in. The letter was a notification that she had two weeks to vacate the property before the bank took possession of it.

Two weeks! How the hell was she going to find somewhere to live in a measly two weeks?

Suddenly it struck her that they would shortly be homeless. They wouldn't have a house to return to.

What the hell was she supposed to do?

CHAPTER 2

Annabelle closed her eyes in frustration before slowly opening them again. It was no good – she hadn't managed to magically transport herself to a nice sunny beach somewhere. She was still in her mother's kitchen, and her mother was still trying to convince her that a holiday in a place called Porthcawl on the South Wales coast, with her aunt, her aunt's daughter, Kate, and Kate's family would be good for her.

Aunt Beverley was backing her mum up, in a kind of two-pronged attack. She was the older of the two sisters, Annabelle's mum being three years younger, and the pair of them were nothing alike. Beverley was rotund compared to her mother's skinniness, and she didn't take as much pride in her appearance. Today Beverley was wearing a pair of navy trousers with an elasticated waist which strained across her tummy, a baggy top and a pair of Crocs. Her hair was dyed an alarming shade of orange, and her face was red and shiny. The eyes looking out of her plump face were the exact same shade of hazel as her mum's and they both had the same shaped nose, but that was where any similarity ended.

Personality-wise, Annabelle's mum was the more

7

uptight of the two, the more reserved and cautious. Beverley was easy-come, easy-go, didn't give two hoots about what anyone thought about her, and had a wicked streak. She loved her dog, her knitting, and her soaps on TV. May loved gin, tennis and going on cruises.

'I don't need a holiday,' Annabelle reiterated for the umpteenth time. It was the last thing she needed. What she actually needed was to get a job and find somewhere to live. She couldn't stay in her parents' house forever. She'd been here six weeks already, three weeks longer than she'd meant to have stayed, but what choice had she had? When she'd finally managed to get hold of Troy to ask him what the hell was going on (part of her hoped it was all a big mistake and that he was in the middle of sorting out) he'd informed her that he'd taken a loan out against the house to fund his new business venture, but it had gone belly up. It wasn't his fault, he'd kept telling her, concentrating more on who was to blame rather than on where his children were to live, until she'd eventually hung up on him. It was at that point she realised she couldn't return to Australia, and they'd have to remain here in her parents' house where they at least had a roof over their heads.

Her mother said breezily, 'Nonsense! It'll do you good. And it'll be good for the children, too. They need to know they've got family here.'

'Kate, Brett and the children don't live in Brighton,' Beverley reminded her. 'They live in Pershore.'

'I know where they live,' Annabelle's mum replied huffily.' By "here" I meant the UK in general, not Brighton in particular. You're not helping, Beverley.'

Beverley squinted at Annabelle. 'Come on,' she urged. 'You'll have a great time. Kate is so looking forward to seeing you. It's been what... twenty years?'

'At least,' Annabelle's mum said.

Annabelle resisted the urge to roll her eyes. She could do without reconnecting with a cousin she hadn't seen for over two decades, especially when she had so many other things on her plate.

Beverley said, 'I know me and Ron are just up the road, but the kids need someone their own age to play with, don't they?' She got to her feet. 'Right, I've made the offer and said my piece, so I'm going to leave you to it. May, when are you and Terence off on your cruise?'

'Saturday.'

'Have a lovely time.' Beverley placed the empty cup she'd been nursing on the draining board, and clambered to her feet. 'And you, my girl,' she said to Annabelle, 'Don't be a stranger. You're welcome to pop round any time.'

Beverley only lived a couple of miles away from Annabelle's parents, but Annabelle had yet to pay her aunt a visit. She'd been meaning to, but after everything that had happened since she'd got on the plane at Cairns, she hadn't felt much like socialising.

'You should go,' her mum insisted, as soon as the front door slammed shut. 'You'll enjoy it, and even if you don't, it'll be a change of scenery.'

'I've had enough changes of scenery recently to last me a lifetime,' Annabelle retorted.

'Nonsense.'

'I hardly know them.' She knew Beverley and Kate, of course, she and Kate having more or less grown up together, but she'd never met Kate's husband, Brett, or their children.

'They're your family,' May persisted. 'There'll be plenty of room in the house they're renting, so you won't all be on top of one another because it's got eight bedrooms.'

'I don't care how many bedrooms it's got, I'm not going. And they might be family, but I've never even met Brett.'

'Oh, you'll like him, he's lovely. I'm not so sure about Ron, though.'

May had a bee in her bonnet about Ron, and hadn't taken to him one little bit. Her mum and dad had returned home from visiting Annabelle and the kids in Australia last Christmas, to discover that he'd moved in with Beverley after having spent a number of years living on the streets.

Her mum had been scandalised, although her dad hadn't batted an eyelid. Annabelle vividly remembered her mum's horror.

Her mother gave her a worried look. 'I hope he doesn't think she's got money and that he might be able to get his hands on it. Could that be why he's with her?' It was a familiar refrain of her mum's.

Annabelle shrugged. 'I don't know, I've never met him.' If her mum hadn't been so unfriendly, Beverley probably would have brought Ron with her today. Instead, she'd left him at home with her dog, who her mum also wasn't too keen on. Apparently the dog was unruly and untrained.

'You'll meet him in Rest Bay,' her mum stated. Her eyes narrowed in suspicion. 'Maybe you could keep an eye on him, see which way the wind blows? Oh, and Brett's mother will be there as well.' She pulled a face. 'She can be a bit trying, from all accounts, so no doubt Kate will welcome a friendly face.'

'If you're referring to *my* face, Kate and I haven't seen each other for years. I doubt she'll even recognise me.'

'Of course, she will. You haven't changed a bit. Another cup of tea?'

'Coffee, please,' Annabelle said, but when her mum took the jar of instant out of the cupboard, Annabelle shuddered and changed her mind. 'On second thoughts, tea will be fine.'

She kept forgetting that she no longer owned a coffee machine. It was back in Australia, along with the rest of her possessions, and she wondered what had happened to it. Her heart gave a nasty lurch at the thought of strangers pawing through her things, and she hastily shoved it away.

Her mother's expression was pained as she tried a different approach. 'I don't like to think of you rattling around in the house on your own, while we're away.'

'I won't be on my own. I'll have the children to keep me company.'

'It's not the same as having another adult around. I wouldn't worry so much, but Beverley will be on the other side of the country so if there's a problem she's not going to get back from Porthcawl in less than four hours, what with the traffic.'

'I'll be fine,' Annabelle insisted.

Her mother carried on, 'If you're determined not to go back to Australia, you need to put down roots in this country, starting with your family. Blood is thicker than water, you know.'

Annabelle wasn't so sure about that. Troy's blood ran in his children's veins, but it may as well have been water for all the interest he showed in them. In his case, blood most definitely wasn't important.

'We are still not going.' How many more times did she have to tell her mother that? 'I'm not uprooting the kids again.'

'I'm sure they understand what a holiday is,' her mum countered, but Annabelle wasn't so certain. This was supposed to have been a holiday, yet it had turned into a permanent relocation.

Jake and Izzie hadn't even had the chance to say goodbye to their friends, and she wasn't sure they'd ever forgive her for that. Or for the weather. It might be summer in Britain, but the weather here was worse than Cairns in winter. It hadn't stopped raining since they'd arrived, which was another reason why she didn't want to go on holiday to Porthcawl for a couple of weeks – it rained even more in Wales than it did here.

'I'm not going anywhere,' Annabelle said firmly. 'You go and enjoy your cruise; the children and I are staying put.'

CHAPTER 3

Ron Masters took a deep breath of fresh sea air and exhaled slowly. He'd always loved the coast, although Worcestershire, and Pershore especially, was his home – *if* you could say that a homeless man had a home, that is. Since Christmas though, Ron had been staying with Beverley and it was now August.

It was strange how things came about, he mused, picking up a piece of driftwood and throwing it for the poodle who, true to form, eyed it with disdain. Pepe wasn't a stick-chasing kind of dog, despite Ron's best efforts. The dog wasn't too keen on balls, either. Sam, however, was, and the boy had brought his football to the beach for a kick about and was currently dribbling it up and down the sand. Every so often he'd look to Ron for his approval and Ron would give him a thumbs up.

The kid was football mad, Ron not so much, but he tried his best to be enthusiastic. Besides, the choice had been to either take Sam to the beach, or stay in the house with Beverley, who was anxiously fussing over the imminent arrival of her niece. The fussing had involved a reshuffle of the sleeping arrangements with Ron offering to sleep in the garden for the rest of the holiday. Beverley had been outraged at the suggestion, but he'd packed up his stuff anyway, cleaned the single room he'd been sleeping in, had put fresh sheets on the bed, then he'd whisked Sam and Pepe off to the beach and left her to it.

Beverley's shock at his suggestion – a perfectly reasonable one, in his opinion – had got him thinking...

A two-week or so visit to Beverley's Brighton home to do some training with a poodle with an attitude, had turned into eight months. It was the longest he'd stayed in one place for years. And it was most definitely the longest he'd had a roof over his head since he'd moved out of his marital home. He couldn't continue to live in Beverley's house indefinitely.

At some point she would want to be rid of him. But each time he'd made leaving noises, she'd been adamant she didn't want him to go.

Sooner or later, though, he'd have to hit the road, and he was worried that he'd gone soft. A comfy bed and a warm house had weakened him, both physically and mentally. It would be hard to live on the streets again. Maybe his offer of bunking down in the garden had been a subconscious acknowledgement that he needed to begin preparing himself, especially since he could so easily kip on the sofa.

'Pepe, heel,' he commanded, spying an enthusiastic and bouncy Springer spaniel tearing across the beach and heading directly for them. Its tail was wagging furiously, but Ron wasn't going to take any chances with Beverley's beloved pet. Obediently Pepe did as he was told, and the poodle even sat without being asked.

'Good boy,' Ron murmured as the spaniel approached, its owner haring after it, calling its name without any effect whatsoever.

'Tink! Tink! Come here, you naughty boy!' the man shouted, and Ron smiled.

'Tink, sit,' Ron said, making a noise and clicking his fingers.

The spaniel hesitated, his headlong rush halted, and he came to a stop a few feet away from Pepe.

'Sit,' Ron repeated, his tone brooking no argument. The spaniel sat, his tail still going nineteen to the dozen, and spraying loose sand in an arc around his wiggling bottom.

'Wow, how did you get him to do that?' the man huffed breathlessly as he hurried over, a lead in his hand.

He bent to fasten it to the spaniel's collar, but Ron said, 'You can leave him free, if you want. Pepe is friendly.'

'Oh, right, OK. If you're sure?'

'I'm sure. I expect Pepe will ignore him anyway. He's getting on a bit and can be quite grumpy.'

'Tink is eighteen months old, and he thinks everyone loves him and wants to play.'

Ron ruffled the spaniel's ears and the dog immediately jumped up on its hind legs. 'Down. Sit.'

Tink sat.

'I can't believe he listens to you like that,' the man said.

'He probably doesn't see you as the pack leader.'

'That's because I'm not,' the chap joked. 'My wife is.'

'Ron, Ron, watch this,' Sam shouted, and Ron's gaze shifted to the boy.

'Well done,' he called back as Sam kicked the ball into the air, then headed it.

'Is that your son?' The man was also looking at Sam, who was now balancing the ball on the top of one of his feet, his expression one of intense concentration. 'My boy loves a game of footie, too.'

'No, he's not mine, he's the grandson of a friend.' Ron tried not to think about his lack of children; it didn't do to dwell on the past.

The guy nodded. 'I'd better get on. I've got miles to go before I wear this one out. Springers are a bit lively, aren't they?'

'Have you tried playing fetch with him? That can sometimes work with dogs who are bred to retrieve things.'

'Are you a dog handler or something?' the bloke joked, and Ron's eyes grew distant.

'I used to be, in another life,' he said.

'OK, well, thanks for the suggestion. I'll definitely give it a try.'

Ron watched him go, his attention mostly on the spaniel. He had a particularly soft spot for Springers; their sheer enthusiasm for life was a joy to see. He'd never known a Springer who didn't have a non-stop waggy tail or a happy expression on its face. Dolly used to have the biggest smile Ron had ever seen on a dog, and the softest eyes.

God, how he'd loved that dog. He'd loved her more than he'd loved his wife – but that had been the problem, hadn't it? He'd not loved his wife as much as he should have done, and although he'd cared for her deeply, he'd been unable to commit fully.

Looking back, he should never have married her, but it had seemed the right and logical thing to do at the time. All his mates were getting married, so he'd tied the knot as well. It was quite telling that only one of those mates was still with the same woman twenty years on.

That's army life for you, he mused. It took a certain kind of couple to make it work. And when he'd realised he was more married to his dog than his wife, he'd walked away. It was just a shame that it had taken him such a long time to realise it. Maybe if they'd had kids—?

All that was water under the bridge. He'd heard that Louise was someone else's wife now, and Ron begrudged her none of it, even though he'd walked away from their union with nothing, not even his job. Or his dog.

Dolly had been killed in the line of duty and his grief had been all-consuming. His mother's death following shortly afterwards had sent his world crashing down around him, like a bomb-damaged building.

Looking back, he believed he must have had some kind of a breakdown. He'd packed a rucksack and left, only returning to sign any documents that needed signing. He'd handed the house over to Louise (his guilt had ridden him hard) and had gone wandering – like a British version of Jack Reacher but without the drama or the violence. Or the army pension. Unfortunately, he wouldn't be able to draw on that until he was fifty-five, so he had a while to go yet.

Since then Ron had seen more of England and Wales than he'd thought possible, and he'd slept in more shop doorways than he could count, but every so often he'd be drawn back to where he grew up, usually arriving in mid-winter and staying until

February or March.

Last winter had been different. Last winter a woman called Kate Peters had shown him a rare kindness by inviting him to Christmas lunch at her house, with her family. And her mother, Beverley, had opened up her home to him.

But now he felt it was time to move on, both for Beverley's sake and for his own. This holiday in Rest Bay would be a farewell. He'd move on from here, and maybe head out to St. David's on the wild west coast. Thankfully, he hadn't lost the habit of travelling light; all his possessions fitted into his trusty Bergen rucksack and he'd brought most of them with him, apart from his tattered old sleeping bag which he'd left at Beverley's house in Brighton. It would be easy enough to buy a new one.

Sam was starting to flag, Ron noticed. The boy was bouncing the ball with his hand as he wandered over to the rock pools and peered into their depths. The tide was on the turn, the amount of available beach was slowly decreasing, and where he was standing would soon be underwater. It was time to go back. Hopefully Beverley would have sorted out the bedroom situation, the new guests would have arrived, and he and Brett's mother, Helen, could prepare the evening meal.

Ron intended to savour the days ahead, when he could pretend to be part of a family. He'd relish the time with Beverley, and he vowed he would do his best to enjoy this holiday with a woman who he had come to love like a mother.

CHAPTER 4

'**I**s Wales a different country?' Jake, Annabelle's eldest child, asked, as she indicated to turn off the motorway.

'Not really. Kind of. It's complicated,' she replied. 'Think of it as going from one state to another, like Queensland to New South Wales.'

'Will there be sharks?'

'I don't think so.'

'Crocs?'

'Definitely not'

Jake nodded, processing the information. One good thing to come out of her agreeing to take the kids on holiday was that they were finally talking to her.

'Can I surf?' he asked.

'I'm not sure.'

They were a bit late to this particular party, because everyone else had arrived on Saturday and today was Monday, but with only about fifteen minutes to go until they arrived at the house that Kate and Brett had rented, Annabelle was suddenly feeling decidedly nervous.

'Why are the houses so small?' Izzie asked, not for the first time.

It was an endless source of wonder to her daughter.

Relocating to the UK had been a culture shock for her kids in more ways than one. The sprawling yards and wide roads of home had been replaced by terraced houses with small gardens and narrow streets. Even Annabelle had taken some time to adjust to how crowded and higgledy-piggledy it was, compared to where they'd lived in Cairns.

The car's satellite navigation system was taking them through a housing estate and Annabelle eyed the houses they passed with trepidation; none of them looked large enough, and she worried that she'd plugged the wrong postcode into the machine. But then she slowed down to negotiate a sharp bend and abruptly the housing estate was left behind and the vista opened up.

'I can see the sea!' Izzie exclaimed, bouncing up and down, and Annabelle's heart lifted.

The ocean had always had that effect on her, and even though today was overcast and the water was a metallic grey and not the blue she'd envisioned, she could already feel some of the tension draining away.

It drained away even further when she noticed the houses lining the coast road. They were big, and one of them was very large indeed, and she let out a whoosh of relief when the Satnav told her she'd arrived at her destination.

Annabelle brought the car to a halt on the drive, feeling incredibly nervous. The rest of the family was already there, everyone else having arrived two days ago, and for a moment she was tempted to turn the car around and go home. But Mum and Dad were already on their way to Southampton. If she went back now she'd only be rattling around the house with a couple of kids who wouldn't be speaking to her again.

With slightly shaking fingers, she switched the engine off and sat there.

Her children were not so reticent. They were out of the car like a shot and Annabelle forced herself to move. When she uncurled her stiff limbs from the driver's seat, the fresh sea breeze slapped her in the face and smiling ruefully at the typical British summer weather, she sucked in a deep breath, tasting the ozone and feeling glad that she'd invested in some Pac-a-Macs. She had a feeling they were going to need them.

Taking a moment to get her bearings, she gazed out to sea, noting the white caps racing across the water and the scudding clouds in the sky. It wasn't cold, despite the stiff breeze, and she took another deep breath. The tide was in and she could see spray rising into the air as the waves crashed against the dark rugged rocks. It looked wild and beautiful, and she was suddenly glad she was here.

In between the sea and the road was a wide strip of land which was covered in grass and gorse, across which people were strolling, many of them with dogs, and as she wondered how far she'd be able to walk, she realised she couldn't wait to go exploring.

That would have to wait, because right now she had her family to meet, so she turned around to face the house, liking what she saw.

Large and detached, it was set back from the road, its nearest neighbours a good couple of hundred feet away, and she liked the sense of space the distance gave. It reminded her of Cairns, of home, where land wasn't at a premium and houses weren't crowded together.

The house itself was three storeys high. The top one had Dorma windows, and the middle floor had huge panes of glass, floor to ceiling, and she imagined the view from there would be magnificent.

Only one other car sat in the driveway, besides hers (or should she say, her *mother's* car, because Annabelle had borrowed it for the duration), and she recognised it as belonging to Aunt Beverley.

It was Jake, on overhearing his grandma tell his mum last night that it wasn't too late to change her mind and it would do the children good to have a holiday before they started school in September, that had persuaded her to come, because Jake had actually spoken to her without her having to say anything first. Since she'd dropped the bombshell that they weren't going back to Australia, he'd not said a word to her unless it was in response to a direct question, and even then his replies had been as brief as possible.

Izzie had followed his lead, although being that much younger she hadn't been able to hold out as long, and had been desperate for Mummy cuddles and reassurance. Make the most of it Annabelle had told herself, as she'd held her daughter close – in a few years Izzie would be a teenager and then she'd hardly want to bother with her mum at all.

With Jake finally talking to her of his own volition, Annabelle didn't want to jeopardise that, so here they were, about to meet a family they only knew through anecdotal stories and snippets of news over the phone.

Suddenly, the children seemed shy, their initial exuberance replaced with wariness as the pair of them hung back. It was up to Annabelle to take the lead, and she did so by retrieving her handbag from the passenger seat, smiling brightly at her offspring, then marching up to the front door and knocking loudly.

It was opened by Aunt Beverley, who took one look at her, let out a cry of delight and spread her arms wide.

'Thank God, you came!' she cried, squashing Annabelle to her, before releasing her and doing the same to each reluctant child.

Annabelle caught her breath and staggered back as Beverley turned her attention to the children. Her aunt was plump and solid, and her hug had been enthusiastic and welcoming.

'She's started already,' Beverley said ominously, after raining kisses on Jake and Izzie's cheeks. Jake grimaced and scrubbed at his face with the hem of his Spiderman T-shirt. Izzie simply looked shell-shocked.

'Who has started what already?' Annabelle asked, bewildered.

Beverley ushered them inside. 'Kate's mother, Helen.' She shuddered. 'Tea? What would you like, kids? We've got pop or squash?'

'Squash?' Jake looked confused.

'Cordial,' Annabelle translated.

Her aunt led them deeper into the house, and Annabelle glanced around with interest. The impressive outside was counterbalanced by an equally impressive inside. White, light and extremely modern, the short hall had a staircase opposite the front door, curling around as it climbed upwards, with huge windows to the side which allowed light to flood in. To the right was a corridor with doors leading off, and another staircase descended into the depths.

'All the bedrooms, apart from one, are on this floor,' Beverley said, noticing her curiosity. 'Those stairs lead to the basement where there's a gym, and a TV room, and whatnot. The main living area is on the next floor.' She leaned in closer and said, 'It's stunning. Wait until you see the view. I could sit and stare at it all day.'

Beverley made her way up the stairs and Annabelle let out a gasp when she emerged into an open-plan living and kitchen area that was very nearly the size of the footprint of the house. The huge windows that she'd seen from the drive were actually bi-fold doors, and they led directly onto a large terrace.

The kitchen was huge, blending seamlessly into a dining area which held a long table with ten slim high-backed chairs. There was a living space with a massive L-shaped sofa plus several other comfy-looking armchairs, but what really stole her breath and made her gasp was the view. It was, as Aunt Beverley said, stunning.

Annabelle could hardly bring herself to tear her gaze away.

'Kate and Brett have got the third floor to themselves,' Beverley said. 'It's not as big as this, but it's got a lovely master bedroom, a study, a seating area that gets the last of the setting sun, and a walk-in wardrobe, although I can't imagine anyone owning so many clothes that they'd need a walk-in wardrobe.'

'It's gorgeous. Thank you so much for inviting us,' Annabelle said.

'I wish I could take the credit, but it was Kate's idea. Right, let me make those drinks.'

Annabelle watched her aunt potter in the kitchen, and she had a moment of coffee-machine envy when she saw the gleaming machine sitting on one of the countertops. That was one of the many things she missed – decent coffee – and as soon as she got herself a job and started earning some money, she vowed to treat herself to one.

'Kids, why don't you go and explore,' Beverley suggested after they'd gulped down their drinks. 'Let your mum and me have a quick chat, then you can help bring your bags in and I'll show you which rooms are yours.' She turned to Annabelle. 'I've had to shift people around a bit because we didn't know you were coming until last night. I've put you and Izzie together in one of the twin-bedded rooms and Jake is in with Sam – they've got bunk beds.'

'I'm sorry, I didn't want to put you to any bother, especially Kate, since she was kind enough to invite us.'

Beverley replied cheerfully, 'There's room for everyone, and you're not putting Kate out at all. As I said, Kate and Brett have the master so they're on the top floor out of the way, although Brett's mother played her face when she thought no one was looking because it is the best bedroom in the house. A leopard doesn't change its spots,' she added cryptically.

'Where is everyone?' Annabelle asked.

'Brett and his mother are on the golf course.' Beverley pulled a face. 'He manages a course near Pershore, so this is like a busman's holiday for him. Apparently, the number one golf course in Wales is just over there.' She pointed in the general direction of the road Annabelle had driven in on. 'Kate and Ellis are at the stables fetching Portia, who has gone riding. Golf and riding!' Beverley snorted. 'They might as well have stayed at home. Only my Ron is doing seaside stuff.' Her voice filled with pride as she added, 'He's taken Sam and Pepe to the beach. He's marvellous with the boy.'

'Sam must be thrilled to have a grandfather figure in his life,' Annabelle said. What with Uncle Vern, Beverley's husband, having died a while back, and Brett's mother also being a widow, it must be nice for Sam and the girls to have an older man in their lives. She remembered her own grandad vividly, his penchant for wearing flat caps, his love of board games, the fossil hunting they'd used to do on Brighton's pebbly beach – they'd never found any but it hadn't stopped them trying.

Annabelle envisioned a kind of Captain Birdseye bloke, with white hair and a grizzly beard, skin weather-beaten after living on the street for such a long time.

Briefly she wondered what his story was. She was about to ask, when the front door banged open and the sounds of voices and a dog barking excitedly floated up to them.

'I'd better put the kettle on. Ron will be parched,' Beverley said, getting another mug out of the cupboard and popping a tea bag into it. She saw Annabelle watching her as she filled the mug with boiling water. 'You ought to see Helen's face when she realised the house didn't have a teapot. She wittered on about it for a whole five minutes, grizzling that it couldn't be advertised as being "superbly appointed" when it didn't have a teapot.'

Oh, dear, Annabelle thought. It appeared Beverley wasn't too keen on Brett's mother, and she guessed the feeling might be mutual. It was going to make for an interesting dynamic if Beverley and Helen didn't get on.

Jake and Izzie burst into the room, their faces alight.

'There's a games room, and gym, and a TV room!' Jake cried. 'And a hot tub.'

'And a little black dog,' Izzie added, and Annabelle guessed that her daughter was referring to Aunt Beverley's poodle.

Annabelle was just saying that she didn't think the dog came with the house, when the dog in question trotted into the room and made a beeline for his mistress, who scooped him up and rained kisses down on his curly little head, as the creature's pom-pom of a tail wagged furiously.

'Did my precious boy have a good time with his Uncle Ron?' Beverley cooed, as though she was talking to a baby.

'He did,' a deep masculine voice said, and Annabelle looked towards the door to see a rather handsome man in his mid-to-late forties stride into the room.

'Hi, I'm Annabelle,' she said, smiling.

The man's gravelly chuckle gave her goosebumps and, as he came closer, holding out his hand, she noticed he had very nice eyes, and a frisson of interest rippled through her.

'So I gathered,' he said. 'I'm Ron.'

As he grasped her hand in his, two things flashed into her mind. The first was surprise at the immediate attraction she felt, and the second was that Ron was considerably younger than she'd expected and far more good-looking.

CHAPTER 5

My word, Beverley's niece is gorgeous, Ron thought, feeling rather on the back foot. Somehow he'd got it into his head that she'd be careworn and dowdy, but the reality was very far from the image he had concocted of her.

The woman standing before him was in her early to mid-forties, with caramel and honey hair falling around her shoulders, a light tan, a pert upturned nose, and startlingly blue eyes. She was quite tall, her figure was trim, and she seemed rather reserved. She was also incredibly pretty.

'I take it these two are yours?' he asked, smiling at the boy and girl who were staring at him and Sam curiously.

'Yes, this is Jake and Izzie. Say hello to Ron,' she instructed.

'Hello,' they chorused.

Sam hung back a little, and Ron placed a hand on his shoulder. 'How about you show Jake and Izzie the games room?' he suggested.

'We've seen it,' Jake said, 'but I'd like to see it again.'

'Can the dog come?' Izzie sidled over to Beverley, who was still cuddling the poodle. 'What's its name?'

'Didn't your Granny tell you?' Beverley asked. 'No? OK, then… his name is Pepe and he's a poodle. He's also Mama's bestest boy, aren't you, my darling?' She put the dog on the floor and he promptly shook himself.

Izzie crouched down and held out her hand. Pepe sniffed it, then gave her fingers a lick. 'Does he like me?' Her little face was hopeful.

'He most definitely does,' Ron said.

'Good, because I like him. I've never had a dog.' She sounded wistful and Ron saw Annabelle wince.

'Run along,' Beverley said, shooing the children away. 'Ron, could you be a love and fetch the luggage in from Annabelle's car?'

'I can do it,' Annabelle said, taking her car keys out of her bag.

'I'm sure you can, my dear, but let Ron do it. He's a big, strong boy.'

'I'm hardly a boy,' Ron objected, giving her a warm smile.

'When you get to my age, anyone younger than fifty is still a kid,' Beverley retorted with a snort.

Ron held his hand out for the keys to Annabelle's car, but Annabelle hung on to them. 'I'll give you a hand,' she insisted, and who was he to argue.

The thought flitted through his mind that she might be worried he was going to steal something, but he shoved it away in irritation. Despite having had a roof over his head for the past eight months, he still couldn't get out of the habit of eyeing people with caution. Beverley's sister, May, would no doubt have told Annabelle all about him. Or, as much as she knew, which wasn't a lot. Even Beverley didn't know the full story.

'This house is lovely,' Annabelle said, following him down the stairs.

He could tell she felt awkward and was trying to make conversation, but that was OK: he was used to people feeling awkward around him.

'It is,' he agreed, although personally he was far more impressed with the view than the building. 'How was your journey?' Listen to him doing small talk!

'Long. The M4 around Newport was horrendous.' She aimed the key fob at the car and unlocked it. He recognised the vehicle as belonging to May.

'Beverley tells me you're staying in the UK for good?' He hoisted one case out of the boot and reached for a second.

'That's right.' Her answer was short, her voice clipped and tight.

It was none of his business and he had no idea why he'd even mentioned it. He'd learned long ago not to pry. Everyone had a story, but not everyone wanted to share.

'I bet the weather is better over there,' he said. Dear Lord, he was doing that small talk thing again.

She shrugged. 'It definitely is, even if it is winter in Cairns right now. We do get rain though. *They* get rain,' she amended quietly.

He noticed her correction. She clearly thought of herself as Australian, and he guessed it must be hard for her to adjust. How long had she lived there? He vaguely recalled Beverley mentioning twenty years or so, but he hadn't taken a great deal of notice at the time.

His response was neutral. 'Rain is good. Cleansing.'

He put one case down and closed the boot.

Annabelle retrieved a couple of rucksacks from the rear seat and he guessed they belonged to her kids.

'The forecast is better for tomorrow. Sunshine with a bit of cloud,' he added.

Her smile was tight. 'That's good to know.'

She locked the car and he followed her inside, admiring the view. She almost caught him staring at her when she glanced over her shoulder, and he hastily looked away. Annabelle might be an attractive woman, but she was off limits. In fact, every woman was off limits, because who in their right mind would want to get involved with a homeless guy?

'Where do you want these?' Ron called to Beverley, and it didn't surprise him to see her trundle down the stairs so she could show him personally.

'In the room Helen was in,' she said.

'*Was* in?' Ron raised his eyebrows, wondering if Helen was happy about the move. Or whether she actually knew about it.

'It's a twin, so I thought Annabelle and Izzie could share. You can't expect them to squash together in a single bed when Helen's room has two perfectly good twin beds. I've put her in the single next to yours.'

It did make more sense for Annabelle and her daughter to have the room Helen had originally chosen for herself, as it was larger, but he'd bet his last penny that Helen hadn't agreed to the move, and when she found out she wouldn't be pleased.

The twinkle in Beverley's eyes told Ron that she was well aware how Helen would react.

The elderly ladies were like chalk and cheese, and from what he'd been able to determine, there had been animosity between them from the very first time they'd met, and it hadn't abated over the years. Last Christmas their squabbling, as well as the typically teenage behaviour of Kate and Brett's daughters, had actually led to Kate disappearing to the south coast for a few days to get away from them.

The family seemed much calmer now and everyone was on their best behaviour. Mind you, Ron thought, it was early days yet and the holiday had only just begun. Time would tell if the good behaviour would continue, and with Beverley moving Helen to another bedroom and taking great delight in doing so, the cracks may already be starting to show.

Ron put both cases in the room Annabelle would be sharing with her daughter – her son was going to sleep in Sam's room because there were bunk beds – and he beat a hasty retreat. For some reason an image of Annabelle's long fair hair splayed across the pillow on one of the twin beds had leapt into his mind, and it made him feel quite peculiar. He should not be having thoughts like that about anyone, and especially not about his benefactor's niece.

It also didn't help his equilibrium when he realised Annabelle was standing directly behind him as he backed out of the door, and when he bumped into her his breath caught in his throat at the unexpected contact.

'Sorry,' he muttered, making a dash for it, feeling the weight of Beverley's curious gaze on his back as he hot-footed it along the hall, heading for the stairs.

Voices coming from beyond the front door told him that Brett and his mother were home.

Brett, he liked; Helen, he wasn't so sure of. Ron didn't think she liked him very much, and whenever she saw him she looked as though she'd caught a faint whiff of a nasty smell. To be fair, the first time she'd met him her expression and distaste probably *had* been due to him having not washed for several days, but with lack of personal hygiene no longer an issue thanks to him having at least one shower a day, Ron could only conclude that Helen simply didn't like him.

He didn't blame her – he often didn't like himself very much, either. But he had a feeling her dislike wasn't so much to do with him as a person, but more to do with the fact that he was still technically homeless. He got the impression Helen thought he was sponging off Beverley, and Helen's mistrust was only thinly veiled.

Annabelle's mother, May, didn't like him much either, probably for the same reason, although her father didn't seem to mind him: though Terence might change his mind if he knew Ron had been ogling his daughter.

Brett gave Ron a wide smile when he spotted him at the foot of the stairs, and his open and friendly face was in direct contrast to the tight jaw and flattening of the lips which was Helen's version of a smile. Although, Ron conceded, she was such a sour lemon of a woman that she tended to wear that expression a lot. The only exception was when she was looking at, or speaking to, Brett: she thought the sun shone out of her son's backside.

'Have you begun preparing dinner?' Helen asked sharply, seeing him halfway up the stairs.

Ron shrugged. 'It's only five o'clock,' he said.

'Nonsense! The others will be back soon, and anyway, Brett is hungry, aren't you, Brett?'

Brett made a face. 'Not particularly,' he said, and Ron could tell he was trying to be diplomatic.

Helen tutted. 'I suppose it's down to me to do the cooking, if no one else can be bothered.' By "no one else", Ron assumed Helen was referring to him.

Ron wasn't averse to doing his share of the chores – in fact, he thought it only fair he did as much as he could to repay Beverley's kindness – but he didn't appreciate Helen's attitude. Whenever he was in her presence he felt very much like a servant.

Beverley, who had followed along behind him, caught his eye and smirked. 'Helen, my dear, I've moved you into the spare room,' she said. 'I know it's only a single, but it's perfectly adequate. Annabelle and Izzie will be sharing the twin.'

Helen shot her an incredulous look. 'You've touched my things?' she spluttered.

'Only to move them to your new room. I didn't know how long you'd be on the golf course, and I wanted Annabelle to settle in.'

Ron turned away so Helen didn't see him trying to hide a smile. The women had a "room-war" last Christmas when they'd visited Kate and Brett at the same time, and it looked like hostilities had well and truly resumed.

'I'll thank you to keep your hands off my things,' Helen snapped. 'I didn't give you permission to touch anything.'

'Oh, dear, I'm sorry,' Beverley said insincerely. 'I thought I was saving you a job. I didn't realise you had things in your room that you don't want anyone to see. Don't worry—' Beverley lowered her voice '— I didn't notice anything, and if I had done your secret would be safe with me.'

'What are you talking about?' Helen demanded. 'What secret?'

34

'Whatever it is you don't want anyone to know about,' Beverley repeated.

'I don't have any such thing.'

'That's good.' Beverley smiled winningly. 'So you don't actually mind me moving your stuff.'

'I *do* mind. I would have preferred to have done it myself.'

'That's a relief,' Beverley said.

'What is?' Helen demanded. Ron could almost see the steam coming out of her ears. The woman was seriously cheesed off.

'That you're happy to move rooms,' Beverley said.

'I didn't say I was happy,' Helen retorted stiffly.

'You did! Didn't she, Brett? Didn't your mother just say that she'd have moved her stuff herself?'

Brett shot Ron a pained look. 'Leave me out of this,' he said to the two women. 'I'm going to grab a beer. Do you want a drink, Ron?'

Glad to escape, Ron said, 'I'd love a Coke, please.'

'I thought you were starting dinner?' Helen called after him, but Ron pretended he hadn't heard.

He'd happily cook tonight's meal, but he didn't need Helen telling him what to do. Two evenings of her looking over his shoulder and issuing commands were enough.

He didn't mind her helping, but her idea of help was to bark orders like a drill sergeant, while he did all the work.

However, for Kate and Brett's sake, and because they had been kind enough to invite him on the family holiday, he held his tongue and kept the peace, whilst being grateful that Helen was no relation of his. In fact, when he was back on the road, he'd probably never see her again.

It was a pleasant thought.

What wasn't so pleasant was the thought of not seeing Beverley.

CHAPTER 6

Annabelle stood in the middle of the bedroom that Beverley had allocated her and Izzie, frozen to the spot and feeling slightly sick. She couldn't believe what she was hearing; if she'd realised Aunt Beverley was going to turf Kate's mother out of her room to make way for her and Izzie, Annabelle would never have agreed to come.

She hadn't wanted to come on this stupid holiday in the first place, but her mother had talked her into it, against her better judgement.

And now look what had happened! She'd already alienated Kate's mother, and it hadn't even been her fault. Annabelle was tempted to bundle the kids and the luggage into the car and drive back to Brighton immediately.

She was about to go looking for her offspring with that very intention, when Jake stuck his head around the door, Sam hovering behind, and cried, 'Sam said there's surfing! Can I go, Mum? Please?' He rushed on, without waiting for an answer. 'And he says there's a fairground and donkeys on the beach and fish and chips and sand dunes.'

He stopped to take a breath, leaping up and down and flapping his arms as though he was a baby bird trying to take off.

Annabelle didn't know how to respond, and something must have shown in her face, because Sam said, 'We don't have to – we can do other stuff, Mrs… er…'

'Aunty Annabelle,' she said. 'I'm your Aunty Annabelle.' The title wasn't strictly accurate, but it would do, and the poor little chap had to call her something.

Jake stopped jumping up and down, and his previously excited expression turned wary and uncertain. He'd frequently worn that same expression since she'd announced that the family wouldn't be returning to Australia. She hated being the one to have caused her previously sunny and exuberant son, who had always run headlong at life despite the way his father had behaved, to suddenly view everything with suspicion. This was the first time in a while that she'd seen him so animated, and it made her heart clench.

Maybe her mum had been right, and this holiday was just what the kids needed?

'Of course you can surf, as long as it's safe,' she said.

'Yay!' he cried, but Annabelle noticed Sam continuing to eye her with caution.

And why shouldn't he? He didn't know her from Adam, despite her and his mother being cousins. It would be good for Jake to get to know him, to understand that he had relatives in the UK besides his Granny and Grandad. And it might be good for Sam to have a boy near enough his own age to play with for the next two weeks.

Whatever her own misgivings, Annabelle decided to make the best of it.

***

'Is there anything I can do to help?' Annabelle asked, a short while later as she wandered into the enormous open-plan living space and saw Ron in the kitchen.

He was wearing an apron and had a wooden spoon in his hand. A large pan was on the stove and the aroma of frying onions and garlic filled the air.

Kate's mother was leaning against the island separating the kitchen from the dining area, and glaring at him. Annabelle took a moment to study her, noticing the set expression on her face. She was immaculately dressed in an A-line skirt in soft lemon, a fine knitted top, a chunky necklace and a pair of pristine white trainers on her feet. Her hair was iron grey and styled to within an inch of its life. Helen couldn't be any more different to Beverley.

She glanced around as Annabelle approached, and Annabelle flinched at the frown on the woman's face. It quickly cleared into a frosty smile as she held out a hand.

'I'm Helen, Brett's mother.'

Annabelle shook her hand. 'Nice to meet you. Thank you for letting me join you.'

Helen's eyes widened a fraction. 'You should thank Kate. It was her suggestion. How do you like your room?'

'Mum, stop it,' Brett warned, coming into the room. Despite he and Kate having been married for over twenty years, Annabelle had never met him. She'd been travelling around Australia at the time, young, single and carefree, and the last thing she'd wanted to do was to return to the UK for the wedding of a cousin she hadn't seen in ages. She'd been having far too much fun.

'Hi, I'm Brett, Kate's better half,' he said as his mother slapped his wrist when he stole a breadstick. 'You must be Annabelle.'

'That's me.' She gave him an awkward little wave and a self-conscious smile. He grinned back, his own smile wide. He was quite pleasant to look at, she thought, late forties, trim, light brown hair, grey eyes. Not a patch on Ron.

Strewth! Had she really just thought that?

'Need a hand?' Brett asked Ron, peering over his shoulder.

'We can manage, dear. You sit down,' Helen said.

Annabelle saw the knowing look that passed between Ron and Brett.

'I was offering to actually help and not just supervise,' Brett said.

Helen pressed her lips together. 'Annabelle has already offered. If you insist on making yourself useful, you can get the garlic bread out of the freezer,' she told him.

'Already done it,' Ron said. Annabelle was certain a smirk was hovering around his mouth and she bit her lip to keep her own smile inside. If nothing else, Brett's mother would provide some entertainment this holiday.

Feeling superfluous to requirements, Annabelle moved towards the enormous windows and gazed at the view.

'See that smudge in the distance?' Brett said, coming to stand next to her. 'That's Devon.' An expanse of sea lay in between, and nearer to the shore the water looked rather choppy. 'Apparently, this channel has one of the highest tidal ranges in the world,' he added.

'Right.' Annabelle wasn't sure how she was supposed to respond.

'Great for rock pooling,' he continued. 'I used to love doing that when I was a kid – maybe Jake would enjoy it?'

'I'm sure he would.' Her son loved anything to do with the sea, although she wasn't sure what he'd make of these cold Atlantic waters. 'He says you can go surfing here?'

'You can.' Brett nodded. 'Just up the coast.' He pointed to the right. 'See that red-roofed building over there? That's the golf course. There's a little bay just there and that's where they surf. You can hire wet suits and boards.'

A car turning into the drive caught his attention and he looked down. Annabelle followed his gaze.

'Ah, here's Kate and the girls,' he said. 'When was the last time you saw each other?'

'Goodness, at least twenty-two years ago, because I went out to Australia then.' She shrugged. 'A couple of years before that, probably.'

'It'll be nice for you to catch up,' he observed.

Annabelle wasn't so sure. She'd hardly known Kate when they were growing up, Kate being a couple of years older. They hadn't had anything in common then, and she wasn't sure whether they would now.

As she waited nervously for Kate to appear, she very much felt the outsider.

Annabelle needn't have worried. As soon as Kate saw her, she gave a squeal and hurried over, her arms wide open, her face wreathed in smiles. Annabelle let out an 'oomph' as Kate barrelled into her and threw her arms around her.

'Long time, no see, cuz!' she exclaimed, hugging her hard for a moment, then Kate pushed her away to gaze into her face. 'You haven't changed a bit! I'd know you anywhere. Ooh, it's so good to see you!' Kate hugged her again, before stepping away and linking her arm through Annabelle's. 'We're going to have such a good time!' she cried, then lowered her voice. 'Or as good a time we can have with a couple of sulky teenagers and a pair of squabbling old ladies around. Where are your two?'

Finally, Annabelle was able to get a word in. 'Downstairs with Sam.'

Kate hadn't changed much either. Her hair was shorter – shoulder-length now – and her face was more angular, but she was still the same Kate, with the same twinkle in her eye and ready smile on her lips. She did look older, admittedly, but then so did Annabelle herself, and wondered what Kate saw when she looked at her.

Annabelle stared curiously at Kate's daughters. Ellis was a tall and willowy eighteen-year-old and Portia was a sporty fifteen. Ellis wore a wafty, floaty dress made out of cream cheesecloth, a pair of gladiator sandals and her hair was long and plaited. Portia was clothed in riding gear and was holding a helmet, and her short black hair was mussed and spiked. Annabelle's mum had said the teenager was a Goth, but apart from the dyed hair and the eyebrow piercing, Annabelle could see little evidence of it.

The girls eyed her for a second, then lost interest and headed for the breadsticks. There'd be none left at this rate, Annabelle thought, wondering whether she should go in search of her children to tell them dinner was almost ready.

Kate beat her to it. 'Portia, change out of your riding gear, wash your hands and go and find Sam and tell him dinner won't be long. Jake and Izzie should be with him. And Portia…?' The girl paused. 'Play nice,' Kate warned.

'I'm always nice.'

Ellis barked out a laugh. 'Yeah, right. Er, not so much.'

Kate sighed and rolled her eyes. 'Teenagers! Who'd have 'em? You've got all this to come. Anyway, enough of that – you must tell me your news. We've got such a lot to catch up on.' And with that, she dragged Annabelle across to the massive dining table, adding, 'As soon as dinner is over, we'll find a quiet spot, crack open a bottle of wine and have a good old chinwag.'

To her surprise, Annabelle thought that was a wonderful idea.

***

Feeling mellow, Annabelle leaned back against the cushions and tilted her face up to the sky. The scudding clouds of earlier had disappeared with the onset of darkness and the night was a relatively clear one. She huddled deeper into her fleece and gazed at the heavens, clutching the remains of her glass of wine. She and Kate had gone out onto the terrace for a good long chat, but it was getting late. The younger kids were in bed, the men were playing snooker with Ellis and Portia in the games room, and the last time

Annabelle had ventured inside, the older women had been ensconced in front of the TV, arguing over what to watch.

Five minutes ago Kate had yawned and had got to her feet, saying that she was knackered, and had taken herself off to bed.

Her cousin had been right, Annabelle thought, it had been fun to catch up, even if it had proved to be a little emotional in places. She had shed a tear or two when she'd recanted what had led her to staying in the UK and, after downing half a bottle of wine, Annabelle was still feeling a little weepy.

It was her children she felt the most sorry for. How could Troy do such a thing to them? What the hell had he thought she was going to do when she found out about the house? It was sheer luck that she'd had their flights booked, otherwise she'd be in Australia with nowhere for her and the kids to live.

She sniffed and wiped her eyes with the sleeve of her fleece, then let out a yelp when she realised she wasn't alone.

'Sorry,' Ron said. 'I didn't mean to disturb you. I didn't know you were still up. I'll go back inside.'

'No need. I'm ready for bed anyway. It's been a long day.'

'Please don't go on my behalf,' Ron said.

She could tell he felt awkward, and she suddenly had the urge to make him feel more comfortable, so she stayed where she was.

'It's beautiful, isn't it?' she said, gazing skywards again, drinking in the twinkling shimmering lights of distant and unimaginable suns.

Ron perched awkwardly on the chair Kate recently vacated. 'It certainly is. I love looking up at the stars. One of the best places to stargaze is in the Brecon Beacons. There's hardly any light pollution. I used to spend hours watching them.'

'Is that before you went to live with Beverley?' She wanted to ask him if he'd watched the stars because he hadn't had a roof over his head, so hadn't had much choice, but she didn't want to be rude.

'Way before. I did my SAS training there.'

'Wow! You were in the SAS?'

He chuckled softly. 'No, I didn't get in. Man, it was tough. I ended up working with dogs instead.' Even in the darkness, she could see a momentary flicker of pain flit across his face and she wondered what caused it.

'My mum said you are good with dogs.' Her mum had said a lot of other things, too, which hadn't been half as complimentary. 'You trained Pepe. I heard he was a bit of a rascal.'

Ron's chuckle was louder this time. 'He still can be when he's in the mood.'

'My daughter has taken quite a shine to him.'

'I think he's taken a shine to her, too.'

Pepe had been glued to Izzie's side all through dinner, but Annabelle suspected it was more to do with her daughter slipping the dog pieces of breadstick when she'd thought her mother wasn't looking. Annabelle dreaded the inevitable question. Izzie hadn't yet asked for a dog, but it was only a matter of time and the answer would have to be no. Yet one more way she could disappoint her children.

Annabelle and Ron sat in silence for a while, but it wasn't an awkward one. There was a stillness about him that made her feel comfortable in his presence. She didn't feel the need to fill the empty air with chat, so she let the peace of the night wash over her, and the pair of them continued to gaze upwards.

Gradually though, Annabelle's attention was drawn to more earthly things, and her eyes gravitated towards Ron. Once again, she marvelled that the guy who Aunt Beverley had taken in wasn't at all what she'd expected. Her initial impression that he was a good-looking man hadn't changed during dinner, and whenever she looked at him she felt a distinct pull of attraction, which she found disturbing.

She hadn't been remotely interested in anyone since Troy had walked out on her and the children and, considering the situation she was in, now wasn't an ideal time for it. Maybe when she'd sorted herself out and the kids were settled, she could think about love again – *if* the right man came along.

If Ron was conscious of her scrutiny, he didn't show it, and she looked away, feeling awkward.

Abruptly she said, 'Sorry, I'm being rude. Would you like some wine? There's enough left in the bottle for another glass.' She could easily fetch a clean one from the kitchen.

'Thanks, but no. I don't drink.'

'Ah, I see.' Annabelle winced. How insensitive of her.

But once again, Ron blew her preconceptions out of the water when he said, 'I haven't drunk alcohol since I was in my teens. Let's just say I got into a bit of bother and ended up in hospital being treated for alcohol poisoning. I vowed never to touch a drop again, and I haven't. Caffeine is my go-to drug.'

'I see,' she repeated, feeling foolish. He must have guessed the direction her thoughts had taken, and her assumption that because he'd been homeless he must have had a drink problem.

'I used to get the mick taken out of me something rotten,' he continued. 'My army mates thought I was a right wuss.'

'I don't think you're a wuss.' She put her nearly empty glass down, unable to work out whether it was a show of solidarity on her part, or fear that she was on the verge of being tipsy. Either way, she didn't feel like drinking anymore.

'Don't let me stop you,' he said, looking pointedly at the remains of her wine.

'I've had enough,' she replied, realising it was true. What she could really do with was a strong cup of coffee.

'Can I make you a coffee?' he asked, interrupting her thoughts.

She smiled. 'You read my mind.'

'Fancy a plate of cheese and biscuits to go with it?'

'That would be lovely.' She watched him go inside, then tilted her head up, resting it on the back of the garden chair, and gazed at the stars once more. It was strange to think that if she'd still been in Australia she'd have been looking at a different sky. Not all of them were different obviously, but many of them were; however she wouldn't have been looking at the stars right at this very moment because it would be late morning there.

Homesickness punched her in the stomach and she let out a gasp.

'Are you OK?' Ron was at her side, a tray in his hands, concern in his voice.

'I'm fine.' She gave him the stock British answer, and he studied her for a moment before putting the tray down on the glass-topped rattan table.

She noticed he'd made black coffees and had brought out a small jug of milk and a bowl of sugar.

'I don't know how to use that infernal coffee machine,' he said, 'So I made it the old-fashioned way with instant granules. Sorry.'

Annabelle laughed, tears hovering perilously close to the surface. 'Instant is fine.' She would make do; any caffeine was better than no caffeine right now.

'How do you take it?' he asked.

'Just milk, please.'

He poured some into her cup, then handed it to her. 'Help yourself to cheese and crackers.' Three varieties of cheeses sat in the middle of the plate, surrounded by several types of biscuits.

'Helen,' he said by way of an explanation when he saw her looking at them. 'She likes things just so. I'd have been happy with a block of Cheddar and a couple of Jacob's crackers.' He picked up a poppy seed cracker and cut off a sliver of oak-smoked Wensleydale. 'Thanks, Helen,' he said. 'I'm going to enjoy this.'

Annabelle followed his example. 'Hmm, tasty.' She hadn't realised she was hungry. The coffee was also good, despite it being instant.

The two of them ate in silence, and once the snack had been demolished and the coffee was drunk, Annabelle got to her feet, feeling suddenly bushed.

'It's been a long day,' she declared. 'It's time I was in bed.' If she didn't get some sleep, she'd be good for nothing tomorrow.

'It has been rather a full one, hasn't it? Goodnight.'

'Goodnight,' she called back as she made her way into the house, feeling better.

Abruptly, she realised that she wanted to make the most of this unexpected holiday; there would be time enough to worry about the future when she returned home.

Home… she meant her parents' house obviously, because although it was her childhood home and her mum and dad had assured her that she and the kids could stay with them for as long as they needed, it wasn't *her* home. Annabelle didn't have a home any more.

Her final thought as she snuggled into the single bed in the room she was sharing with her daughter, was that she and Ron were in the same boat. Both of them were technically homeless. If it hadn't been for her parents, she too wouldn't have anywhere to live. And an old saying flitted through her mind – "there but for the grace of God…"

CHAPTER 7

Ron laced his trainers up and grabbed his Bergen. Brett would carry the other rucksack, because although the walk to Kenfig Pool wouldn't take all day, they would be out of the house long enough to warrant taking some refreshments with them. He noticed Annabelle also had a small bag on her back. It had a picture of a cartoon hero on it, and he recognised it as belonging to Jake.

'If you want to leave that behind, I've got room to spare in my rucksack,' he offered.

'It's OK. I'd feel lost without a bag of some kind.' Despite her rejection, her smile was warm.

The sadness he'd seen in her eyes last night was gone – for the moment, at least, although he guessed it would probably return. Beverley had filled him in as to Annabelle's circumstances and his heart went out to her. It couldn't be easy for her, with two children to care for. The shock and the upheaval must be horrendous, and he could only imagine what she was feeling. At least she had May and Terence, and a roof over her head.

He'd met her parents on several occasions, and whilst he got on well enough with Terence, he was aware that her mother viewed him with suspicion.

'Are you sure about coming with us?' he asked Beverley. It was a fair old walk to the lake, at around three and a half miles, so Sam had informed them when he'd asked if they could go. Set in a nature reserve of rolling dunes and boasting the largest natural lake in the area, it promised to be a beautiful walk.

'I'll manage,' Beverley insisted. 'I'm not old and decrepit yet.'

'I never said you were,' Ron replied, with a chuckle.

'We'll be fine, won't we, Helen?' Beverley insisted.

The contrast between the two women was never more apparent than this morning. Beverley wore black leggings with a flowery tunic over the top, a pair of well-worn trainers on her feet and a cardi slung around her shoulders. She'd borrowed one of Sam's baseball caps which, being slightly too small, was perched on the top of her orange-haired head. She was gripping her handbag in one hand and holding Pepe's lead with the other, the excited poodle dancing about on the end of it.

Helen, on the other hand, was dressed in a pair of white linen trousers, a pale blue long-sleeved top ("because it wasn't that warm out, you know") and had a navy cable-knit sweater draped around her neck with the sleeves tied artfully across her chest. Big sunglasses, a floppy-brimmed hat, and deck shoes completed her outfit. One of them looked as though she was taking the dog for a quick walk around the block, the other as though she was going to spend the day on a yacht, sipping martinis.

There was a similar contrast between the teenage girls, with Portia only gradually emerging from her

Goth phase and still favouring black clothes and heavy make-up, and Ellis looking like a 1960s hippy chick with her white floaty skirts and flowing blonde hair. Winter and summer, dark and light...

Annabelle's daughter was clearly in awe of both of them and Ron felt a little sorry for the child. The sisters had each other for company – although you wouldn't think it to listen to them squabble – and Sam and Jake had bonded instantly. Izzie was the odd one out, and she had yet to find her feet within the family.

'Can I hold his leash?' Izzie asked Beverley shyly, and beamed widely when Beverley gave her the lead.

'Put your hand through there,' Beverley instructed, 'and wrap the lead once around to make sure you've got a firm grip.'

'Tell him "heel" and he'll walk just behind your left foot,' Ron said. It had taken the poodle a while to get the hang of the heel command; not because the dog couldn't grasp what was being asked of him, but because he didn't want to obey. Pepe had been a stubborn little so-and-so. He still was when the mood took him, and Ron felt a pang shoot through his chest when he thought about not seeing the irascible little dog again. Or its equally irascible owner.

'Are you OK?' Annabelle asked, and he realised his sadness must have shown on his face.

Hastily he rearranged his features into a smile. 'I'm fine,' he answered, echoing her reply when he'd asked her the very same thing last night.

A look passed between them, full of something he couldn't identify, and even after he had turned away, her face continued to linger in his mind. He wasn't drawn to her just because she was pretty. There was something deeper, more— Gah! He didn't know how to explain it, or whether he should even try. She was out of his league; why would a woman like her look twice at a man like him? But even if she hadn't been, she was Beverley's niece and that put her off limits. Whatever the reason, he was in no position to even think about acting on his attraction to her.

Without another word he hoisted the rucksack onto his back and stomped outside. He'd do well to remember to keep his distance.

***

The mid-morning sun was already warm, and the breeze blowing off the sea was gentle. With hardly a cloud in the sky, the day promised to be a lovely one and perfect for a stroll along the coastal path.

Apart from the dunes themselves, which undulated, the path running beside the high tide mark was mostly flat. The first section had been overlaid with a kind of boardwalk, providing easy access for any kind of wheeled user, whether it be pram, wheelchair or bicycle, and was quite busy with people strolling along, enjoying the sunshine. But as the walkway came to an end and the terrain grew rougher underfoot, so the number of people walking along the coastal path dwindled.

Sam and Jake took the lead, scampering ahead, the two older girls behind them, chattering amicably, rather than being at each other's throats for a change. Then came Kate, Annabelle and Izzie. Pepe was off the lead but wasn't ranging too far ahead, and behind them came Beverley and Helen, with Ron and Brett bringing up the rear.

For some of the way, the path rang alongside the golf course, and Brett's attention had been on the numerous games being played, the state of the green, and the condition of the bunkers, and he'd shared his thoughts freely with Ron. Once they'd left the course behind and began walking through open meadow-land on their way to the next bay, talk turned away from golf and onto more interesting things.

'Did Kate tell you that she's been asked to run her own shop in Worcester?' Brett said. 'She turned them down, though – she likes it where she is and doesn't want the extra responsibility, or the extra hours. Then there's the travelling to consider.'

Kate worked in a charity shop in Pershore. It was where Ron and she had met: he'd been sleeping rough in the shop's doorway and she used to supply him with coffee, food and, on occasion, clean clothes from the shop, which he knew she used to pay for out of her own pocket. Ron was indebted to her. He knew she would be hurt when he left Beverley, as would Beverley herself, but he would undoubtedly see Kate again.

He'd grown up in Pershore and the surrounding area, and wherever he roamed, he was always drawn back there. He'd certainly bump into Kate again, although he'd think twice about kipping down in the shop's doorway as he didn't want her to feel obligated or awkward.

Ron's thoughts drifted to living on the streets again, as he considered his options. Maybe moving on from Rest Bay wouldn't be the best idea – he didn't want to spoil Beverley's holiday – so perhaps he'd wait until they returned to Brighton before he told her he was going back on the road.

Oh, what did it matter? A few more days were neither here nor there. It wasn't as though he had anywhere to go or a burning need to be anywhere else; his appointment with a park bench in Pershore could wait.

Brett was saying, 'Kate and Annabelle seem to be getting on like a house on fire. I must admit, I was a bit anxious when Beverley asked if her niece and the children could join us. After all, Kate and Annabelle might be cousins, but they haven't seen each other for years, and I don't think they were particularly close as kids. But she seems nice enough.'

'She does,' Ron agreed.

She was also sad, worried, and clearly apprehensive about her future (not that she'd said anything, but he'd picked up the vibes last night) but nice all the same. Although "nice" was too bland a word to describe her, it was the only word he was permitting himself to use. Nice was maiden aunt, the woman serving tea and cake in the church hall, the librarian who let you borrow a book even though it was against the rules.

Annabelle, however, was more than nice.

Pushing her to the back of his mind, Ron tried to lose himself in the beauty around him, and his heart lifted when they crested a rise and saw the next bay ahead of them. A length of wide gold sand stretched into the distance, edged by white-topped waves rolling in to break on the gently shelving shore. There were a few dog-walkers, their excited charges dashing around in delight, a lone couple, shoes in their hands, walking through the water's edge, and three riders on horseback cantering through the shallows, the spray cast up by their hooves catching the sun.

To the right of the beach lay an undulating mass of grass-covered dunes, wildflowers sprouting up between the sparse vegetation, and to either side of the path tiny wild strawberries grew. It was unexpectedly exotic and breathtakingly beautiful, and Ron greedily drank it in.

Everyone had stopped to look, even the boys, who were standing with eyes wide, tongues stilled.

This was what life was all about, Ron thought: not mobile phones, or the latest car, or the trendiest clothes.

This was food for the soul and the senses.

However, the mood was soon broken by a flurry of photo-taking and exclamations of delight, accompanied by the excited chatter of the boys and barking from Pepe.

Only Annabelle was still and silent, gazing at the view, and he suddenly realised that she felt it too, the connection with nature and the pleasure of immersing oneself in the moment.

Then he almost laughed out loud at his silliness. She could be thinking about her next dental appointment for all he knew; or comparing the view in front of her to one in Australia and finding it wanting.

As though she felt the weight of his stare, Annabelle glanced back at him and caught his gaze. The light in her eyes and the wide beam of her smile told him she felt the same as he, and in that nano-second of contact a zing flashed through him.

Unable or unwilling to think about what it meant, Ron hastily dropped his gaze, but not before he'd seen an answering flash in hers.

'Are we nearly there yet?' Sam tugged at his sleeve.

'Ron? Did you hear me? I said, are we nearly there yet?'

Relieved to be distracted, Ron looked down into the boy's hopeful face. 'You tell me, Map Boy. You're the one who told us about this place, you're the one who worked out how to get to it.'

Sam puffed up his chest with the responsibility of leading them to the lake. 'I think we need to walk down to that dune there, where there's a path going over the top, then walk along that.'

Ron nodded. 'Lead on!' he cried, although he wasn't entirely sure Sam knew the way. The dunes were criss-crossed with paths going to God knows where, but he was fairly sure that if they got lost all they needed to do was to head towards the sea, to get them back to Rest Bay. Anyway, a little adventure never hurt anyone.

He glanced around the group to check everyone was all right, caught Annabelle's eye once again, and bit his lip. He must stop looking at her like that. She might get the wrong idea (or the right one – that he fancied her something rotten) and he didn't want to cause her any distress. The last thing she needed was to feel uncomfortable because he was ogling her. She was here to enjoy a holiday with her family, and he would hate to think that she might wish she hadn't come.

As soon as they turned inland and dropped into the lee of one of the tussocky dunes, the breeze immediately subsided, and the air was still. It was getting warm, and Ron paused for a second, shrugged off the rucksack and held out his hand to Beverley.

'Give me your cardi and I'll pop it in here,' he said.

When she handed it to him, he cocked his head at Helen, whose face had grown pink. He guessed she might be sweltering with that sweater wrapped around her shoulders.

'No, thank you,' she said, lifting her nose.

'Let me know if you change your mind,' he offered, and she gave him a look he interpreted as being that she'd rather collapse from heat exhaustion than be beholden to him, even for something as simple as carrying her sweater for her. Which was surprising considering she had a tendency to treat him like a servant when at the house.

'Silly cow,' Beverley muttered in his ear. 'She acts like she's strolling along the front in Monaco, and people actually care what she looks like. Give me comfort any day.'

'How much longer?' Izzie, being the youngest of the group, was starting to flag.

'Sam?' Ron asked. Although he knew the answer, he also knew that Sam was revelling in the responsibility he'd been given.

Sam squinted into the distance and pointed towards a stand of scrubby trees. 'I think the lake is over there.'

'It is,' Brett confirmed, moving alongside Ron. He stepped closer and lowered his voice. 'I checked it out before we left.' He eased his own backpack off and said in a louder voice, 'Anyone want some water?'

The three youngest had a drink, but the others were eager to move on.

'Can we swim in the pool?' Jake asked, as everyone started walking again. 'I've got my swimmies on.' He pulled at the waistband of his shorts to reveal his swimming trunks.

'It's not recommended because it's a nature reserve and you might disturb the birds,' Ron said. He'd done his homework, too. 'There's another reason you can't swim in the pool,' he added, when he saw the boy's disappointment. 'It's dangerous. There's a whirlpool in the middle.' He lowered his voice and the three youngest children slowed to listen. 'According to local legend,' he continued, 'the pool is bottomless. It's rumoured to be fed by seven springs, and these swirl and converge to form a whirlpool in the middle. Any boats that get too close are dragged into it and sucked down into the depths.' He gave a theatrical shudder and made a sucking gurgling noise.

The three youngsters listened with wide eyes and gleefully horrified expressions on their faces. Even Ellis and Portia looked mildly interested.

'Stuff and nonsense,' Ron heard Helen mutter, followed by, 'Fancy scaring the children like that.' But Kate gave him a wink, so he carried on. 'Another legend has it that there was once a town called Kenfig which stood on the very spot where the pool is now. Long, long ago, a young man fell in love with a lord's daughter, but he was poor and the lord refused to let him marry her. The young man was desperately in love, and because of that he did something unspeakable.' Ron paused dramatically.

'What, did he do, Ron?' Sam demanded.

'He killed a wealthy man, stole all his money, and buried the man's body. Then he asked the lord's permission to marry his daughter, and the lord gave it because the young man was now very rich indeed. But during the wedding celebrations a huge storm blew up, and in the wind a voice could be heard, and do you know what it said?' He paused again, and saw

Izzie slip a hand in her mother's. 'It cried "vengeance will come!". The storm raged all night and by morning the town was no more. It was underwater – all that could be seen of it were two chimney pots belching out black smoke. And sometimes in the darkest middle of the deepest night the bells of the drowned church can still be heard.' He finished his story, and there was silence for a moment. Even the insects had stopped buzzing.

Then Sam asked, 'That's not really true, is it?'

Ron shrugged. 'Who knows? But there really was once a town called Kenfig and it's not here any more, so...' He shrugged again. 'Look, I think we're almost at the lake.'

Whilst they were listening to his story, the grassy dunes had given way to scrubby bushes and small trees, and a few minutes more saw the path wind through much taller ones before it abruptly opened out into a clearing.

'Told you I knew how to get here!' Sam cried, as he shot down the small gently shelving beach towards the water.

'Wow, this is beautiful!' Kate exclaimed, and Ron had to agree.

The lake was larger than he'd expected and was surrounded by trees, and the beach they were standing on had a couple of picnic tables dotted around it. It was also completely theirs, as there was no one else in sight.

With the blue, cloudless sky overhead, the call of water birds, and the utter tranquillity of the place, it was magical.

Pepe rudely broke the spell by dashing to the water's edge and barking at the rippling wavelets.

'What if he goes in?' Izzie asked, turning her worried little face towards Ron. 'The whirlpool might get him.'

'He'll be fine. It's OK to paddle near the shore,' he assured her. 'And if anyone wants a swim later, I'm happy to take a quick detour to the sea. That beach we saw earlier looked fabulous.'

'Yay!' Jake leapt up and down in excitement.

'He loves the water,' Annabelle said, as Ron put the rucksack down on one of the benches. 'Thank you,' she said to him.

'For what?'

'Most people would have just said no when Jake asked if he could swim in the lake. No explanation, nothing. And your story took Izzie's mind off the final part of the walk.'

'It was nothing.' Ron reddened and hoped she hadn't noticed his embarrassment at the praise.

'I think it was. Their father—' She stopped abruptly and looked away.

He couldn't be certain, but he thought she might have had tears in her eyes, and a wave of sympathy swept through him. 'Sandwich?' he asked, changing the subject.

Her grateful look stirred a feeling of protectiveness in his chest.

'That would be lovely,' she said.

Ron unpacked the rucksack, laying out a veritable feast, whilst Brett took out towels, a ball, and sun cream, and everyone settled down to refuel and enjoy the view.

It really was a fantastic spot, Ron thought, munching on a mini pork pie and gazing around. But its scenery failed to hold his attention for long as his eyes kept returning to Annabelle. She was half-turned away, a sandwich in her hand, wearing a pensive look on her face, and he wished he could take her sadness away.

Then he snorted in disgust at his ridiculousness. He wasn't able to help *himself*, so how on earth could he help anyone else? He was in a worse position than she was!

The noise he'd inadvertently made attracted her attention, and he found her looking at him curiously, her head tilted to the side. Giving her a smile, he popped the last morsel of pork pie into his mouth and chewed. It was like eating cardboard and he swallowed with difficulty, wondering what was wrong with him.

It really was time he moved on, he decided. He was getting far too comfortable living with Beverley, and he suddenly had the awful thought that maybe she wanted him gone but didn't like to say. Eight months he'd been living in her house – eight months! It was only supposed to have been a couple of weeks.

In the early days, whenever he'd mentioned leaving, Beverley would persuade him to stay, and he'd let her. He got the impression she was lonely, and long after he'd instilled some manners into Pepe and should have been on his way, she was finding things to do to keep him there. Eventually, though, he'd run out of odd jobs and DIY, yet still he'd lingered, believing her when she'd appeared horrified at him going.

This holiday though...

He didn't belong here. This wasn't his family, these weren't his people. No matter how welcome they made him feel (Helen aside), he didn't belong.

Had Beverley only asked him to come with her out of duty, a sense of obligation because she'd taken him in and didn't know how to extricate herself from the situation? He knew she genuinely cared for him, but was she taking altruism too far?

His gratitude to her was endless and he cared for her too, more than she'd ever know, but emotions which he had no business feeling were starting to surface, and they scared him. Even before Annabelle's arrival, he'd made the decision to go back on the road. Meeting her had now made it imperative.

A sudden loud shriek had him leaping to his feet, fear surging through him, and he quickly scanned the shocked faces to make sure that the children were OK. After his cautionary tale, he didn't think they'd go in the water, but—

He sighed with relief when he saw that everyone was present and correct, and no one appeared to be in any danger.

Apart from Pepe, who was haring down the little beach with a sandwich flapping in his mouth and Helen in hot pursuit.

Ron laughed and shook his head in despair.

Maybe his attempt at teaching the poodle some manners hadn't been quite as successful as he'd hoped!

CHAPTER 8

'No, thank you!' Helen shuddered. 'If it's all the same to you, I'll stay here. I don't like fairground rides.'

Annabelle was secretly relieved. She found Brett's mother hard work. The woman hadn't stopped going on about Sandwich Gate all afternoon, and whenever she brought it up Annabelle got the impression that she was having a snide dig at Ron.

Ron, bless him, had been stoic in the face of the woman's disgruntlement, and hadn't said a word. Mind you, Annabelle thought, he hadn't needed to with Aunt Beverley in his corner championing him.

So it was with a certain amount of relief that Annabelle heard Helen say she wouldn't be accompanying them to the amusement park this evening.

'And don't be thinking you can leave that animal with me,' Helen said, jabbing a finger in Pepe's direction. 'I'm not looking after it.'

'I wouldn't trust you to,' Beverley snapped back. 'You don't like him.'

'It's hardly surprising, is it? The dog's a menace.'

'He doesn't like you, either,' Beverley added, in a so-there tone of voice.

'I don't care whether that creature likes me or not.' Helen pursed her lips. 'All I care about is whether he's adequately trained – and he definitely isn't.'

'It was just a sodding sandwich.' Beverley's face was purple.

'He snatched it out of my hand and nearly bit my finger off.'

'Don't be so dramatic. He was nowhere near your finger.' Beverley scooped Pepe up and cradled him in her arms. 'You shouldn't have been waving your sandwich around. He thought it was for him.'

'I wasn't waving it – I was *eating* it.'

'Ladies! Enough.' Brett clapped his hands and the two women ceased bickering long enough for Kate to hustle Beverley out of the room.

'Go get ready,' she said to her mum. 'We'll leave in about ten minutes, yeah?'

Still muttering and grumbling, Beverley trotted down the stairs and everyone else scrambled to sort themselves out.

'We'll drive into Porthcawl,' Kate said a short while later when they were all assembled in the hall. 'I think we've done enough walking for today. My legs are killing me.'

Annabelle was also feeling a bit weary and could quite happily have curled up in a chair and watched TV for the evening, but when Portia said she wanted to go to the shows, Jake, Izzie and Sam had staged a concerted effort to persuade the adults to let them go, too. And because they were too young to go on their own, it was decided that everyone should go. Apart from Helen, who had poured scorn on the idea.

'We'll take our car,' Kate was saying. 'Annabelle, do you think you can take yours? Mum and Ron, if you go with Annabelle, Ellis and Portia can come with us. Sam and Jake, if you go with Annabelle, maybe Izzie can come with us, too?'

Izzie, wide-eyed and uncertain, looked to her mum for guidance, but Portia got there before Annabelle could reply.

'You can sit in the middle,' Portia said. 'Do you like rides? I think they've got a merry-go-round and a rollercoaster.'

Izzie nodded, and slipped her hand into Portia's.

'Thank you,' Annabelle mouthed to the teenager as she caught her eye. With Jake having found a friend in Sam, Annabelle had been worrying that Izzie might feel left out.

'Everyone ready?' Kate asked, bustling around, making sure people had fleeces, hoodies or cardigans, and delving into her bag for her car keys.

Annabelle followed Kate and Brett's car, acutely conscious of Ron's lean form in the passenger seat next to her.

She could almost feel his body heat, and once, when her hand brushed up against his leg as she changed gears, she almost jumped a mile, for which she apologised profusely. Not for the jumping, because she hoped he hadn't noticed her reaction, but for inadvertently touching him.

He apologised back, shifting in his seat and edging his thigh away.

She could smell him too, an outdoorsy, fresh male scent with a vague hint of soap and laundry detergent, unmasked by aftershave or cologne. It made her feel a little light-headed, but she put the woozy feeling down to having been out in the sun all day.

She was still feeling a little out-of-sorts when she clambered stiffly out of the car.

'Are you OK?' Ron asked.

'I'm fine.' His lips twitched at her answer, and she made a face. 'It's what you say when people ask, isn't it?' she added.

'Don't say you're fine if you're not,' he said.

'Just like you don't?' she arched an eyebrow.

'Touché.' He hesitated. 'Seriously, if there's anything I can help with...?'

'Unless you can magic me a house and a job—Shit!' Annabelle felt awful. 'Sorry, I didn't mean— I wasn't thinking—'

'No worries.' His smile was sad. 'I can't manage to magic a house up for myself, so I'm hardly likely to magic one up for you. I do, however, have a job, of sorts. You're welcome to share it.' His smile became teasing.

'Mum didn't say. What do you do?' Annabelle wondered if her mother knew, and if not, would the information change her opinion of him.

'Odd jobs. Your aunt rents me out now and again.' Another sad smile. 'You'd be surprised how many elderly people there are who need a leaky tap fixing or a bit of decorating done. It's not much, but it means I can pay my way.'

'I'm not implying that you don't.'

'I know you're not, but some people think that.'

'Helen?' Annabelle hazarded a guess. She thought her own mother could also be added to the list, and shame pricked at her.

'OK,' Kate called. 'If anyone gets separated, wait at the entrance to the shows. Do not – I repeat – *do not* leave the fair. Sam, I'm looking at you.'

'Mum...' Ellis rolled her eyes. 'I'm eighteen, not eight.'

'Obviously that rule doesn't apply to the adults or to Ellis and Portia. But please can everyone be at the entrance by ten o'clock?'

Without replying, the two older girls moved off, clearly eager to ditch their relatives. Annabelle didn't blame them; she would have felt the same at their age. But when she saw Izzie staring sadly after them, her heart went out to her daughter.

Annabelle wasn't the only one to notice.

Ron said, 'I know you can borrow Pepe when you're here, but how about if I try and win you a toy dog of your own?'

Oh, my goodness! What a lovely thing to say to a little girl who'd had to leave nearly all of her toys behind, Annabelle thought. Granny and Grandad had bought her a few more, but toys hadn't been at the top of anyone's list when Annabelle had been packing for what she'd assumed would be a three-week holiday.

'We'll take a stroll around, and you tell me which one you'd like me to try to win for you. There's no guarantee I will, though,' Ron warned, and Izzie nodded solemnly.

'Thank you,' Annabelle said, gratitude flooding through her.

He waited for Izzie to catch up with the boys, who were skipping ahead, before saying, 'I hope to God I can actually win one for her. I should never have promised.'

'It's the thought that counts,' Annabelle replied, 'and I'm sure Izzie will understand if you don't.' She wasn't sure at all, but she'd deal with that if it happened. For some reason, she didn't think it would – she had every faith that Ron would come through for her daughter.

As they walked along the promenade, Annabelle tried to let go of her ever-present worry about the future, and enjoy the evening.

Her children seemed happier than she'd seen them since she'd given them the news that the UK would now be their home, so that was a step in the right direction. And their happiness was her main concern, followed by where they were going to live, how she was going to support herself, would they settle into their new schools, would they make friends—?

Argh! Stop it, she admonished silently.

'You're fine again, aren't you?' Ron's tongue-in-cheek comment made her smile.

'Absolutely,' she agreed. 'Never better.'

'Good. I'd hate to think of you as not being fine.'

'We'll be OK,' Annabelle stated firmly.

'I know you will. You're tough, independent, resourceful…'

'Keep going,' Annabelle joked. 'I need the pep talk.'

'Intelligent, determined, beautiful.'

Annabelle faltered. Did Ron just say she was beautiful? She sneaked a glimpse at him out of the corner of her eye, but he was looking straight ahead, and she wondered whether he was simply being polite – after all, she'd practically invited and encouraged him to say nice things about her – or whether he'd actually meant what he'd said.

Interestingly, she rather hoped it was the latter.

***

'That one!' Izzie declared. 'I want that one.'

'Are you sure?' Ron asked.

The cuddly toy she was pointing at was small and fairly nondescript. It was a beanie type dog, roughly resembling a black Labrador puppy, and was small enough to sit in the palm of Ron's hand, should he succeed in winning it.

Annabelle was also surprised at her daughter's choice of toy. She would have expected her to go for something larger.

Izzie was emphatic. 'That's the one I want.'

'What about that one there?' Ron pointed to a huge brown and white dog which was almost as large as Izzie herself. Its face wore a manically cheerful expression.

Izzie shook her head. 'No. That one.'

'What's so special about that little dog?' Annabelle asked. The inner workings of her children's minds was an endless source of fascination to her.

'He's little, like Pepe, so I can take him with me.'

'Even if Ron won you the big one, you can still take him with you,' Annabelle pointed out.

'He's too big for the plane. The little one will fit in my rucksack.'

'Oh, my sweet girl, we won't be flying anywhere. We won't be going back.' A stab of pain to the heart caught Annabelle unawares and she stifled a sob, blinking away the bitter sting of tears. She thought she'd explained it to her children, but she realised that Izzie hadn't fully grasped the situation.

'Shall we see if I can win the little guy?' Ron said, handing some money over to the bloke manning the booth and picking up the three darts he'd been given in exchange. He sent Annabelle a slightly panicked look, and she had a feeling Ron had never thrown a dart in his life. Why couldn't Izzie have chosen a toy from the stall with the rifles and the ducks? He'd been in the army, so surely he could point and shoot?

Ron stood as close as he could and leaned forward as much as possible. The aim was to burst a balloon. How difficult could it be, right? But if it was as easy as it looked, the stallholder would be out of business in an afternoon, so what was the catch?

Despite not wanting to look, Annabelle couldn't help herself. The two boys were entranced, but Izzie had her hands over her face and was peeping through her fingers. Annabelle seriously considered doing the same.

Ron shuffled, getting his balance, one foot in front of the other, his focus on the yellow balloon in front of him. He pulled his arm back slightly, then slowly moved it forward, repeating the process twice more before he finally let the dart fly.

It bounced harmlessly off the balloon and dropped to the floor, and all three children let out a groan of disappointment.

'Go on, Ron, you can do it!' Sam urged, and Ron pulled a face.

The stallholder whipped forward to snatch the failed dart up, then stepped safely to the side as Ron prepared to throw again.

The same thing happened.

Ron muttered under his breath, and Annabelle looked away. She didn't want to see her daughter's face when the third and final dart clattered to the ground.

Another groan told her the outcome of his final throw, and when she looked at Izzie her daughter had her thumb in her mouth – something she'd grown out of when she was about four or five, but had started doing again since she'd learned that her whole world had been turned upside down. Over the past couple of weeks the thumb-sucking had eased off a little, and Annabelle had been starting to hope that Izzie was losing the habit. However, it was back with a vengeance today.

'What a shame,' Annabelle said. 'Ron did his best.' She shot him an apologetic look, and he mouthed 'Sorry,' back at her.

He was clearly as disappointed as she, and she guessed he was kicking himself for having said he'd try to win the toy in the first place.

Izzie looked up at her, her eyes brimming with tears. She took her thumb out of her mouth for long enough to say, 'I know,' then she shoved it straight back in again, and Annabelle realised just how badly her daughter had wanted the toy.

'There's got to be a shop or two selling cuddly toys,' Annabelle said, draping her arm around Izzie's thin shoulders and pulling her into a hug as she drew her away from the stall. They could have a look along the front, where she'd noticed loads of kiosks and shops – one of them must surely have a similar toy for sale.

Maybe some candyfloss would help take Izzie's mind off it, or a ride on the Ghost Train?

'Wait up,' Ron called from behind, and Annabelle stopped. She was surprised to see him grinning from ear to ear, and when she saw what he was holding she was amazed.

'I did it!' he said, handing Izzie the stuffed dog. 'I had one more go…'

Izzie cradled the toy, cuddling it to her chest. Her face was beaming. 'Thank you. I love him. I'm going to call him Pepe,' she announced.

'Won't that be confusing, having two dogs called Pepe?' Ron asked.

Izzie shook her head emphatically. 'His name is Pepe. He looks just like Aunt Beverley's Pepe,' the little girl insisted.

Annabelle thought that the only thing the real Pepe and the toy Pepe had in common was their colour, but she didn't say anything and her smile was indulgent as she watched her daughter scamper off to show Jake and Sam her prize.

'You didn't actually win it, did you?' she asked Ron out of the side of her mouth, her smile still in place, her eyes on Izzie.

'No.'

'How much did you pay for it?'

'As much as I needed to.'

'I suspect you paid much more than it was worth.'

'I paid what it is worth to Izzie,' Ron said quietly, a small smile playing about his lips.

Annabelle narrowed her eyes. 'You paid that much, eh?'

'To Izzie it's priceless.' Ron's grin widened. 'Look at her!'

Annabelle hadn't stopped looking. She couldn't take her gaze off her daughter. 'She's thrilled to bits you won it for her.'

'Exactly!'

Annabelle abruptly stopped walking and Ron came to a halt. 'You're a nice man, Ron,' she said, leaning towards him and kissing him on the cheek.

Ron looked stunned.

Annabelle was fairly stunned herself because as her lips touched his skin, she'd felt a tingle shoot down her body, ending at her toes.

Ron's eyes bored into hers, and he lifted his fingers to touch the place on his cheek where she'd kissed him.

Gosh, had he felt it too?

Unlikely, Annabelle concluded. He was probably just wiping away the moisture left by her sloppy peck.

But she couldn't drag her eyes away from his, and she had a feeling he wanted to kiss her back. A proper kiss.

'Can you win *me* something?' Sam's voice was a welcome interruption and Annabelle broke Ron's gaze with relief.

'I've used up all my luck for one day,' Ron told the boy. 'How about I take you and Jake rock pooling tomorrow, if Jake wants to come?' Ron glanced at her, questioningly.

'I'm sure he'll be delighted,' she said.

'Izzie can come as well,' Ron added. 'I don't want her to feel left out.'

'That's very kind of you, but please don't feel sorry for us. We'll be fine.'

'So you keep saying. Anyway, I don't feel sorry for you.'

Annabelle looked away. Of course he didn't. From where he was standing, he probably thought she had a fair bit going for her: a roof over her head, parents who loved and supported her emotionally and financially, two gorgeous children...

'I'll buy the lads some buckets and nets,' she said, spying a stall selling colourful beachy stuff and kiss-me-quick hats. Anything to get away from the depths of Ron's eyes. Whenever she looked into them, they did funny things to her insides.

Thankfully, just then the others caught up with them, and the strange atmosphere between her and Ron dissipated, and for the rest of the evening she studiously avoided looking in his direction.

Not because she didn't like him. It was the exact opposite.

But it would benefit no one, least of all her, if Ron were to suspect she was developing feelings for him. Especially since she had no idea what to do with them and even less intention of acting on them.

CHAPTER 9

Ron heard Beverley's shriek coming from inside the house just as he was getting out of Annabelle's car.

Without stopping to think, he ran towards the open front door and bolted inside, his heart in his mouth. His first thought was that someone was injured, but as he scooted to a halt in the hall, he was thankful to see that neither Beverley, Kate, Brett nor Helen appeared to be hurt.

'Where are the girls?' he demanded, failing to see Ellis or Portia.

'What?' Kate looked at him with a distracted expression.

'Ellis? Portia? Has something happened? Are they OK?'

'They're fine. They've gone upstairs.'

'Then why—?'

'You had no right!' Beverley cried, glowering at Helen and cutting off Ron's question. She put a wriggling Pepe down on the floor, and the dog immediately scampered up the stairs.

Ron was dimly aware of Annabelle, Sam and the other children crowding in behind, as he tried to work out what was going on.

Helen had the look of a cat that had got the cream, and his heart sank. Even before she opened her mouth, he guessed what had happened. No wonder she'd wanted to remain behind this evening – she must have been planning her revenge ever since Beverley had ousted her from her original bedroom.

'I just thought you'd be better off in the room next to the bathroom.' Helen dropped her voice to a whisper which could clearly be heard by everyone. 'What with your bladder problems.'

'I don't have a bladder problem.' Beverley was indignant.

'But isn't that why you said you should have had the twin room I was in? I'm sure I heard you say that was the reason you wanted it. Remember? When we arrived and we were deciding who should sleep where? Because it has an en suite?' Helen's smile was triumphant.

Not again, Ron thought. Hadn't the pair of them caused enough trouble last Christmas when they'd feuded over who was going to sleep in Kate and Brett's spare room? And now they were at it again.

Ron risked a quick peep at the double bedroom that Beverley had ended up with. Pepe's basket was no longer next to the bed, and he felt like groaning. Dear God, did these two never learn?

Kate looked at Brett, and Brett looked at Kate. As one, they shrugged and headed for the stairs.

'Kate! Where do you think you're going?' Beverley demanded. 'You have to sort this out.'

'No, Mum, I don't. The two of you need to grow up.'

'But she's moved my things.' Beverley was determined not to let it lie.

'You moved hers,' Kate pointed out reasonably.

Annabelle pushed past him. 'I think it's better all round if we left,' she said, gesturing to her children. 'Then you can go back to the rooms you had before we came.' She looked upset, and Ron wanted to knock the old ladies' heads together.

'Now look what you've done!' Beverley cried, her hands on her hips, her mouth a thin line as she scowled at Helen.

'Stop it!' Brett yelled from halfway up the stairs. He came back down them, his eyes flashing with annoyance. 'I've got a better idea. If you two can't stop arguing, you can bugger off home.'

'Brett!' Helen sounded aghast.

Beverley opened her mouth, then closed it again, obviously thinking better of it.

'I mean it,' Brett said. 'You're not spoiling this holiday the way you spoiled Christmas.'

Beverley took a deep breath, walked over to Annabelle and caught hold of her hands. 'Please don't go. I'm happy to have the single room. I was just a bit shocked, that's all.' She glared at Helen.

Helen glared back, but Ron saw the smugness in her eyes.

Beverley continued, 'Brett, I'm sorry about Christmas, but I wouldn't change what happened for all the tea in China, because otherwise I wouldn't have met Ron.' She looked across at Ron and gave him a watery smile.

Aw, knickers, Ron thought, his emotions churning and tumbling. He nodded at her, and bit his lip. 'I'm, erm, shattered,' he said, wanting nothing more than to escape the supercharged atmosphere. 'I'll have to say goodnight.'

He headed to his room, giving Beverley's arm a pat as he went, and darted inside. His was also a single, but unlike the squabbling old ladies, he didn't care which room he had – he was just grateful for a roof over his head and for being asked to come on this holiday.

Flopping down on the bed fully clothed, the mattress bouncing underneath him, he felt perilously close to tears. He knew Beverley had become as attached to him as he was to her, but what she'd just said made his heart ache.

He knew he had to leave, he couldn't stay with her forever, but he now realised how much it was going to hurt her when he did, and the last thing he wanted to do was to cause the kind, cantankerous, thoughtful, irascible old lady any pain.

He lay there until the house fell silent, then with a muttered curse he swung his feet off the bed. The walls were closing in on him and he needed to get some fresh air. Being outside, away from the lingering tension, would give him a chance to think.

Ron crept out of his room, careful not to make a noise, and padded upstairs to grab a throw from the back of the sofa, then let himself quietly out of the house.

As he was pulling the front door closed behind him, he thought he heard a muffled woof from Pepe and he held his breath for a moment, but when he heard nothing further he headed down the drive.

He'd only gone a few paces before he immediately felt calmer and more grounded. He knew he'd made the right decision as his feet took him in the direction of the dunes, and with each step he took, he breathed a little easier.

The night was a warm one, the air still, and the further he walked from Rest Bay, the darker it became and the quieter it grew. The only sounds were that of the rhythmic pounding of the waves, like the earth's steadily beating heart, the occasional rustle as some small creature moved through the grass, and his footsteps.

When he felt he'd gone far enough, he slowed, looking for the best place to snuggle down in the sand, and when he found a sheltered spot in a dip between the dunes, he sank down and draped the throw over him.

Breathing deeply, he let the peace of the night soothe him, and he gazed up at the stars until sleep eventually came.

***

'Whaaa?' Ron grunted as something snuffled in his ear and a wet tongue slobbered up his cheek. A weight settled on his chest and he grunted again. 'Geddofff.'

Without opening his eyes he knew he was being assaulted by a happy dog, and from the feel of its curly coat and the lingering smell of Anais Anais, Beverley's favourite perfume, he was fairly confident it was Pepe.

Ron pushed the persistent poodle off and sat up, blinking the sleep from his eyes. For a second he wondered where he was and what he was doing here, until last night's shenanigans came flooding back and he flopped back down with a sigh. Pepe, delighted to find his human companion down on his level once more, launched another enthusiastic attack.

Ron fended the dog off, then abruptly sat up again as a thought occurred to him. 'What are you doing here?' he asked him. 'I hope you're not on your own?'

Clambering to his feet and brushing the sand off his clothes, Ron scrambled to the top of a dune and gazed around.

Apart from the dog, a bee or two and several seagulls wheeling overhead, he was alone. Wondering what the time was, he turned to face the east, and took a guess that it was no earlier than about five am, and no later than about eight.

'Where's your mistress?' he asked Pepe, shading his eyes with his hand as he squinted in the direction of Rest Bay. 'Have you escaped?'

Pepe sat on his haunches and gazed up at him, his brown button eyes giving nothing away.

'You have, haven't you? I bet your mum is going frantic. Heel,' he commanded, and the dog obediently followed him as he began to make his way back.

Wishing he'd thought to bring some water, Ron trudged over the dunes and cursed himself for not waking up sooner. He'd intended to return to the house before anyone was up, but stargazing until the silver light of pre-dawn streaked the sky had scuppered that plan. Flipping heck, he was out of practice at sleeping outside. For Pepe to have sneaked up on him and practically licked his face off, would have once been unthinkable. He never used to sleep very deeply – he hadn't risked it – but eight months in a comfy bed with a securely locked front door had softened him.

Feeling irked, he grizzled to himself under his breath, until the dog's whining made him stop. 'Sorry, boy, am I getting on your nerves?' he asked, then he came to a halt as he realised that it was something else that had made Pepe whimper.

Ron listened intently, his head swivelling from side to side.

It took him a moment to hear it too.

'P-e-e-e-e-p-e-e-e-!' It was a drawn out call, the kind of call a person had been making for some time.

Pepe whined again.

'That's Kate,' Ron said to him. 'But I expect you already know that. Hurry up, we'd better tell her you're safe and well.'

Ron broke into a jog, and soon spotted her in the distance.

She waved, then cupped a hand around her mouth. 'Have you seen Pepe?' she yelled.

Ron pointed at his feet his movements exaggerated. 'He's here. I've got him,' he shouted back, and he saw her sag with relief as she bent forward at the waist and put her hands on her hips.

She was still in the same position when he reached her. Pepe, unconcerned, wagged his tail at her, then found a fascinating smell to sniff.

Kate straightened up, still panting. 'Bloody hell, we've been looking all over for him. Where did you find him?'

Ron was saved from an immediate reply by the sound of Brett hollering in the distance, as he made his way towards them.

'You've found him!' Brett exclaimed when he grew close enough not to have to shout. 'Where was the little blighter?'

'In the dunes,' Ron said. '*He* found *me.*'

'Thank God! Beverley has been worried sick. She was on the phone to the police when we left. Not that they can do anything, but at least if someone did find him and hand him in, the police would know where we are staying.'

'How did he get out?' Ron asked, hoping to goodness it hadn't been his fault. He didn't think he'd left the door open, but he'd been so keen for some alone time that he mightn't have been paying enough attention to shutting it properly.

Kate said, 'Mum got up at around five-thirty to go to the bathroom, and she let Pepe out for a wee. He was standing by the front door, so she opened that instead of making him go into the garden at the back. She assumed he'd cock his leg and come straight in, but the little sod ran off.'

'I'm sorry,' Ron said, then felt even more guilty when he saw Annabelle approach with the three younger children and noticed Izzie's tear-streaked face.

'Pepe!' Izzie sobbed, running towards them and throwing herself to the ground when she got within cuddling distance. She was clutching her toy Pepe tightly, he noticed, and he guessed the cuddly dog would be going everywhere with her.

Pepe seemed equally pleased to see the child, smothering her face in kisses, very much as he'd done to Ron.

'Sorry, Kate, I tried to persuade Beverley to remain at the house but she insisted on coming to look for him,' Annabelle said, as Beverley's rotund figure hurried into view. She was panting and her face was red.

Concerned, Ron dashed forward, took the old lady by the arm and guided her to the nearest bench, Izzie following, carrying a wriggling poodle in her arms, as well as her toy dog. Izzie solemnly deposited her charge onto Beverley's lap.

'Ooh, you naughty, naughty boy!' Beverley wheezed. 'You gave your mama such a fright. Don't you dare do that again.' She wagged her finger at him. Pepe licked it, then struggled to get down. 'Here,' she said to Ron. 'Put his lead on him. I don't trust the little bugger not to run off again.'

Ron actually did trust him, because Pepe hadn't actually run off – the dog had come looking for *him*. But he did as he was asked and clipped the lead to Pepe's collar.

'You are out early,' Beverley said. Her gaze was penetrating. 'He must have heard you go and decided to follow you when I let him out for a pee.'

'Sorry,' was all he said. He didn't want to admit to sleeping outside all night, but the way Beverley was scrutinising him made him think she'd guessed anyway.

It took her a few minutes to get her breath back, but finally Beverley was ready to make the trek back to the house. She was such a determined and robust lady, that he had to keep reminding himself she was no spring chicken, and he felt an immense sense of guilt that he was the cause of her distress. If he could have slung her over his shoulders and carried her back to the house, he would have.

On the return journey, Ron hung back, feeling awkward.

'Early walk, was it?' Annabelle fell into step beside him. She stared pointedly at the throw he was carrying.

'Not really,' he admitted.

'I didn't think so.'

'I had to get away for a bit.'

'You should have said – I'd have joined you. I almost packed up and went home last night after yet another bedroom fiasco. If it wasn't for the kids, I would have.'

'It did get a bit fraught,' Ron said. 'I don't understand why Beverley and Helen don't get on.'

'They're totally different people, I guess,' Annabelle said. She was quiet for a moment. 'When you weren't in your room, I wondered whether you'd left for good.'

He tilted his head to the side as he thought about what she'd just said. Most people would never consider the possibility that he might have gone back to living on the streets. A homeless man being given a roof over his head, three meals a day, all the baths or showers he could wish for? It would never occur to them that he would give it all up and go back to sleeping rough – because who in their right mind would swap a house for a park bench or a shop doorway?

But it had occurred to Annabelle, and he was grateful to her for not assuming that he thought he had it made living with Beverley. He knew her mother thought that, and Helen clearly did.

'It did cross my mind,' he admitted.

'I'm glad you stayed.'

Ron turned shocked eyes to her and his heart missed a beat.

'Beverley would miss you if you went,' she added, and he swallowed and coughed as his heartbeat returned to a more normal rhythm when he realised what she'd meant was that *Beverley* would miss him, not that Annabelle herself would.

'Was it cold without a tent or a sleeping bag?' she asked.

'No, not last night. It was quite warm. Sand retains a lot of the sun's heat.'

He could see her thinking, and he fully expected her to ask about the trials of sleeping rough.

'It was a clear night,' she said instead. 'I sat in the garden for a while.'

'The stars are even better when you get away from the street lights,' he said, as though trying to persuade her it was one of the reasons for him doing a bunk last night.

'I bet they are. It must have been magical.'

'It was.'

'I'd love to see them sometime. If you do it again, could I come with you?'

'If you like,' Ron said. He meant it, but he didn't think she did. She'd forget she'd asked.

Ron wished he could forget too, but an image of them lying on their backs, their faces turned towards the heavens, was to stay with him for a long time.

CHAPTER 10

This morning Annabelle was taking the children to the beach, and she was really looking forward to it, even though it would be vastly different to the beaches she'd spent the last twenty or so years on. This one was a British beach – a completely different bucket of sand to the ones she was used to.

Whenever Annabelle remembered days on the beach when she was a child, it usually involved her parents trying to balance fold-up deckchairs on the ever-shifting pebbles of Brighton beach, often still wearing their coats, whilst she ran back and forth to the water. Blue with cold and shivering fit to burst, they would dry her off and warm her up, then she'd do it all over again.

There had been some gloriously hot days, of course, but when they occurred so many people flocked to the beach that her parents tended to stay away, though when Annabelle was older, she used to lie out on a towel with her friends, all of them wearing the skimpiest of bikinis, to watch the world go by.

Those were the days… young, carefree, with the future sprawling ahead of them like an unexplored city, none of them knowing what direction fate might take them in, but all of them convinced that it had to be better than going to school and living at home under their parents' watchful eyes.

Huh! Look at her now: she was once again living with her parents, and they nagged just as much as they'd done when she was a child. At least, her mum did, although her dad wasn't so bad. She loved them to bits, but she needed her own space. As soon as she'd sorted herself out with paid employment, she'd find somewhere to live, she vowed.

Annabelle took a couple of towels out of a bag and flicked them expertly, so they drifted down onto the sand, then she held onto Beverley's arm as her aunt lowered herself slowly onto one of them. Pepe staked a claim on the other.

Ron dropped his rucksack next to the towels. 'I've brought a couple more to dry the kids off,' he said, 'and both the flasks are in there as well, along with some cold drinks.'

'Marvellous.' Annabelle smiled at him, before quickly turning her attention to the children. Izzie was on her knees, making a hole by scooping out handfuls of sand, and the two boys were dancing on their toes, eager to be off for the promised rockpool expedition.

'Come on, Ron,' Sam urged, making swinging motions with his net. He bobbed it onto Jake's head and Jake returned the favour.

'Careful with those, you'll have someone's eye out,' Beverley cautioned, wrapping her hand firmly around Pepe's leash. 'Pass me the flask with the tea in, will you, lovey? I'm parched.'

Annabelle undid Ron's rucksack and brought out the two flasks.

'Do you want a drink before you go?' she asked him.

'I'd better not. This lot might lynch me if I keep them waiting any longer.'

She watched him round up the children and her gaze followed him as he led them across the sand towards the recently exposed rocks. The tide was going out, and even in the few minutes since she'd laid out the towels, more people had ventured onto the sand. So far, most of them were clustered near the lifeguard station and the slipway, because that was where the sand was the driest, but Ron had aimed for a damper patch to the left of it, nearer to the rocks, and that was where Annabelle, Beverley, and Pepe now sat.

'It's going to be hot again today,' Beverley declared, as Annabelle poured them both a cup of tea. 'I hope you've brought plenty of sunscreen.'

'I have, and spare clothes and hats.' She was used to being beach ready, and so were her children.

Jake and Izzie, after checking that they were indeed going rock pooling as promised, had lathered themselves in Factor 30, and had plonked hats on their heads. Jake had encouraged Sam to do the same, although Kate had also made sure her son had creamed up before she left. She was dropping Portia off at the stables, then she and Ellis were having a spa day. Kate had begged Annabelle to come with them, saying that Ron was perfectly capable of supervising the younger ones, and Brett and his mother would be back from golf by lunchtime, so Brett would take over childminding duties, but Annabelle had refused. Not because she didn't trust Ron to look after her children (despite knowing him for less than two days, she did) or that she wouldn't enjoy a spa day (she would), but she couldn't justify the expense. She might be living rent free with her parents who didn't expect her to contribute anything to the bills, and she might still have some dollars left in her bank account – her final wages from her employer, plus a bit she'd saved up for their trip to the UK – but she was acutely conscious that she needed to be careful with money. Paying for the kids to go on the rides last night had made her wince, and she was aware that Jake was desperate to go surfing. In fact, there were several wetsuit-clad people already playing in the waves, boards at the ready.

'Didn't you want to go to the spa?' Beverley asked, reading her mind. She sipped her tea and smacked her lips. 'Ah, that's the ticket,' she sighed.

'Not really.'

'If it's because of Ron, you can trust him with the kids. Whatever your mother has said about him, you should take with a pinch of salt. You can tell her from me that he's not after my money.' Beverley barked out a laugh. 'He knows I haven't bloody got any!'

'I didn't think he was,' Annabelle replied, mildly. She could see Ron and the children on the rocks, Ron holding a hand out to help Izzie now and again. Occasionally a faint shout reached her as one or the other of them spotted something lurking in the depths of a pool.

'He's a good man,' Beverley continued, following Annabelle's gaze. 'He's brilliant with Sam. I wish Brett had come to the beach with us this morning – he'd be better off spending more time with the boy. And it might have done Helen more good if she'd gone with Kate to the spa.'

'I'm not sure Kate would have been too happy, though,' Annabelle said with a wry grin. 'If I'm not mistaken there seems to be a bit of an atmosphere between them.'

'Helen's a right cow,' Beverley said cheerfully. 'She played me at my own game all right. One all,' she crowed, as though she was calling out a football score. 'I didn't expect her to do that.'

'You were a bit upset last night, but you appear to be OK about it now,' Annabelle replied tentatively.

'Don't worry, I'll get her back. I'm good at biding my time. Anyway, if we don't play nice Brett may very well tell us to sling our hooks. It wouldn't be the first time.'

'Oh?' Despite not wanting to take sides and feeling that she should probably keep an open mind, Annabelle couldn't help being curious.

Beverley shook the dregs of tea out of her plastic cup and set it to one side. 'You know that I usually go to your mum's for Christmas?'

Annabelle nodded.

'Well, last year she and your dad went out to visit you, so I decided I wouldn't spend Christmas on my own – I'd go to Kate and Brett's. The problem was, Helen always goes to them for Christmas, and she wasn't pleased that I was there, too. We had a bit of a tussle over rooms, because Kate's only got the one spare bedroom, and Ellis and Portia were being right little madams and showing off about having to share to free up another room. There was some argy-bargy and tempers got frayed. Season of goodwill, my peachy arse! Pepe didn't help, either – he stole a leg of lamb that was meant for our evening meal, and he peed on Brett's shoes. Oh, and he did a whoopsie on the carpet in Kate's bedroom.' Beverley bit her lip and pulled a face. 'You were a naughty boy, weren't you?' Pepe pricked his ears but didn't look up – he was quite happy snoozing in the sun, curled up next to his mistress.

'Anyway,' Beverley continued, 'to cut a long story short, it all blew up when Kate overheard Helen saying that Brett should never have married her. See what I mean when I say Helen is a cow?'

Annabelle was shocked. If what Beverley said was true, Helen was even worse than Annabelle thought. However, she told herself, she was only hearing Beverley's side of the story. Before she passed judgement, she really should hear Helen's side – but she couldn't imagine asking her for it. 'What happened then?'

'Kate buggered off. She just upped and left. Went to Paignton or somewhere near there. Left us to get on with Christmas without her.' Beverley shrugged. 'I don't blame her. All of us except for Brett and Sam were fighting like cats and dogs. Me and Helen were at each other's throats, the girls were being right brats, and Brett was about as much help as a chocolate fireguard. He buried his head in the sand and hoped it would all go away.' She fell silent, her eyes narrowed against the glare of the sun on the water as she stared out to sea.

'*And?*' Annabelle was agog. Beverley couldn't just leave it there!

'Kate had had enough. She disappeared and didn't tell anyone where she was going. It wasn't permanent – just for Christmas. She wanted to see how we managed without her. When Brett realised what his mother had said and how Kate must be feeling, he read us the riot act and went to fetch her back.'

'Wow, that's some story.' Annabelle thought for a moment, then said, 'How does Ron fit into all this?'

'He was the one who gave Brett a clue as to where she might be. See, Ron used to like kipping down in the doorway of the shop Kate works in. Kate used to buy him food now and again, and supplied him with coffee and clean clothes. They got to chatting one day near Christmas and she told him she felt like running away, and that the south coast sounded good. Anyway, after she did a runner, Brett was trying to find out where she'd gone, and he bumped into Ron. The rest is history. Oh, apart from Brett inviting him to Christmas lunch as a thank you.'

'That doesn't explain how he came to live with you.'

'Pepe,' Beverley said with a purse of her lips. 'I love him to bits, but that dog can be a menace. Ron used to be a dog handler, you know. In the army.'

'He did mention it.' Annabelle was intrigued. 'Do you know what happened? Why he ended up living on the streets?'

'Not the full story, no. It's something to do with his marriage breaking up, his mum dying, and there's a dog in there somewhere, but I don't know the details. It sounds to me like he had some kind of a breakdown.'

'The poor man.'

'He was only supposed to come to me for a couple of weeks, just until he taught Pepe some manners, but I've got used to him being around the place.' Beverley shot Annabelle a look. 'I know what you're thinking – that he hasn't done a very good job with Pepe – but I assure you he has. Pepe running off this morning was

93

him. I don't know what got into him. He
heard Ron go out for a walk and thought
have gone too. The little sod.'

'Ron or Pepe?' Annabelle asked dryly.

'Ha ha.' Beverley scratched behind the dog's ears
and he let out a groan of pleasure.

Annabelle shaded her eyes with her hand. The four
figures could still be seen clambering about on the
rocks. 'Kate and Brett seem to be OK now.'

'They are.' Beverley's reply was emphatic. 'They
appreciate each other more, and Brett's got a new job
as the manager of a golf course, which means he's
happier. He helps around the house now as well,
instead of leaving it all to Kate, and the girls also do
their share. Don't get me wrong, Ellis and Portia still
fight, just like me and Helen, but we all try to get on a
bit better.'

Annabelle gave her aunt a sideways look.

'OK, me and Helen have a tendency to revert to
our old ways – I mean, you've met her, so you can't
blame me for winding her up – but we are trying to
get along, hence the holiday. Helen is uppity and
frosty, and I appreciate that she can be hard work, but
it's not all her fault. I sometimes go out of my way to
annoy her, especially when she forgets herself and
treats Ron like the hired help.'

Annabelle leant back on her hands and stretched
her legs out in front of her, suddenly feeling pleased
that her mum had talked her into coming on this
impromptu holiday.

It was nice getting to know Aunt Beverley
properly. When she was younger, Annabelle hadn't
had a great deal to do with her, content to leave the
chatting to her parents. She hadn't been interested in

the lives of her elders – she'd been too wrapped up in her own life, she supposed.

But now, though, she was enjoying talking to her.

'What about you, lovey?' Beverley asked, breaking into her thoughts. 'How are you coping?'

Annabelle sat up and tucked her legs in. She made a seesaw motion with her hand. 'So, so.'

'Do you miss Australia?'

'Er, actually, now I come to think of it, not as much as I thought I was going to. I miss my house, but I think I only miss it because it was mine and I could do what I liked in it. I miss my job, but not because of the job itself but because of the independence it gave me, and I miss my friends.' But apart from the odd text or two, none of them had really reached out to her. She missed Pauline the most. They messaged each other a couple of times a week, but it wasn't the same as having a proper chinwag over a coffee.

Beverley tutted. 'It's the children I feel sorry for. How could their father do that to them?' She shook her head and covered Pepe's ears. 'The bastard.'

'Exactly. I don't know what he was thinking.'

Beverley said, 'He probably wasn't thinking at all. Or at least, he didn't think his business would go under.'

'Any sensible person would realise that's a possibility,' Annabelle pointed out. 'And he should have told me he'd taken out a loan against the house. At least I could have prepared myself.'

'Oh, lovey, it must have been a shock.' Beverley patted her hand, and Annabelle felt tears gathering behind her eyes.

'It was. I don't know if I told you, but I only found out on the plane. We were just about to go to the airport, when the mail came. We were already out of the door, so I stuffed it in my carry-on and forgot about it until one of the kids went in my bag. I nearly howled when I read it.'

'But what about all your things? Your furniture? Your clothes? The kids' toys?'

Annabelle thought about her daughter wanting Ron to win her the little dog rather than the great big one, and the reason why, and a knife twisted in her heart. 'We had to leave everything behind. My neighbour had a key to the house, and as soon as I got to the UK I rang her and told her what had happened, and asked her if she could let herself in and box up the personal stuff – things like the kid's birth certificates, and other important documents. She also rescued my jewellery – not that I have a lot – and stuff from when the children were little that are precious to me. She posted it all off, bless her, and the parcel arrived a couple of weeks ago.'

Annabelle was still tracking Ron and the children, and she noticed that Sam and Jake had gone for a swim. Izzie was holding Ron's hand and the two of them were up to their knees, the buckets and nets on the sand behind them.

'Have you thought about where you're going to live?' Beverley asked, adding, 'I know you're welcome to stay with May and Terence for as long as you need, but I get the feeling you'll want a place of your own sooner rather than later.'

'Too right! Mum and Dad have been fab, but it can't be easy for them to suddenly have their adult daughter and her two kids living in their house.'

Beverley patted her hand again. 'It will sort itself out. You're still in shock, so be kind to yourself. You don't have to do everything at once. One step at a time, eh? At least the children are enrolled in school, so as soon as the term starts you'll have a bit more time to yourself to decide what you want to do. And if there's ever anything I can do to help…?' Beverley left the sentence hanging.

'Thank you; I really appreciate it.' Those treacherous tears were close to the surface again, and Annabelle blinked them away.

She was about to pour them another cup of tea, thinking that after the conversation they'd just had they could do with one, when a scream made her drop the flask on the towel.

Dread surged through her when she realised the sound had come from one of the children.

Without stopping to think, she leapt to her feet and raced down the beach, fear lending speed to her legs.

Sam was lying on the sand, Ron crouched next to him. Jake and Izzie were standing, watching. Jake had his head bowed.

Oh, God…

She skidded to a halt, her feet making trenches in the sand. 'What happened?' she cried, then she saw what her son was doing and she immediately knew why he was doing it.

Sam had been stung by a jellyfish.

Suddenly, a small black form rushed past her, aimed itself at Sam, and before she realised what was happening Pepe had cocked his leg and was contributing his watery offering by weeing over Sam's leg, too.

Sam leapt to his feet with a shriek, and danced around, his expression one of horror.

'Jellyfish,' Ron said, confirming her suspicion. He stood up slowly.

'Oh, my God, has he definitely been stung?' A bolt of fear struck her in the chest. Please no, not a jellyfish… It could be fatal.

'Thankfully not, but it came close enough to give him a fright,' Ron said.

'Are you sure? Jellyfish stings can—' She stopped abruptly not wanting to scare the children any more than they were already. Jake and Izzie were aware of how serious a sting from certain species of jellyfish could be, but Sam probably wasn't.

Then she caught herself, remembering that they were no longer in Australia, where being stung by a jellyfish could have very serious consequences indeed. They were on a beach in South Wales, and the odds of being stung by that kind of jellyfish were very slim. The wave of relief which washed over her made her feel weak and slightly shaky.

Sam abruptly dropped to the ground again, grabbed a handful of sand and began scrubbing furiously at his leg.

'It's all right, Mum – I peed on it.' Jake announced.

Annabelle swallowed and took a deep breath. 'You know that's a myth, right?'

Izzie slipped a hand in hers, her little face white, and said, 'It didn't really sting him, Mum. It swam close to him, and he got scared. He shouted, and Jake thought he'd been stung so he peed on him.'

Sam stopped scrubbing and turned a disgusted face towards her. 'Jake peed on me, and so did Pepe. Ew.'

He made retching noised and grabbed another handful of sand.

'Why don't you wash it off in the sea?' Ron suggested.

Sam looked even more horrified. 'I'm not going in *there*. There's a jellyfish.'

'There are loads, probably,' Jake told him. 'They swarm, like bees.'

Sam backed away from the water, shaking his head.

'They're venomous,' her son continued, and Annabelle gave him a look to shut him up.

'That's only in Australia,' she said. It wasn't strictly true, but Sam hadn't actually been stung, so it was a moot point, and she didn't want him to be scared of the sea.

'Listen to your Aunty Annabelle,' Ron advised. 'She knows what she's talking about.'

Sam stood up, holding his leg out to the side, his nose wrinkling in disgust. 'Are you sure?' he asked her.

She said, 'Totally sure.'

'But Jake peed on me, and so did Pepe,' he wailed.

'They were only trying to help,' Annabelle said. 'There's an old wives' tale that if you urinate on a jellyfish sting it can stop it from hurting as much. They can be excruciatingly painful.'

Pepe, having played his part, scratched at the sand with his hind paws, kicking up a spray of wet granules, then trotted off up the beach in the direction of his mistress, who was calling frantically for him.

'There's a standpipe on the causeway,' Ron said. 'You can wash your leg there, and there's a change of clothes in one of the rucksacks. OK?'

Sam nodded. 'Aunty Annabelle, I've got a starfish and a crab in my bucket,' he told her, and she was pleased to see that the incident didn't seem to have had a lasting effect.

'Let's get you cleaned up, then you can show me,' she said. 'Are you hungry? Aunt Beverley has made us a lovely picnic.'

The children raced off to collect their buckets and nets, leaving Annabelle with Ron.

She glanced at him and noticed his lips twitching, and when he turned away she realised that he wanted to laugh but daren't – not when Sam was still in earshot.

'I can't believe how calm you were,' she said. 'I was freaking out.'

'You're probably still in Australia mode. From what I can gather, nearly everything out there wants to kill you.'

'Not everything,' she argued.

'Duck-billed platypus,' he stated flatly. 'A mammal with enough venom to incapacitate a grown man for weeks. I rest my case.'

'Fair point,' she conceded. 'Although, I don't think they can kill you.'

'I wouldn't want to find out, would you?'

Annabelle giggled, feeling quite giddy now the fear had gone. 'Definitely not!'

'Now that's settled, shall we sort the kids out, then grab a bite to eat? All this excitement has given me an appetite.'

Annabelle fell into step alongside him, but it wasn't food on her mind; it was the way he'd dealt with the children, Sam especially. He'd been calm and level-headed, and once again she had the feeling that he was trustworthy and dependable. The contrast between him and Troy was glaring.

And there was something else: when he'd said, "shall we sort the kids out", she'd had a fleeting image of what it might be like if he was her children's father. Quickly followed by what it might be like to have him in her bed.

Because no matter how much she tried to deny it, or how much she didn't need or want a man in her life, Ron Masters was starting to bore his way into her heart.

CHAPTER 11

'**M**um says that peeing on a jellyfish sting is an old wives' tale,' Jake said.

'It is,' Annabelle replied. 'Here – look it up for yourself.' She handed Jake her mobile phone.

'Even if I had been stung, Jake would have peed on me for no reason because peeing doesn't work,' Sam said. He rolled his eyes, and there were chuckles around the dinner table. The boy was recounting his story yet again, and with each retelling the size of the jellyfish grew and the episode became even more dramatic. Sam was playing to his audience and loving it, and Annabelle smiled indulgently. He seemed to have recovered, and was even talking about having a go at surfing.

When Ron rose to start collecting the dirty plates, Kate waved him back down.

'Stay there,' she instructed. 'You and Brett cooked, so me and Annabelle will clear up. If that's OK with you, Annabelle?'

'Of course it is.' Annabelle got to her feet, and the younger children made a dash for the door and the lure of the games room downstairs.

Kate called out, 'Hold it right there, kids! You're not in the clear yet. Put your plates on the counter next to the dishwasher, please. You, too, Ellis and Portia. What are your plans for this evening?'

Ellis shrugged, but Portia said, 'She'll be Facetiming Riley, like she does every night.' Portia made a kissy face and Ellis elbowed her.

'You're just jealous because you can't Facetime your horse,' Ellis countered.

'Yeah, because Starlight is way better looking than Riley,' Portia countered.

'Are you saying my boyfriend is ugly? At least I've got one!' Ellis pulled a face.

'I don't want one,' Portia replied loftily.

'Oh yeah? What about that boy in your geography class? Dillon, is it? I heard you talking to…'

Their voices became indistinct as the girls left the room, still bickering, and Kate blew out her cheeks.

'When they are babies you have this idea that they'll be great friends and will keep each other company and stick together no matter what. Now look at them.' She began rinsing the plates and stacking them in the dishwasher.

Annabelle made a start on the saucepans. 'I notice Sam stays out of it.'

'He has his moments, but for the most part he's just their annoying little brother. Your two seem to get on, though.'

'They have their moments, too. Right now they're on their best behaviour. I think it's because they feel they've only got each other.'

'They've also got you,' Kate pointed out.

'I'm not so sure they see it that way. Jake hasn't totally forgiven me – he blames me for not going back to Australia.'

'He'll come round. He's getting on really well with

Sam, and I'm sure he'll make new friends once he starts school. It's a pity we don't live closer. Maybe we can sort out a visit when you get back? You can come to us in Pershore.'

Annabelle was touched. It would be something to look forward to. The kids got on well, and she had to admit that although she loved her mum and dad to the moon and back, living with them could be a little stifling. And cramped: she was in the single room whilst the kids shared the far more generously proportioned double room that had been hers when she was a child. It wasn't ideal, but with only three bedrooms it was the most practical solution. The sooner Annabelle and the kids had a place of their own the better.

'I'd like that. Thank you for asking us,' she decided. 'I expect Mum and Dad would appreciate a break from us, too.'

'Have you heard from them? They're cruising around the fjords, aren't they?'

'Now you come to mention it, I haven't heard a peep since they let me know they'd arrived at the port safely. I'd better send them a message and check they're OK.' She patted her pockets, before remembering she'd given her phone to Jake. It wasn't on the dining table and neither could she see it anywhere else, so he must still have it.

'Jake, what did you do with my phone? 'Annabelle asked, poking her head around the games room door. 'I want to message Granny and Grandad to see how they're enjoying their holiday. Oh, and Kate's invited us for a visit later in the year, if that's OK with you?'

Jake and Sam were playing table tennis, while Portia and Izzie were watching a Disney film in the

TV room. Portia was plaiting Izzie's hair and trying out different styles.

Jake shrugged. 'Sure.' Then he caught the ball and looked at her, his face wary. 'We won't be going to live with them, will we?'

'Definitely not. It'll be a little holiday, just like this one.'

'You said that before,' he muttered.

'I know Jake, and I'm sorry. I truly believed it was, but your father—' She halted abruptly, not wanting to bad-mouth their dad.

Troy might have behaved like a total shit, but the kids still loved him. She had tried to explain what had happened in the simplest of terms and without making Troy out to be a villain, but Annabelle wasn't sure they fully understood.

'It won't be for a couple of weeks,' she continued, 'because we've got to go back to Granny and Grandad's so you can get ready for your new school.'

'I liked my old one.' Jake's expression was sullen.

'I'm going to a new school in September,' Sam told him. 'It won't be too bad.' He didn't look convinced either, but at eleven he was moving to secondary school. 'And Ellis is going away to university. I'm going to have her room.'

'I heard that,' Ellis said, wafting into the games room on a cloud of floral perfume and a layered chiffon skirt. 'You are *not* having my room.'

'I am, too! Mum said.'

'Great. She might have asked me first.'

Ellis didn't look pleased and headed for the stairs muttering darkly under her breath.

'What about me?' Portia asked, emerging from the TV room, Izzie behind her. 'Ellis's room is nicer than mine. As the next oldest, I should get it. I'm going to speak to Mum.'

Oh, dear, Annabelle thought as the girls left. Rooms really did seem to be an issue in that family.

'Phone?' she reminded her son, who reluctantly handed it over. He'd been trying to persuade her for months that he should have a mobile phone of his own, but she wasn't keen on the idea.

Hastily she tapped out a message to her mum, then hurried upstairs after hearing raised voices coming from the living room, to find a heated discussion in full swing.

From what Annabelle could gather, Kate had said nothing of the sort about Sam having Ellis's room, but Sam was trying to argue that it was only fair since Ellis was going to university and wouldn't be home half of the time. And Ellis, whilst vehemently insisting that she kept her room, was also claiming that she couldn't wait to go to university if it meant getting away from her annoying brother and her horrid sister.

Finally, Kate managed to assure all three of her children that just because Ellis would be away during term time, it didn't mean she was moving out permanently, and that everything would stay as it was. This was received with glee by Ellis, and mutterings by the other two, Sam especially, who rumbled on about it not being fair as he retreated to the games room.

'Phew,' Kate said, as she switched the kettle on. 'Crisis averted. Tea or coffee?'

'Coffee, please. I'll make it. Hang on, a sec!' Her phone pinged and she pulled it out of her shorts pocket. 'It's from Mum,' she read. 'They're having a wonderful time.'

Annabelle was just about to slip the phone back into her pocket when she noticed she had a missed call, and her heart sank when she saw who it was from. The last person she wanted to speak to was Troy.

Briefly she debated not phoning him back, but duty won. After all, he *was* her children's father…

'Troy, it's Annabelle,' she said, walking onto the drive where she wouldn't be overheard. 'What do you want?'

'What do you mean *what do you want*? You called *me*.' The voice which had once had her hanging on every word, now sounded nasally and whiney. She knew where Jake got his whiney tone from.

'You called me first,' she retorted, beginning to lose patience.

'Whatever. Stop playing games. How are the kids?'

The last thing she wanted to do was to play games with Troy. Unless it was hide and seek, and he'd go hide for a very long time indeed. Preferably forever. If it hadn't been for the kids…

'Nice of you to ask.' Annabelle was unable to prevent the ooze of sarcasm. 'We've been gone nearly seven weeks and you've not once—'

'If you're only ringing to have a go, I'm hanging up. Do you know what time it is here?'

'I don't care. Look, this isn't productive. If you don't want anything, I'm ending this call.'

'Bella, wait a minute.' The whine had turned to wheedling. 'It doesn't matter who called who, we're speaking to each other now.' He paused and when he spoke again his tone was more confident. 'I *do* want something. I want you to come home.'

'*Excuse me*?'

'Come back to Stralia. I miss you. The kids too'

Annabelle barked out an incredulous laugh. 'Troy, we've been divorced for over a year, and we were separated for a year before that. You're with Sallie now, remember?'

'Sallie and I split up in May.'

'Really?' Annabelle wasn't sure she believed him – he'd not mentioned it before. Uncharitably she wondered who had ended it, and she hoped it was Sallie, to give Troy a taste of his own medicine.

'Bella, I admit it – I made a mistake. A big one.'

'With Sallie?'

'With you, you daftie. I should never have let you go.'

'You didn't *let me go* – you went to live with someone else.' Her laugh was scornful.

'I was a wally.'

'You've got that right.'

'Please come back. If not to me, then come back to Australia.'

Annabelle snorted. 'And where are we supposed to live? The house has been repossessed, thanks to you.'

'It was a blip,' Troy protested.

'Some blip! Anyway, if you really miss the kids as much as you say you do, you would have made some effort to contact them before now. They deserve an explanation.'

'I didn't want to speak to them until I knew what was happening. Everything was a mess for a while.'

'And it's not now? It bloody well looks it from where I'm standing.'

'Look, Bella, I made a mistake, but I'm sorting it. Give a fella a chance, eh?'

'You had your chance. The kids are settled. I'm not uprooting them again.'

You've only been there a couple of months. Just tell them it was an extended holiday.'

'No. Absolutely not. We're not going back to Australia and that's final.'

'Mum? Are you talking to Dad?' Jake's voice made her jump and she looked around to find the front door wide open and her son standing a few feet away from her.

Dam! Without saying goodbye to Troy, she ended the call and stuffed the phone into her pocket. 'Er, yes, but he's got to go, he's busy. He'll call you another time.'

'I want to speak to him *now*.' Jake looked mutinous. His chin was jutting out and his eyes brimmed with tears.

When the phone rang, Annabelle didn't need to look at the screen to know it was Troy trying to call her back. With Jake glaring at her, she dumped the call.

'That was Dad again, wasn't it?' he demanded. 'You said he was *busy*.' He spat the last word out.

'It… er…' She wanted to deny that the call had been from Troy, but she couldn't lie to her son.

'I hate you!' Jake shouted. 'You don't care about me and Izzie – all you care about is yourself! I want to go home. I hate it here. And I want to live with Dad, not you!' And with that, he spun on his heel and stormed back inside.

Annabelle felt sick. Her stomach churned and her pulse raced, and when she tried to follow her son she discovered that her legs were shaking.

Leaning against the nearest car for support, she

began to cry. What had she done? She should have let Jake speak to his father, but she hadn't felt able to deal with the fallout once Jake knew that his dad wanted them to go back to Australia.

Instead of containing the situation, she'd gone and made things worse.

She had known as soon as she'd read the letter which had blown her life apart, that it would be one step forward and two steps back when it came to the children and their feelings, but she hadn't expected it to be so hard. She certainly hadn't expected her previously easy-going and sunny son to tell her he hated her.

Jake and Izzie needed to speak with their father, but she didn't want Troy filling their heads with nonsense about going back. How could they return to Australia? She didn't trust her ex-husband as far as she could throw him, and she noticed that he managed to dodge the question when she'd asked him where they were supposed to live. Anyway, even if she did take the children back, she had nothing to live on and no job, so she could hardly pick up the threads of her old life as though nothing had happened.

They were better off staying here, even if Jake didn't think so. She was the adult and she could see the bigger picture, so it was up to her to decide what was best for them. And if it wasn't what Troy wanted, then tough luck. He'd made his bed and now he had to lie on it, however thorny he found it.

Unfortunately, she was also forced to lie on a bed he'd made for her, and those damned thorns were sharp enough to pierce her aching heart.

CHAPTER 12

I'm *turning into a midnight prowler*, Annabelle decided, after slipping out of bed yet again to check on her sleeping son. Jake had refused to speak to her or even meet her eye for the rest of the evening, remaining ensconced in the games room with Sam. He didn't appear to have said anything to Izzie though, which Annabelle was grateful for. She was only just able to cope with Jake's animosity – if her sweet, innocent little daughter discovered that her mum was refusing to allow her to speak to her father it would devastate her. It would devastate Annabelle, too, and with tears so close to the surface, she feared she might break down.

It had taken Annabelle a long time to calm down, and her distress had been obvious when she'd returned to the living room.

Tactfully no one had mentioned anything, although she'd caught Kate's concerned glances, and Ron had gazed at her steadily, but she'd been unable to decipher the look in his eyes.

Eventually Kate had managed to get her on her own and had asked her outright if she was all right.

About to reply that she was fine, Annabelle had changed her mind. 'It's Jake,' she'd said. 'He wanted to speak to his father and I told him no, and now he hates me.'

To her surprise, Kate hadn't been at all concerned. 'I'm sure he doesn't,' she'd said. 'My kids tell me they hate me all the time, but they don't mean it.'

'Jake does.' Annabelle was convinced – if she hated herself, how could Jake not? 'He's never said anything like that to me before.'

'Count yourself lucky. Seriously,' Kate had continued, 'he doesn't mean it. He's scared and hurt. He's lashing out, and you're the one closest to him, so…'

Chatting to Kate had put things into perspective. Jake might be angry with her, but deep down she knew he loved her. He also loved his father, and she'd have to be careful how she handled that. She didn't want to prevent her children from speaking to Troy, or even seeing him if he ever deigned to visit the UK, but she had to make it clear to her ex-husband that they wouldn't be going back and that he wasn't to give their children false hope.

Someone was still up, she noticed, as she slunk out of the room she shared with Izzie, because there were voices coming from Ellis and Portia's room, and she could hear the shower running in the family bathroom.

Quietly she opened the door to the boys' room and peeped inside. Both bunks had hunched duvet-covered forms lying in them and she recognised the soft snuffle from the boy on the lower bunk as coming from her son.

Relieved that he, at least, wasn't lying awake fretting, Annabelle studied him for a while then she gently pulled the door closed.

As she did so, the bathroom door behind her opened and out came Ron.

She hadn't realised the shower had stopped, so intent had she been on Jake, that she let out a shriek of surprise and clapped a hand to her mouth.

'Sorry,' he said. 'I didn't realise you were still up.'

'I'm not,' she squeaked. 'I'm in bed. I mean, I *was* in bed, but I got up to check on Jake.' She knew she was blabbering, but seeing Ron had thrown her – mainly because he was semi-naked.

All Ron was wearing was a towel around his waist and a concerned expression. 'Is everything OK?' he asked.

'Hmm?' Annabelle murmured. Blimmin' heck, he was fit. He had one of the nicest chests she'd ever seen on a man in his mid-forties – and living in Cairns, she'd seen her fair share over the years.

'Is there anything I can help with?' he persisted.

Annabelle snapped into focus. What on earth was she doing, drooling over a man, when her son thought she was the devil incarnate?

'Not really,' she said, 'but thanks, anyway.' She cut herself a bit of slack for her reaction to him – it had been purely animalistic, a healthy female response to an attractive man. That she'd felt a jolt of desire shoot through her at the sight of the smattering of hairs on his chest, his muscled shoulders, the curve of his collarbone, and skin still glistening with moisture, didn't detract from her being worried about Jake.

But Jake was sleeping like a baby at the moment, and Annabelle hadn't felt the strength of a man's arms around her in a very long time. She longed to be held and comforted, cherished and desired. Yes, *desired*, because she'd forgotten what that was like.

'Can you take me now?' she asked, not wanting to return to her cold, sleepless bed just yet.

'Pardon?'

Oh, Lord! Annabelle blushed furiously as she realised what she'd just said. Slowly she drew in a deep breath, closed her eyes, then opened them again.

Ron was studying her with a wary expression.

'Stargazing,' she said distinctly.

Understanding flared in his eyes and it was his turn to be embarrassed. 'Ah, right. Um.... now?'

'Would you mind? It's a beautiful night.'

'It certainly is. If you're sure?'

She made a face. 'I can't sleep, so...?'

'Give me five minutes to throw some clothes on. You might want to change out of your PJs, too.' He gave her a meaningful look.

Annabelle had forgotten she had her nightclothes on, and she was abruptly aware that she was naked underneath. 'Yes, good idea. I'll... um…be right back.'

Hastily she returned to her room and pulled on jeans and a sweatshirt, and stuffed her feet into a pair of trainers. She wasn't going to bother checking her appearance in the mirror, even though she knew her hair was probably a bird's nest. This wasn't a date, and Ron wouldn't care what she looked like, but she couldn't resist running a brush through it anyway.

He was waiting for her in the hall, and although he was fully clothed, her gaze lingered on his chest and what she now knew lay underneath the T-shirt he wore.

'Are you ready?' he asked.

She didn't answer. Instead, she unlocked the front door and stepped outside.

Rest Bay was a different place in the depths of the night. Gone were the dog walkers, the joggers, the people out for a stroll. In their place were the heightened sound of the waves, the rumble of an occasional car in the distance, and the sigh of the wind through the grass. The sea was black against the sky, and stars glittered in the crisp darkness.

'It gets better,' Ron said. 'Come on.'

To her surprise, once her eyes had adjusted she found she could see well enough, although she did stumble once or twice, and Ron's hand shot out to steady her.

Each time he did so, she felt a thrill pulse through her at his touch. It was fleeting, because he quickly withdrew his hand, but the contact shocked her; she'd not reacted like this to a man since... never?

It was like a punch to the gut, yet when he let go of her she felt unbalanced, as though she was about to fall. She put it down to not being able to see exactly where she was putting her feet, but she suspected she was lying to herself.

Neither of them said anything as they made their way along the path, and she was grateful for the silence; the sound of the waves and the answering beat of her heart was noise enough.

Boardwalk soon became an undulating sandy meadow as the path turned slightly inland, and the night grew darker and more still. As they walked, Annabelle turned her face to the sky more and more frequently, until finally she came to a halt and pivoted in a slow circle, her arms outstretched as she stared in awe at the heavens.

Softly Ron said, 'We don't have to go any further, if you don't want.'

She knew he was looking at her, and not the stars. She could feel his gaze, as weighty and as soft as a caress, and she shivered. 'I think we do,' she said, but she wasn't referring to the dunes.

She lowered her head, her mind filled with glittering sparks of light, and she took a step towards him.

He was close enough to touch, to smell, and she wondered what he tasted like.

Annabelle put out her hand, her palm resting on his chest, and she felt the thud of his heart, and his soft exhalation stirred something deep within her. He wanted her, she could sense it. And she wondered if he'd take her here, in the springy grass.

Ron remained motionless, apart from the rise and fall of his chest, and she slowly closed her eyes and leaned into him, her chin lifting as she offered him her mouth.

She almost thought she imagined the first flutter of his lips on hers, as she felt his breath on her cheek, and when she opened her eyes her gaze met the dark depths of his own.

Her lips parted, inviting him in, and with a barely-heard groan, he crushed her to him, and suddenly she was being thoroughly and expertly kissed.

Losing herself in the heady sweetness of it, she closed her eyes again and wrapped her arms around his neck, drawing him to her. Then his hands were cupping her face as his mouth explored hers, and desire shot through her, making her pulse race and her senses reel, until all she could think about was his lips, his tongue, the strength of his fingers, his ragged breathing.

Abruptly, he dragged his mouth away and released her, and as he took a step back, she almost lost her balance with the shock of it.

He stood there, breathing hard, a dark shape against an even darker landscape. But she could see his eyes, and they glittered with hunger.

So why wasn't he...?

His voice was gruff as he said, 'I'm sorry, I shouldn't have done that. Please forgive me.'

When he dropped his gaze, the connection between them was abruptly severed and Annabelle felt like crying. She turned away in shame. She'd practically thrown herself at him, and he was the one apologising.

Despair replaced lust, rejection replaced heady excitement, and her desire turned to ashes in her mouth. He didn't want her. Not in the way she needed to be wanted. Ron was too nice a man to take her simply because she'd offered herself. It could have been so easy for him to have lowered her into the grass and had sex with her, when what she'd wanted was for him to *make love* to her. Instead, he'd pulled away.

She ought to thank him for preventing her from making a big mistake, but all she wanted to do was cry.

'Can we go back?' she croaked, her voice hoarse with unshed tears and unrequited need.

'Of course.' He didn't say anything further. He didn't have to. He'd already said enough – words weren't necessary.

When they arrived back at the house, he paused before unlocking the door, and when she risked a glance at him, wondering at the delay, he stroked her cheek with the back of his hand, and said simply, 'We can't.'

Annabelle fled to her room, a plethora of emotions swooping through her mind: because he was right – they couldn't.

But that didn't prevent her from wishing that they could.

CHAPTER 13

'R on, where are we?' Jake's expression was earnest, as the boy came running up to him, chasing the football.

'Erm, I'm not sure what you mean.' Ron stopped the ball with his foot and picked it up. He, Sam, and Jake had been having a kick-about on the beach. Ron had offered to take the boys out because they'd been restless and, if he was honest, he wanted to get out of the house and away from Annabelle for a while. The events of last night weighed heavily on his mind.

He'd lain awake for hours after they'd got back, mulling the whole thing over and over until he was sick of thinking about it, and had arrived at the conclusion that he was ashamed of himself for having taken advantage of a woman who was clearly vulnerable.

At this moment Ron didn't like himself very much, because he hadn't thought he was that kind of man.

'Where are we?' Jake asked again. He was still gazing up at him, Sam by his side.

'On the beach?' Ron hazarded a guess, not sure what the boy was getting at, and thinking this might be some kind of a riddle.

'Bigger,' Jake said.

'Rest Bay?' Is that what he wanted to know?

'Bigger!' Jake opened his arms wide.

'Porthcawl.'

'Bigger,' the boy urged.

'South Wales,' Ron replied with gusto, joining in with the game.

That gave Jake pause. '*South Wales?*'

'That's right.'

'But we're not in Australia.' Jake's face scrunched up into a frown.

'This, here, is the original South Wales,' Ron explained, leading the boys along the beach towards the slipway. 'When Australia was first colonised by the British, part of it looked similar to South Wales, where we are now, so they called it *New* South Wales.'

'Is there a North Wales, an East Wales and West Wales?' the boy wanted to know.

'Yes to North and West, but the other bit is usually called Mid Wales.'

'That's silly.'

'I suppose it is. Why do you want to know?'

'Wales has lots of castles,' Sam piped up. 'We learned about them in school. King Edward built them to scare the Welsh.'

'That's right, he did,' Ron said.

'Can we go and see a castle?' Sam asked. 'I've been to Warwick Castle on a school trip, but it's not the same as a ruined one.'

'You'll have to ask your mother. I'm not sure where the nearest one is.'

'There's one in Cardiff,' Sam said. 'That's Wales's capital city. I saw signs for Cardiff when we were on the motorway.'

'Is Cardiff big?' Jake asked.

'I suppose it is.' Ron wondered at this sudden interest in geography.

'Is it far?' the boy asked.

'About thirty miles, I believe.'

'OK. Rest Bay, Porthcawl, Cardiff, old South Wales,' Jake muttered, then suddenly lost interest in the subject. 'Can you take me surfing?'

'I don't think that's a good idea,' Ron laughed.

'Why not?'

'I don't surf.'

'Never?'

'No.'

'Even Izzie surfs.' Jake sounded scornful about Ron's lack of wave action, until Sam said that he'd never been surfing either. 'I can teach you!' Jake cried excitedly. 'It's easy. Mum says we can rent wetsuits and boards.' His face closed in. 'I don't want to rent a suit or a board. I've got my own, but they are at home.'

Ron was fairly sure the boy wasn't referring to his grandparents' house in Brighton, and his heart went out to him.

'Tell you what,' Ron said. 'Why don't we pop along to that building over there?' He pointed to a glass and steel structure above Rest Bay. I think that's where the surf school is based. We can find out a bit more about it, then we can tell everyone over lunch?'

'OK,' Jake agreed, but he didn't look as pleased about the suggestion as Ron assumed he would. 'Ron, can I borrow your phone?' he asked, instead of pursuing the subject of surfing.

Ron said, 'I don't own one.'

'Not at all?' Jake was astounded, and even Sam looked shocked.

'Nope,' Ron said.

'Everyone has a mobile.'

'I don't.'

'Why not?'

'I don't need one.'

'What if you want to speak to someone?'

'I do it face-to-face.'

'But what if they're far away?' Jake asked.

'All the people I want to speak to, I see every day – namely your Aunt Beverley.'

Jake blinked owlishly at him, the concept of an adult not owning a mobile phone clearly an alien one. 'A phone's not just for phoning people,' Jake said. 'You can play games on it and listen to music, you can take photos, you can look things up. I want a phone,' he added plaintively.

'So do I,' Sam said. 'My mum said I can have one when I start big school, but that's ages away.'

Ron smiled. They were already halfway through August, and the start of a new term was a mere three or so weeks away – just a blink of an eye for him, but "ages" to an eleven-year-old boy. Suddenly Ron felt rather old.

The lack of a mobile phone must have played on Jake's mind all morning because as soon as they got back, the boy cornered Ellis who was sprawled out on a lounger on the sun-trap of a terrace, and Ron watched as she handed her phone over. Jake didn't get to play with it for long though, because Ellis soon held her hand out for Jake to give it back. Ron was surprised she'd let Jake have it in the first place, considering how attached to it she was. He didn't think he'd seen her without it for more than ten minutes, and only then because Kate didn't allow electronic devices at the table during mealtimes.

'Where is everyone?' he asked, spying Brett in the lounge, reading.

Brett closed his book and put it down. 'Kate, Annabelle, and Izzie have gone for a walk, and have taken Pepe with them. Portia is at the stables, naturally; Beverley is boiling herself in the hot tub, and my mum has gone to have her hair done. Oh, and Ellis is whispering sweet nothings down the phone to her boyfriend. She can't leave the poor lad alone for five minutes. God help it when he's in one uni and she's in another – she'll be a basket case wondering what he's getting up to with all those freshers. Did you go to university?'

'No, I joined the army.'

'I didn't go either. Wish I had now, seeing how excited Ellis is. Still, I wouldn't have liked to rack up all that student debt. Fancy a spot of lunch? I was just about to make some ham sandwiches, and I dare say the boys are starving. Sam eats like a horse. I don't know where he puts it all.'

Ron was happy to let Brett prattle on without expecting much in the way of an answer. His mind was on Annabelle, and he couldn't believe how disappointed he was when Brett told him she was out. He'd been looking forward to telling her that he'd booked the kids in for a surfing lesson – all of them, Ellis and Portia included, although if one or both of them didn't want to go, he'd happily take the vacant spot.

Jake hadn't been too keen on having "a lesson", arguing that he'd been surfing since he was five, but the chap who had taken the booking had insisted he assessed everyone's level of ability first. Despite Jake's incredulity, Ron could tell that the boy was thrilled to bits and was looking forward to getting into the water.

***

'You shouldn't have,' Annabelle objected when Ron shared the news with her after she'd returned from her walk. He'd hoped she'd have been pleased; instead she looked put out. They were sitting on the terrace, the bi-fold doors wide open, and he shaded his eyes against the sun, trying to see her face.

He shrugged. 'I can always cancel, if you want.' He'd lose the deposit, but he didn't care.

Annabelle's eyes bored into his. 'I think Jake might never speak to you again, if you do. But I insist on paying.'

'I can afford it, so let me treat them.'

Her expression was sceptical, so he added, 'Remember those odd jobs I told you about?' and when she nodded, he said, 'Well, then, let's leave it at that, shall we?'

He could tell she still wasn't happy but that was hard luck, Jake was desperate to resurrect some remnants of his old life Down Under, and Annabelle needed to keep hold of her money. Ron had enough for his immediate needs, although he may well regret spending his hard-earned cash so recklessly when he was back on the streets.

But, darn it, it had been a long time since he'd been in a position to spoil anyone, except for Beverley, and if ever there was someone who could do with being spoilt it was Annabelle and her children.

Annabelle was off limits, though, so that left Jake and Izzie. And he couldn't leave Sam out and neither would he have wanted to, which meant that it was only fair to include Ellis and Portia.

The cost of those five lessons had gouged a big chunk out of what little money he had, but it had been worth it to see Jake's face. Ron sensed that the little guy was finding it more difficult than his sister to adjust to the new situation he'd found himself in and his heart went out to him.

'Do you know if they had any spaces left?' Annabelle asked and Ron shrugged.

'No idea. Why? Are you thinking of having a go?'

'Absolutely! I haven't surfed in ages.' She gave him a sly look. 'You should give it a go, too. You might enjoy it.'

'Enjoy what?' Brett asked, coming up behind them.

'Surfing,' Annabelle said. 'Ron has arranged for all the children to go tomorrow, and I said I wouldn't mind hopping on a board.'

'Can you surf?' Brett asked her.

'A bit. I'm nowhere near as good as Jake, though. He misses his surfing.'

'Is Brighton any good for it?'

Annabelle frowned. 'When I was a kid, there used to be a few surfers around, but that was mostly in the winter. I don't think there's much wave action in the summer. I'll have to look into it.' She gave a slightly bitter laugh. 'I'm not sure Jake will like the chilly English Channel in November. The wave pool back home is considerably warmer.'

'Wave pool?' Brett asked.

Ron noticed that she still referred to Australia as home.

'There's no beach at Cairns,' she explained. 'The nearest ones that are good enough for surfing are a thirty-minute drive away, but you've got to watch out for jellyfish and saltwater crocs, so I won't let him go in the water there. He has done some surfing in the ocean, but not locally.'

Brett whistled. 'If there were crocodiles in the UK, I don't think I'd paddle in the sea ever again. It was bad enough Sam having had a close encounter with a jellyfish yesterday.' Brett turned to Ron. 'Are you going to have a go?'

Ron sniggered. 'Only if you do.'

Brett stuck out his hand. 'It's a deal.'

Ron took it and they shook. 'Will you ask Kate if she wants to come?'

'I'll ask, but it's not her kind of thing.'

However, Kate surprised her husband by agreeing to join in. 'You only live once,' she said, cheerfully, and with the two girls also up for it, tomorrow was shaping up to be a fun family day out.

Ron found himself really looking forward to it, and not just because it was something he hadn't tried before. He had an image in his head of how gorgeous Annabelle would look in a wetsuit, and he simply couldn't shift it.

CHAPTER 14

A t least Ron was speaking to her, Annabelle thought as she helped clear away the dinner things later that evening. When he'd suggested taking the boys for a kickabout on the beach earlier, she'd assumed it was because he wanted to avoid her. And it was terribly kind of him to have booked surfing sessions for the younger members of the group, even though she suspected he couldn't afford it.

Despite his protestations that he had a job, she guessed that odd-jobbing didn't pay much, which made his gift even more special.

'Board games, anyone?' Kate asked. She was holding several boxes in her hands, and Annabelle recognised some old favourites from her childhood.

All the kids were downstairs, either watching TV, playing table tennis, or glued to their phones (Annabelle was referring to Ellis and Portia here) and the adults were settling down for the evening, an open bottle of wine on the table. They were gathered on the terrace, enjoying watching the sun go down, and mostly chatting. Helen had a book of puzzles and crosswords in her hand and was spending most of her time tutting crossly at it, concentration etched on her face, and Beverley was knitting, Pepe curled in a ball at her feet, exhausted after his long walk that morning.

Kate placed the boxes on the table. 'We've got Scrabble, Monopoly, Twister, Cluedo, Hungry Hungry Hippos, Trivial Pursuit, or there's a compendium with Snakes and Ladders, chess, and so on.'

'Not for me, thanks. I don't like board games,' Helen said. 'I'll stick to my Sudoku.'

'And I'm happy just watching,' Beverley said, holding up her knitting. 'I want to get the back of this finished.'

'What are you making?' Annabelle asked.

'A nice thick winter jumper.' Beverley hesitated as Ron got to his feet and went inside, then lowered her voice. 'It's for Ron, for Christmas.' She caught Annabelle's look. 'Yes, I know Christmas is ages away yet, but I'm not as quick a knitter as I once was. Arthritis, you know.'

Annabelle glanced at Beverley's hands. Her fingers were moving non-stop as she wound thread around the needles, and they looked dextrous enough to her.

'Just the four of us, then?' Kate said, adding, 'Are you up for a game?' to Ron as he reappeared with a fresh glass of lemonade in his hand.

'Depends on what we're playing,' he said.

'Don't worry, strip poker is off limits,' Brett joked. 'I'm not flashing my moobs for anyone. It's all right for you, you're ripped.'

'You think?' Ron looked amused.

'Don't you think he's ripped, Annabelle?'

'Oh, um, yeah.' Heat rushed into her cheeks and she wished Brett would stop talking.

When Kate threw her husband a stern glare, Annabelle had the feeling that Brett had known exactly what he was doing, and her face flamed even more.

And when she caught Kate's eye, Annabelle realised she hadn't been as good at hiding her feelings as she'd hoped.

Her eyes flew to Ron's, but he was studiously avoiding looking at her.

She didn't blame him. Not only had she thrown herself at him last night, but now the whole world seemed to know that she fancied him. Great.

'I'm leaning towards Scrabble, or maybe Cluedo,' Kate said. 'Shall we take a vote?'

'Cluedo,' Brett said. 'I've always fancied myself as a detective.' He gave Annabelle an innocent smile.

She narrowed her eyes at him. 'OK, Inspector Clouseau, let's see if you can win a game.'

'Bagsie Professor Plum. I can see you as Miss Scarlett,' Brett said to Annabelle, reaching for the box and pulling it towards him.

'That leaves me with Mrs Peacock or Mrs White,' Kate said, sitting down and picking up the wine. 'Fancy a refill?' she asked Annabelle.

Annabelle held out her glass.

'I fancy Ron as Colonel Mustard,' Brett said, laying out the pieces, a grin playing about his mouth.

Annabelle frowned. Why was the word "fancy" popping up all of a sudden? She had no doubt it was deliberate. It suddenly struck her that she and Ron mightn't have been as quiet and as unobtrusive as they'd hoped when they'd slipped out last night, and she had a sneaky suspicion that they might have been seen.

Suddenly she remembered that Kate and Brett's penthouse bedroom also had a small balcony, and the whole suite on the top floor had views to the front of the house.

Stonily, she picked up the dice. If only they knew how the night had ended and that Ron had rejected her, they wouldn't be so free with their unsubtle comments.

Her attention was only half on the game – the other half was trying not to look at Ron sitting opposite – so it was no surprise when she didn't win. And she didn't win at Scrabble either. What she did seem to be winning at was wine drinking, because her glass seemed to be constantly full, despite sipping from it steadily. As a result, she was a bit unsteady on her feet when she went downstairs to round her children up and put them to bed.

Izzie was already half-asleep on the couch in the TV room, as she watched her brother and Sam play on the X-Box, so Annabelle only faced a small protest as she ran her daughter a bath, then supervised teeth-cleaning.

'Can I read for a bit?' Izzie asked.

'Of course you can.' Annabelle bent over to tuck her in and give her a kiss. 'I won't be long before I come to bed.' She brushed a stray lock of hair off Izzie's face. 'The boys are just about to go to bed, too.'

She'd let her children stay up longer than she would have done if they were at home because they were on holiday, but she didn't want them to stay up until all hours, so ten pm was a reasonable compromise she thought, as she headed back upstairs.

When she returned to the living room, she wasn't prepared for the sight of Brett on all fours with his backside in the air and Kate's limbs entwined around his. They were playing Twister, and her heart sank because she knew what was coming next as Kate and Brett tumbled over, giggling hysterically.

'Your turn,' Kate said to her, getting her feet and brushing herself down.

'I'm off to bed,' Helen announced.

'Me, too. I'm too old for all these shenanigans.' Beverley wrapped her knitting up and put it in the basket by her feet. 'You want to be careful you don't break something,' she warned.

Yeah, my heart, Annabelle thought dryly, as she resisted the urge to glance at Ron. Goodness knows what he must be thinking.

Annabelle watched the two ladies leave and was just about to say that she should retire too, when Kate grabbed her arm and dragged her over to the plastic Twister mat laid out on the floor.

'Go on,' she urged. 'It's fun. Here.' Kate shoved her wine glass at her. 'Drink this. There's no point in wasting it.'

There had only been a couple of sips left in the bottom when Annabelle had put Izzie to bed, but now the glass was full again.

Annabelle put it down without tasting it. She didn't dare drink any more.

'Come on.' Kate was urging Ron to his feet.

Annabelle could sense his reluctance, but he got up anyway, and allowed himself to be pulled over to the mat, where he smiled uncertainly at her.

'We could always tell them to bugger off,' he murmured.

Maybe it was the wine, maybe it was pure devilment, or maybe she was so desperate to feel close to him that she was willing to take whatever she could get, but she found herself saying, 'Remind me, how do you play this game?'

Ron lifted an eyebrow, the rest of his face blank. 'You put one foot there, and one there. The referee spins the spinner, and you move whichever body part to whatever colour circle it tells you to. Are you sure you want to play?'

'I'm sure. I'm going to beat you – I'm quite bendy.' Oh, God, she'd definitely had too much to drink.

'I'm sure you are,' he said, and she couldn't work out whether he was agreeing that she'd win the game, or whether he thought she was supple.

'Ready?' Kate called.

'As ready as I'll ever be,' Annabelle muttered, as she got into position.

Ron did the same.

'Annabelle, you go first,' Kate told her, and she spun the spinner. 'Left hand, blue,' she announced when the spinner came to a stop.

Annabelle crouched down and did as she was instructed.

'Ron, your go. Right foot, red.'

Ron moved his foot. He was still upright, and Annabelle felt rather strange being almost on her knees at his feet.

She risked a swift glance up at him, and looked away hastily when she saw he was gazing down at her, his expression unreadable.

'Annabelle, left foot, green,' Kate said.

Annabelle moved her foot, feeling the stretch in her thigh.

A few moves later, she was feeling more than a stretch, because her face was centimetres from Ron's. Her one arm was underneath his leg and the other… she actually tried not to think about what part of his anatomy her shoulder was touching because it was making her giddy.

Suddenly she muttered, 'I can't do this,' and dropped her knee to the floor. 'I'm out,' she cried. It came out as a squeak, and she cleared her throat before adding, 'Ron won.'

She waited for him to straighten up so she could get out from underneath him, then she scrambled to her feet, pretending not to notice the hand he held out for her. If she touched him now, she might explode.

'Fancy a nightcap?' Kate asked, smirking.

'Not for me, thanks,' Ron said. 'I think I'll take a stroll before I turn in.' His departure was so abrupt that Annabelle knew he wanted to be on his own.

Brett, however, didn't take the hint. 'Wait up,' he called after him. 'I'll come with you. I could do with stretching my legs.'

Annabelle waited for Brett to dash out of the room before picking up her wine and taking a long swallow. 'You did that on purpose,' she said to Kate as she wiped her lips.

'Yep. Fun, wasn't it?'

'Not for me, and I don't think Ron appreciated it, either.' Annabelle stalked onto the terrace and flung herself into a chair.

Peering into the darkness, she could see two figures striding along the pavement. Ron and Brett. They didn't appear to be talking, but it was difficult to tell.

Kate packed away the game and joined her. 'We saw you last night,' she said, picking up her own glass and taking a mouthful.

'I thought you might have. Is that what this evening has been about? I mean… Twister? *Really*?'

Kate smirked. 'I saw the way you've been looking at him, and it's obvious you fancy him.'

'Ha! Did you and Brett have to keep dropping the word "fancy" into the conversation?'

'Sorry. But it's clear you fancy each other rotten, so we thought we'd help things along a bit.'

Annabelle tipped her head back and poured the rest of her drink down her throat. She couldn't believe she was about to tell Kate this— 'I kissed him. Last night, among the dunes.'

'How romantic,' Kate said dreamily.

'Yeah, you would have thought.' Her small laugh was sorrowful. 'I would have let him take me there and then, sand and all, but he didn't want me.' She pulled a face. 'He apologised and said he shouldn't have kissed me.'

'I see. But it doesn't explain why he looks at you like he wants to throw you over his shoulder and run away with you.'

'He does not look at me like that.'

'Believe me, he does. You look at him the same way.'

'And there I was, thinking I was doing a good job of hiding it. God, Kate, I've only been here four days. I don't *know* the guy, yet I'm drooling over him like a flipping teenager.'

'You don't have to know someone to fancy them.'

'There's that word again.' Annabelle snorted. 'It's a bit more than that – I really, really like him. A lot.

How can that be? Four ruddy days. Four! I think I'm losing the plot.'

'Love strikes at the oddest times.'

'Flipping heck! You don't think it's *love*, do you?' Annabelle snorted in disbelief.

'I don't know; you tell me.'

'It can't be. It's lust. Sheer animal lust.'

Kate sniggered. 'Yeah, I could tell. At one point, you almost had your nose in his—'

'And who's fault was that?' Annabelle interjected hurriedly. She didn't need any reminders, thank you. 'You insisted we play the stupid game.'

Kate looked contrite. 'Sorry. I thought it might help bring the two of you closer together. I didn't expect him to storm off.'

'He didn't exactly storm. I don't think Ron is the type to storm anywhere. Not that I really know, of course, considering I've only just met the fella, but that's the impression I get.'

'He is rather reserved, isn't he?' Kate paused, then added, 'I don't know the full story, and even if I did it's not mine to tell, but he seems like a good man, an honourable man.'

'I think that's why he didn't make love to me last night. I understand that you don't want to talk about him, but can you tell me one thing – has he got a girlfriend?'

'Definitely not. He was married once, I think.'

'It's not that, then.' Annabelle shook her head. 'Other men would have taken what was on offer, but Ron didn't. I wonder why?'

'He must have had his reasons, but it's not because he's not attracted to you.'

'And you say he's not in a relationship... so?'

Annabelle had run out of ideas.

'Maybe it's because of Mum?' Kate mused.

'It could be. Aunt Beverley thinks the world of him, so maybe he doesn't want to enter into a relationship with her niece in case it goes belly up. Not that I want a relationship,' Annabelle added hurriedly. 'I don't need any more complications in my life.'

'You just want a bit of fun? A holiday romance?' Kate nudged her.

'Yes. No. Oh, I don't know. Anyway, it's a moot point. He's not interested– or if he is,' she added, seeing Kate's expression, 'He's not going to act on it.'

'I think I might be right about my mum,' Kate said slowly.

'Possibly. Do you know, before I joined you here that my mum asked me to find out what was going on with him and Aunt Beverley. She's got it into her head that he's up to no good – that he's after her money.'

Kate barked out a laugh. 'Ha! If he was, he'd be in for a shock – she hasn't got any, and she's already signed the house over to me.'

Annabelle raised her eyebrows, so Kate explained. 'In case she ever has to go into a care home. Not that I'd let that happen if I could help it, but if she needed specialist nursing care, she might have to, and if she did she'd be forced to sell the house to contribute to the care home fees. This way, I own it, so officially she doesn't have any assets.' Kate paused. 'Tell you what though, having Ron living with her has done her the world of good. She's so much happier now. She used to be so miserable. No doubt you've heard about the fiasco that was last Christmas?'

'A bit.' Annabelle didn't want to say too much. What Beverley had told her, she'd keep to herself.

'Part of the problem was that the kids, the girls especially, couldn't deal with both their grandmothers coming to visit at the same time. Helen is so particular and interfering, always telling the kids off; and my mum was just so miserable. She wasn't happy unless she was complaining. Such a killjoy. Between the pair of them, the run up to Christmas was a bit of a trial.'

'Really? Beverley seems quite happy now.'

'She does, doesn't she? It's as though she's got a new lease of life and has found joy in living again. God help her if Ron ever moves out.'

'Do you think he will?'

'I hope not. There's no real reason for him to leave.'

Annabelle thought back to the morning Pepe had escaped. Ron had spent the night outside, and although the reason for that was because of the bickering between Beverley and Helen, Annabelle had the impression there was more to it.

She hoped she was wrong, and not only for Beverley's sake, but for her own, too, because Beverley only lived a short distance away from her parents, and Annabelle was harbouring a secret hope that she could see more of Ron when the holiday was over.

Kate had got it wrong when she'd suggested that Annabelle might be up for a holiday romance. Annabelle wasn't the sort of woman to have a fling then forget about it, no matter how turned-on she felt. She was more like a loyal puppy – if she gave herself to someone it was because she cared deeply for them. And the fact that she'd been prepared to make love with Ron, was very significant indeed.

She might have only known Ron for four days, but Annabelle was smitten.

CHAPTER 15

'Surfing with a hangover is so not a good idea,' Ron heard Annabelle groan as she walked down the beach with Kate. She was wearing a wetsuit and carrying a board under her arm.

Ron watched her go and tried not to eat her up with his eyes. She looked phenomenal. He'd already noticed her gorgeous figure (how could he not?) but to see her every curve and dip outlined in sleek black neoprene was almost more than he could bear. And after the events of last night, when she'd been so close that she would have been blind not to have noticed how he felt, he was more conscious of her than ever.

Brett had tried to talk to him about her when he'd insisted on going for a walk with him, but Ron had made it clear that he didn't want to discuss it. It hadn't prevented Brett from trying though, and Ron had come to the conclusion that the man was almost as stubborn as Helen.

'We saw you last night,' had been Brett's opening gambit. 'You like going for midnight strolls, don't you?'

'Sometimes.'

'You and Annabelle looked pretty close.'

Ron knew that Brett and Kate couldn't have seen much. For one thing, the kiss had taken place well out of sight of the house, and for another all he'd done when they'd got back was to stroke her cheek. Hardly sensational, was it?

'Did you go back out again?' Brett had asked.

'No – why?'

'I could have sworn I heard the front door… Meh, it was probably my imagination.'

'Along with you imagining that Annabelle and I are close?' Ron had asked, his eyebrows raised.

'Go on, admit it, you two fancy each other,' Brett had teased.

Ron had said nothing. And he'd continued to say nothing until eventually Brett had given up, and they'd strolled in silence as they'd made their way back to the house.

Thankfully, by the time they'd got back, Annabelle was nowhere to be seen and Ron guessed she'd gone to bed.

It had taken him a long time to fall asleep and his dreams had been filled with images of her limbs wrapping themselves around his to the sound of the waves pounding against the shore. It didn't take a professional to interpret what that meant.

The sight of her in a wetsuit today didn't help, and he wished he'd never booked the windsurfing sessions. But then he saw Jake's face, and knew it was worth every penny. Ron would have been willing to put up with far worse if it meant seeing Jake's sheer joy at being on a board again.

It became clear pretty swiftly that neither Annabelle, Jake, nor Izzie needed much instruction, so they went off to catch some waves (Ron felt pleased that he was starting to pick up the lingo), whilst he, Brett, Kate and the other children were treated to the beginner's session.

He felt a right idiot lying on his board on the sand, then hopping to his feet and pretending he was riding a wave, but he could see the sense in practicing the manoeuvre. Some of his embarrassment stemmed from being a total novice whilst kids barely out of nappies looked like pros in the water (*Izzie, that means you*, Ron thought), and also from wearing the wetsuit itself. It was probably the least forgiving piece of kit he'd ever worn, showing off every lump and bump, and he couldn't wait to get into the water to hide.

Once he was in, though, he soon discovered that all his concentration and effort was taken up with trying to stay upright on his board, and there was nothing left to think about how ridiculous he looked.

Brett, he noticed with satisfaction, was also finding it hard to make the transition from lying flat to balancing on two feet, and the pair of them spent more time falling in than they spent on the board itself.

'Look at Jake go!' Brett cried, while they were taking a much-needed breather. Ron hadn't had this much exercise in years – walking didn't count – and he was grateful for the brief respite.

Jake and Izzie made surfing look easy, and Ron watched the children with envy. Sam was doing rather well for a beginner too and so was Portia, while Kate and Ellis were struggling as much as Ron and Brett, but seemed to be having far more fun if all the giggling and shrieking was any indication.

Brett and Ron were slightly less fun-orientated and more on the competitive side, so it was probably for the best that the two of them were as bad as each other.

However, it was Annabelle who stole the show as far as Ron was concerned.

Utterly graceful, she balanced on the board with all the skill of a gymnast, and he watched her over and over again as she paddled out to beyond where the swells were breaking, searching for a decent wave.

Suddenly, he wanted to be out there with her, to experience what she was experiencing, and grabbing his board he waded into the water and paddled out to join her.

'Are you having fun?' he asked, spluttering as seawater splashed him in the face.

'Absolutely!' Her eyes were shining and her smile was wide. She'd worn her hair in a ponytail, and it was wet and sleekly plastered to her head, making her look incredibly young. 'Are you?' she asked.

He was, although surfing, like many things, was harder than it looked, especially when watching a competent person do it.

Annabelle was paddling whilst looking behind her, her board at a slight angle to the incoming waves. 'Get ready here's a good one!' she cried, expertly turning her board.

Ron tried to follow suit, and he was kind of in the right position when he felt the wave lift him. He scrambled to his knees, hoping he could get from there into a crouching position in time, but he couldn't. One minute he was balancing and hoping for the best, the next it was as though he was in a giant washing machine, and he was under the wave with a mouthful of salt water, not knowing which way was up.

It briefly flashed through his mind that this might be the end of him. Even though he was a fairly competent swimmer, he could feel the board tugging at his ankle where it was lashed to his leg, and he prayed to God he wasn't going to be dragged out to sea with the outgoing tide. Panicking, he flailed upwards, then felt someone grab his arm and pull, and abruptly his head broke the surface and he took a welcome gasp of air.

He felt like he'd been under for minutes, but he guessed it was probably only seconds.

Spluttering, he saw the wave crashing to the shore, and felt the suck as another one prepared to tumble over his head.

Annabelle was holding onto him tightly, but she let go when she saw he was all right.

'Come on, let's get you closer in,' she shouted, and she grabbed the board that was bobbing around behind him and pushed it towards him. Ron grasped it and crawled halfway across it, using his feet to propel him closer to the beach.

'Are you OK?' Annabelle asked when their feet touched the bottom.

Ron wiped the water from his face and sat down in the shallows. 'I think so,' he panted. 'I'm getting too old for stuff like this.'

'Nonsense,' she cried. 'You're only as old as you feel.'

'Right now I feel about a hundred and six,' Ron told her. 'I don't know how you do it.'

'I've had a lot of practise, but I must admit I haven't been surfing in a good many years. It's a bit like riding a bike, you don't really forget, and these waves are only babies.'

Only babies? Ron would hate to see a fully grown one.

'Are you coming back in?' she asked.

Ron shook his head. 'Nope, I think I'm done. I'll sit and watch, if you don't mind.'

Annabelle chuckled. 'I don't mind at all,' she said. 'You stay there, I'll catch a couple more waves, and then I think I'm finished too. I'm not as young as I used to be, either. I wouldn't mind going out for a little swim afterwards though, if you're up for it, considering you've still got your wet suit on. I thought the water was going to be freezing, but it isn't too bad once you get used to it.'

Ron was more than happy to sit and watch. Eventually though, she'd also had enough, and after a particularly successful wave, she aimed her board at the shore, still standing on it, and brought it to an impressive halt.

Picking it up, she carried it up the beach and put it next to Ron's. 'Come on, let's go for that dip before the tide changes. Race you!' And with that, she whirled around and shot back into the sea, splashing through the waves and kicking up water.

Ron didn't need asking twice. He leapt to his feet and charged off after her, powering through the water until it reached his thighs, and then he dived straight in.

Not only was Annabelle a decent enough surfer in his opinion, she was also a good swimmer, strong with a smooth action, and she drove forward in a powerful front crawl.

It was hard to keep up, and he was panting by the time she decided to tread water. They were well out beyond the breaking waves, and he bobbed next to her and looked out to sea, the gentle swells almost filling his vision, and he felt as though they were the only two people on earth.

'I'm glad I came on this holiday,' Annabelle said, out of the blue.

'I'm glad you came, too,' he said.

She turned in the water to look at him, and now they were face-to-face, a metre or so apart, and he would have given everything he owned, which admittedly wasn't a lot, to kiss her right there in the sea.

He didn't know whether his hunger and his desire for her had shown on his face, or whether she'd had the same idea at the same time, but suddenly they were in each other's arms and were kissing, her warm lips on his, her arms around his neck, both of them kicking to keep afloat in the water.

It only lasted for a heartbeat or two, and then she pulled away and looked guiltily towards the shore. Ron could see Jake riding one of the swells, his back to them, and he scanned the beach to see where everyone else was.

Kate Brett and the two girls were sitting on the sand, but he couldn't tell whether they were watching him or not.

'I had better check on Izzie,' Annabelle said. They could just make out the little girl's head bobbing in the water. 'I didn't realise we'd come quite so far,' she added. 'Are you going to get in OK?'

Ron grinned. 'Race you,' he dared her, and before the words had even left his mouth, she was off, and once more he had to work hard to keep up with her. Goodness me, but he hadn't been swimming in such a long time, he was out of practice.

She beat him to the shore with only half a metre or so between them, and waded through the shallow waves, almost falling, giggling as she ran. Then she threw herself down on the sand next to Kate, gasping, a big grin on her face.

Ron noticed Kate giving her a sideways look, and he was aware that Brett's eyes were on him, but he didn't care. That kiss had been... magical. His only regret was that it hadn't lasted longer, and he so desperately wanted to do it again.

What the hell was he thinking? Only the other night he'd pushed her away, telling her that they couldn't, that a relationship wasn't a good idea, and now he was practically throwing himself at her. What had gotten into him?

He didn't know, but he was enjoying it. He hadn't felt so lighthearted or so carefree in such a very long time.

Even as those thoughts were going through his head, he was also telling himself that this was not a good idea, that he had nothing to offer her, but both Kate and Brett were beaming at him, and when Brett gave him a thumbs up he knew they approved.

It put a whole different perspective on what was happening and how he was feeling. If they were happy about it, surely he could allow himself to be, too? They knew his circumstances, were well aware that he didn't have a home of his own, and that he was living off Beverley's charity, but they didn't seem to mind.

It was an interesting and enlightening thought. He'd been so convinced that no woman would ever want him, and that he didn't deserve to have another relationship, that this was a novel way of looking at things for him. He still wasn't convinced, but neither was he quite so dead set against a romantic relationship.

Even if he had been, he wasn't sure how well he could control his feelings for Annabelle: his brain might say no but his heart and his body were screaming yes. That far too brief contact in the water had been enough to send his pulse soaring, and he couldn't wait to kiss her again. If she'd let him. And he hoped with everything he had that she would.

CHAPTER 16

As the first week of the holiday slipped by, it was becoming harder and harder for Annabelle not to give in to temptation and snog Ron at every opportunity. She didn't know what had happened the other day when they'd gone surfing, but he seemed to have lost his inhibitions and he'd kissed her as eagerly as she'd kissed him – with the added bonus of him not pushing her away this time and telling her that they couldn't.

She was a bit hesitant, uncertain whether now was the best time to be diving headfirst into a new relationship, considering that her life was a total mess. But she had been single for a while now, and before she'd even booked their flights to the UK she had been thinking it was about time she started dating again. Not because she needed a man in her life, but because she missed having a special someone. She missed the companionship; she missed coming home from work and chatting about her day; she missed someone to mull over her problems with, to share her concerns and her highlights; and most of all she missed having someone in her bed. Sex wasn't the be-all and end-all, but it was certainly something to be considered. And she'd definitely been considering it –

or the lack of it – for quite some time. She had been planning on dipping her toe into the dating pool as soon as they returned from the UK, but that idea had been shot out of the water by her abrupt change in circumstances.

She knew she had a great deal to sort out – namely a place to live and a job – before she could start thinking about romance, but it seemed to have been thrust upon her regardless. She'd not gone looking for it, yet the minute she'd set eyes on Ron something had clicked inside.

The click had transformed into a fizzing and a tingling, until now she couldn't even look at him without her heart leaping out of her chest and desire running rampant.

It wasn't just desire that she felt, because if it had been she could have simply scratched the itch and walked away with her heart intact. She actually liked Ron tremendously. He was so thoughtful and kind, and he was great with her kids, too. She liked him as a *person,* and not just as a potential lover.

Lover… the word swirled around in her head, making her skin tingle, and the little dip at the base of her throat throb in time with her heartbeat.

She and Ron had been sending each other lingering glances when they thought no one was looking, and she was finding it harder and harder to deal with the tension humming between them.

Although Kate and Brett were aware of what was going on, thankfully Beverley and Helen seemed oblivious, as did the children, and Annabelle wanted to keep it that way. The less the kids knew about her growing feelings for Ron, the better. Until she was utterly sure what was happening, she wanted to keep them well out of it. Luckily Ron seemed to understand, because he made no further move towards her, just sending her the occasional deep and meaningful glance instead.

If it hadn't been for those looks, she might have thought he wasn't interested and that the kiss had been a one off, but every time she caught his eye she was aware of the hunger and the desire that lurked in their depths, and it made her heart squeeze with excitement and longing. At some point in this holiday she knew she would go to bed with him, and the anticipation was exquisite.

As was the fear.

The crunch came on Sunday afternoon, a full two days since that magical kiss in the water.

Kate and Brett suggested going to the cinema, then a meal out, which Annabelle was totally up for (although the money she'd be spending made her cringe), but she'd developed a migraine and the thought of sitting in a room with a huge screen and lots of colours and noise, made her feel quite faint.

Annabelle was hiding in the bedroom, the curtains drawn, wishing her head wasn't hurting when Kate had come to find her.

Kate offered to remain behind to keep her company, but Annabelle insisted she go.

'You'll enjoy it,' she said. 'I'll be fine.'

'I don't like leaving you on your own,' Kate protested. 'Mum isn't too keen on going because she doesn't want to leave the dog for that length of time, so how about if I ask her to—?' She stopped as a thought occurred to her. 'Ron!' she exclaimed, clapping her hands, the noise sending a bolt of pain through Annabelle's head. '*He* can stay with you,'

Kate continued. 'Mum will be happy leaving Pepe for most of the day if she knows Ron will take him for a walk. After all, she couldn't ask you, not the state you're in. Perfect.'

Kate clapped her hands again, and Annabelle let out a groan.

'Oops, sorry,' Kate said, lowering her voice. 'But you've got to admit, it's the perfect opportunity.'

'For what?' Annabelle croaked.

'For you and Ron to spend some time together. *Alone.*'

'If you haven't noticed, I'm feeling like crap,' Annabelle said. 'I think it's a migraine.'

'Do you get them often? How long do they last?'

'This is my first,' Annabelle admitted.

'It's probably just a headache,' Kate said.

'It feels like more than just a headache.'

'Helen always has an assortment of pain killers in her bag. I'll ask her to give you some.'

Annabelle didn't usually like taking tablets, but the way her head felt right now, she'd happily take anything if it relieved the pain.

'Gimme,' she said feebly, when Kate returned with a couple of capsules and a glass of water, and she downed them eagerly. 'I suppose I should have asked what they were.'

'Who cares as long as they do the trick?' Kate replied. 'Now, Ron is around if you need him—' Kate winked at her '—and Brett and I will take good care of Jake and Izzie, so there's no need for you to worry about anything. I'll text you when we're on our way back – just in case.'

'In case of what?'

'You never know…' Kate said vaguely.

Annabelle would have shaken her head in disbelief if she hadn't been too scared to move it. Instead, she lay back down on the pillows and closed her eyes.

The last thing she remembered was Kate softly closing the door.

***

Disorientated, Annabelle struggled into a sitting position. She had no idea where she was or what day it was, and it took her a minute or so to gather her wits, and remember that the kids were at the cinema and that she had a headache.

Except… the headache had gone, leaving her with a slightly muzzy feeling and a dry mouth. God knows what was in those tablets, but they'd worked a treat.

Gingerly, she got out of bed and padded into the en suite, taking the empty glass with her. After filling it up from the tap and downing its contents in one, she felt slightly more human, so she had a quick shower and changed into fresh clothes.

Surprised to find she was hungry, she headed upstairs, wondering if Ron was around. He might have taken Pepe for that walk Kate had mentioned, but Annabelle was delighted to discover him sitting on the sofa, staring through the picture window.

He leapt to his feet when he saw her. 'How are you feeling? Can I get you anything? Tea? A cold drink? More painkillers? Actually, you'd better not have any more just yet.'

'What's the time?' She'd left her phone in her bag, and she fished it out, hoping she hadn't missed any calls from Jake or Izzie. 'Gosh, I thought I must have been asleep for hours, but it's only half-past five.' She made her way over to the kettle, but as she began to pick it up, Ron gently nudged her out of the way.

'I've had strict instructions to look after you,' he said. 'I'll make the tea. Or would you prefer a coffee?'

'Tea is fine. Will you allow me to make myself something to eat? I'm starving.'

'I certainly will not. If you're hungry, I'll make it. What do you fancy? I can do you lasagne, chicken breast and salad, a baked potato with something…?' He looked at her expectantly.

'A piece of toast or a sandwich will be fine,' she said.

'Oh, no! If Kate finds out you only had a sandwich for dinner, she'll have my guts for garters. Let me cook you a proper meal.'

'I don't think I can wait that long,' she said. 'My tummy feels like my throat has been cut.'

'That's a Beverley saying, if ever I heard one,' Ron chuckled. 'OK, how about pizza? I can have it on the table in about fifteen minutes. Can you wait that long?'

Annabelle giggled. 'I suppose I'll have to. Where's Pepe? Have you taken him for a walk?'

'He's been out twice, but not for long, as I didn't like to leave you.'

'I'm fine,' she said.

'So you keep saying.' He took a pizza out of the freezer and showed her the box. 'Will this do you?'

Annabelle nodded, adding, 'I really am fine: I'm not fibbing.'

'Are you sure your headache has gone?'

'I'm sure.'

'Good, that's a relief. After we've eaten, how about taking the dog for a longer walk across the front?'

Annabelle gazed at Ron and a strange feeling swept over her. God, he was sexy. There was something very attractive about him taking care of her, and seeing him in the kitchen wearing a T-shirt and faded jeans, stubble on his chin and nothing on his feet, was doing funny things to her insides.

She paused as Kate's words swam into her head. She and Ron were alone in the house. The others weren't due back for hours. It was now or never...

'Wait,' she said huskily, as he was about to pop the pizza in the oven. 'Turn it off.'

'Have you changed your mind? No worries, I'll—'

'Come here.' She beckoned him with a finger and caught her bottom lip between her teeth, the butterflies in her stomach flitting about crazily. She didn't take her eyes off him as he put the pizza on the counter and switched the oven off,

Her gaze captured his and his pupils dilated. He licked his lips, and she watched the flick of his tongue and shivered deliciously, her knees weak with anticipation and excitement.

Not letting him get too close, she backed away towards the stairs. He followed her slowly, his eyes dark pits of desire. She realised he wanted this as much as she, and the knowledge stoked the fire inside her.

Turning, she tiptoed down the stairs, hearing his bare-footed tread behind her, and she ached to feel his hands on her skin and his body next to hers.

When she reached his room, she faced him, her back against the door. 'Are you sure?' she asked.

'I'm sure. Are *you*?'

'Hell, yeah.' Then she opened the door and stepped inside.

Dinner could wait – Annabelle Litton had a more urgent hunger to satisfy.

***

Single beds weren't designed to hold two adults, and the only way Annabelle could get comfortable was if she lay on top of Ron. To be fair, she'd already done that, and it had led to the most wonderful half hour of her life.

Then they'd switched places, leading her to experience the second most wonderful half hour of her life.

Now though, Ron was tired. He needed to rest for a while, which was a shame, because Annabelle was rested enough already and could quite happily have gone for round three. Then her tummy rumbled loudly, reducing her to giggles and reminding her that she was hungry.

'I'm supposed to be looking after you,' Ron said, kissing her on the tip of her nose.

'You did. Twice,' she retorted cheekily. 'When you're ready for a third go, be sure to let me know.' Her eyes widened as she felt a twitch of interest from down below, and she cocked her head to one side, a question on her face.

'No, definitely not, lady,' he said. 'I need time to recover.'

'Wimp,' she teased, easing off him and perching on the side of the bed. 'Your problem is that you've got no stamina.'

'Oh, really?' He leapt up and pushed her back down onto the crumpled covers. 'I don't need stamina for this,' he said, kissing her deeply. 'Or this.'

His lips moved lower, and Annabelle, to her delight, discovered that he hadn't been lying – because what he did to her next didn't require any stamina whatsoever.

***

'We can't stay here much longer,' Ron said, when they finally came up for air and checked the time. 'We'd better go upstairs and pretend we've been watching TV all evening.'

Annabelle would have loved nothing better than to stay in his bed for the rest of the night, but she knew he was right. The others would be back shortly and she didn't want to be caught in a compromising position.

'I've no intention of lying,' she said primly. 'If anyone asks, I'm going to say that I spent most of the day in bed.' She smirked at him, and he sent her a warning look.

'Behave yourself,' he groaned. 'Come on.' He got to his feet and held his hand out to her.

She took it, and he hauled her upright.

Slapping her on the backside, he said, 'Get dressed. I don't know about you, but I'm starving. I'd better put two pizzas in the oven, because I intend to eat a whole one all by myself.'

Annabelle reached for her clothes, which were scattered over the floor of the small room. As she dressed she said quietly, 'I wish we could stay here forever.'

'Me, too.'

'I don't want you to think I hop into bed with just any—'

'Shh. I don't. This is special. *You're* special.'

She thought he was about to say something else, but the sound of an engine pulling into the drive and the sweep of headlights through the glass, had the pair of them scrambling to get dressed and rush upstairs.

But before the front door opened and the family surged in, he held her gently and kissed her deeply once more. 'I know I said we can't, but we did, and it was indescribable. I don't want this to end in Rest Bay,' he said.

And when she replied, 'Neither do I,' the smile that lit his face set her soul on fire and she hoped with all her heart that this truly was the start of something new and wonderful.

CHAPTER 17

Margam Country Park was only a fifteen-minute drive from Porthcawl, so an early start wasn't needed, although a substantial breakfast was, especially for the younger members of the family because they were going to need bags of energy for the day ahead. The older ones managed to pack away a decent amount as well, and even Helen, who was generally careful about what she ate, scoffed a bacon and cream cheese bagel and a croissant at the breakfast table, and Ron also spied her sneakily scoffing another croissant when she thought no one was looking.

Beverley, on the other hand, made no secret that she enjoyed her food, and neither did Annabelle. For such a slim woman, Annabelle had a hearty appetite. Ron didn't skimp, either. There was something about being at the seaside that made him feel constantly hungry. Or maybe it was because he was expending much more energy than usual, because Annabelle had been sneaking into his room every night since the first time they'd made love. And he'd enjoyed every second of it, even if he was exhausted.

Finally, with everyone fed and watered, they were off. Ron rode with Annabelle, with the three younger children in the back, while the rest of the family piled into Brett's seven-seater Peugeot. Smiling, he let the kids' excited chatter wash over him as the car pootled along, their sheer enthusiasm lifting his spirits.

Aware that this was the last-but-one day of the holiday and that once everyone returned to their respective homes, Ron didn't know when he'd next see Annabelle, he was determined to make the most of today.

It was less than two weeks since he'd first set eyes on Annabelle Litton, and Ron couldn't believe how thoroughly she'd burrowed under his skin and pierced his heart. This holiday had been magical, purely because he'd shared it with her, but he was under no illusion that things would be quite so wonderful when they were back in Brighton.

Both their situations were in flux: he would still be relying on Beverley's charity, and Annabelle needed to find a job and a place of her own. The future of their budding relationship was far from assured, but if both of them were determined enough, he was confident they'd make it work. It was scary, though; Ron was acutely conscious of how badly his last relationship had ended. However, there was a significant difference this time around: this time Ron was in love. Properly, deeply, irreversibly in love.

The feeling was poignant. If he had loved Louise the way he loved Annabelle, his life would have been vastly different, and he couldn't help feeling a certain measure of guilt that he hadn't loved Louise as deeply as he should have done. Wherever she was, whoever she was with, Ron hoped she was happy. She deserved it. The last he'd heard, she was engaged to be married to a chap who owned a company which manufactured car parts for the luxury end of the market, but Ron didn't know how accurate the information was. Regardless, he wished her well.

Cross with himself for thinking about the past when he should be concentrating on the present, he came out of his reverie to find Brett's car turning off the road, Annabelle following.

'We're here!' Sam cried, bouncing up and down in his seat. The other children joined in, and Ron clapped his hands to his ears at the deafening noise until Annabelle shouted at them to calm down, otherwise no one would be going on anything.

By "going on", Annabelle was referring to the main attraction for all the youngsters, which was something called Go Ape. Even Ellis, who at eighteen definitely wasn't a child, was keen to have a go at swinging and clambering about through the treetops.

Ron and Brett had volunteered to keep an eye on them if the women wanted to explore some of the less energetic parts of the extensive park, but Kate and Annabelle decided to go with them, while Beverley and Helen, in a rare show of solidarity, decided to have a look around the sections of the impressive manor house that were open to the public, then take a gentle stroll around the gardens. Pepe would stay with the main party at Go Ape, as he wouldn't be allowed in the house.

So, with an agreement to meet up for lunch, the elderly ladies strolled off.

'From this distance they look as though they actually like each other,' Brett muttered in Ron's ear.

'I think you could say it's the lesser of two evils', Ron said chuckling. 'I honestly couldn't see Helen tottering through the woods, could you? And

Beverley might be game, but she hasn't got the energy.'

'I'm not sure I have either,' Brett said.

'Nonsense! You're on your feet all day, and what about all those rounds of golf you play?'

'Hmm, I'm not so sure I'm as fit as you think I am,' Brett replied. 'You seem to have kept in trim, though.'

'When you're constantly being moved on by the police, and when most of the food you eat goes towards trying to keep you warm, you don't get to accumulate a lot of fat.'

'Oh, Lord, I'm sorry, I didn't mean it like that.'

Ron hadn't taken offence and he told Brett so. 'It's just the way it is,' he said shrugging. 'It's a fact of life. Besides, I never stay long in one place. I'm always on the move, and all that walking keeps you fit.'

Brett gave him a quizzical look. 'Except for now. I don't want you to take this the wrong way and it might be a silly question, but you do like living in a house, don't you?'

Ron barked out a laugh. 'Yes, I do.'

'And you like living with Beverley?'

'I like that, too,' Ron said. 'She's a lovely lady: very kind, very generous.'

'Do you miss it at all?'

'Being homeless?'

Brett looked sheepish. 'Not being homeless as such, but being on the road. When I was going through my really dark patch just before Christmas and before I started my new job, I had a fantasy of buying a camper van, selling the house, and touring the world.'

'Some people do it,' Ron said, 'but I suspect it's not as idyllic as it looks.'

'Not with three kids it wouldn't be,' Brett said. 'At least not with my three. Sam isn't so bad, but can you imagine Ellis and Portia squashed in a camper van and being on top of each other all day, every day? There'd be hell to pay.'

'I don't think Kate would be too keen, either,' Ron observed.

'Ah, that's where you're wrong. She can be a bit partial to running away, can Kate.'

The two men shared a smile. It was Kate running away, albeit only for a couple of days, that had brought Ron into the fold of the family.

'Look, look! Deer!' Izzie's eyes were wide as she turned to the others.

She was right, there were deer, and there were loads of them.

Sam, who as usual had done his homework, pointed out that the park had a herd of six-thousand, and a lively discussion followed over which species they might be.

The debate kept the younger kids occupied as they made their way toward the Go Ape centre. Typically, the older girls had taken a couple of photos (Ron noticed Jake's envious glances at their phones) and then had become much more enthralled by their mobiles than the actual sights around them.

This pattern was followed more or less throughout the course of the day, as selfie after selfie was taken and shared with goodness knows who. However, both girls had to stop playing with their phones when they were on the zip wires or the Tarzan swing (blimey, six metres was one hell of a drop!), or scrambling through the nets, because they were scared in case they fell out of pockets and were lost. Kate and Brett had been under strict instructions to take loads of photos and forward them to the girls. Annabelle took a fair few too, when she wasn't wincing at the speed the kids were travelling at, or the height they reached, or both.

It must have been exhilarating for them, and Ron wished he'd had a go. It was a very long time indeed since he'd done anything like that – possibly not since his SAS training.

When the session was at an end, the kids were eager for their lunch, and they chattered non-stop on the way to the café, comparing stories and sharing the experience.

As they walked towards the rendezvous point, Ron let the children go on ahead and he fell into step beside Annabelle.

'I think they had a whale of a time,' she said. She was smiling as broadly as Izzie, who was skipping ahead, clutching Pepe's lead. 'You'd think she'd be worn out,' Annabelle added, looking pointedly at her daughter. 'But oh, no, she's still got bags of energy. I wish I had half of what she's got. It makes me tired just watching her.'

'She's definitely a live wire,' Rion agreed. 'Were you like that at her age?'

'According to my mum I was, but I can't remember being overly energetic.'

Ron bit his lip, checked that none of the kids were looking, then moved closer to her and murmured in her ear, 'Oh, I don't know – you were energetic enough last night.' He nibbled on her earlobe, making her squeal.

'Stop it! she hissed, pushing him away, but she was laughing as she did so. 'You need to get your mind out of the gutter,' she added demurely, and Ron snorted.

'You're a fine one to talk,' he said, grinning wickedly, and he had the satisfaction of seeing her blush.

She still had quite a bit of colour in her cheeks when they arrived at the cafe. Beverley and Helen had already bagged a table and had pushed another up to it, along with some more chairs.

'How did it go?' Beverley asked. 'Did you have a good time?' Her gaze scanned the children, Ellis and Portia included.

'It was fab!' Sam cried, and then the others joined in, all speaking at once.

Helen pulled a face at the noise, and Ron saw Beverley's lips twitch. The naughty madam had done it on purpose, knowing what the children's reaction would be. It seemed that hostilities between the old ladies weren't at an end after all.

Once the chatter had died down and everyone had decided what they wanted for lunch, Brett took the bull by the horns and asked his mother how they'd enjoyed looking around the manor house and its grounds.

'I would have liked to see more of the gardens,' Helen sniffed, 'but someone wasn't quite up to all that walking.' She shot Beverley a look out of the corner of her eye.

'My arthritis was playing up,' Beverley said.

Ron bit back a laugh. As far as he knew Beverley didn't suffer from arthritis: she used it as an excuse now and again when she didn't want to do something, or fancied preferential treatment.

'So we came here,' Helen continued, 'and had a cup of tea.' She sounded quite put out.

'How about if we take a walk after lunch?' Kate suggested.' There's lots more to see and do.'

Sam piped up, 'They've got a fairy-tale village, farm animals, a woodland trail where you can play music on the *trees*, and an adventure playground. Can we go, Mum?'

'I don't see why not,' Kate said. 'We might as well take advantage of everything and have a good look round while we're here. I doubt if we'll come this way again.'

'Aw.' Sam looked crestfallen. 'I've really enjoyed this holiday,' he said. 'It beats silly old Menorca any day.'

Ellis huffed. 'Hardly!'

Ron could see that Portia was torn, and he guessed that on previous holidays she might not yet have been of an age where she wanted to flop down on a sunbed to top up her tan, but neither would she have wanted to take part in the children's activities.

'I won't be coming with you next year,' Ellis announced casually.

'That's a shame,' Kate said. Her tone was mild, but Ron could see that she was hurt.

'I'm going to go away with my friends,' Ellis added.

Portia decided to try her luck. 'I'm going to go with my friends, too,' she said.

Kate stared at her youngest daughter. 'I don't think so.'

'I'll be sixteen! I'm allowed.'

'No, you won't be allowed. Sixteen is not old enough to go on holiday with your friends without adult supervision.' Kate was adamant.

'It's not fair! You never let me do anything.'

'I tell you what,' Brett said. 'To save all the bickering, none of us will have a holiday at all next year. How does that grab you?'

Sam looked mutinous and Portia rolled her eyes.

'I don't care,' Ellis said, 'because I'll be going with my friends.'

'How are you going to afford it?' Brett asked and Ellis blinked at him. She clearly hadn't considered how she was going to fund it.

'Mummy, if Auntie Kate and Uncle Brett go on holiday next year, can we go with them?' This was from Izzie. 'It's been fun. I don't want to go home yet.' The little girl bit her lip.

'Neither do I, love, neither do I,' Annabelle said.

Ron noticed that Jake didn't say anything. His face had closed up like a flower turning away from the sun, and Ron wondered what the boy was thinking. Ron had spent quite a lot of time with the three younger children, the boys especially, and he could have sworn that Jake had enjoyed himself. Maybe he was wrong? Maybe Jake hadn't enjoyed himself at all and couldn't wait to get back to Brighton.

Although Annabelle wasn't looking at him, Ron could sense her intensity, and he hoped that the reason she didn't want to go back to Brighton yet was because of him. Because of *them*.

He felt the same way, and every time he thought about the days and the weeks ahead, his heart sank, because he couldn't live with Beverley forever and he also needed to get a proper job. Annabelle and her children deserved a nice house and nice things, and at the moment he could provide neither. Admittedly, he did have his little handyman business, but it was hardly a proper business, was it? He just pottered about doing odd jobs for people who couldn't manage to do them themselves. He could hardly support a family on what he earned.

Once again he pushed the dismal thoughts to the back of his mind, and reminded himself that he was going to enjoy the next day or so. Saturday would come soon enough, but for the moment he wanted to live for the present.

***

'Fish and chips anyone?' Beverley smacked her lips together. 'How about rounding the day off at Beales?'

Kate clapped her hands. 'Ooh! We haven't been there yet. I've been told they do the best fish and chips for miles around.'

Ron held the car door open for the kids to pile into the back, and his mouth watered at the thought of crispy batter and hot, vinegary chips. He was knackered and didn't feel like cooking. Not that he was *expected* to do it, but he usually seemed to end up wielding a wooden spoon.

'A perfect end to a perfect day,' Brett said. 'I don't know about anyone else, but I've had a wonderful time.'

There were murmurs of agreement and nods all round.

Today had been great fun, Ron thought. After lunch, they'd explored the rest of the park, and even Beverley and Helen had stopped bickering after a

167

while. Beverley's arthritis had miraculously disappeared once all the family were together, and she'd walked around the grounds without a murmur. Ron had even managed to grab a sneaky kiss with Annabelle as they rooted around the ruins of an old abbey, hanging back behind one of the tumbledown walls to snatch a swift embrace when no one was looking.

'Later,' she'd promised him, and his whole body had tingled with anticipation.

Right now though, he needed some dinner, otherwise he might well keel over from hunger.

The chippie had two parts to it – a takeaway section and an eat-in area – and when the majority decided that they preferred to eat in, Ron offered to grab his food to go, and walk over to the park opposite to eat his meal there. It wasn't fair to leave Pepe in the car, and someone had to look after him because he wasn't allowed inside the chip shop.

'You don't want to be eating your supper alone in the park,' Brett told him.

Ron shrugged and smiled. 'I'll have Pepe to keep me company. Anyway, it wouldn't be the first time, mate.'

'I'll join you,' Brett offered, but Kate tugged at his arm.

'Maybe Annabelle would appreciate a few minutes peace?' she suggested, and it took Brett a second to get what she meant.

'Oh, right, yes, good idea. Come on you lot,' he said, rounding up the children. 'Let's go find a table.'

Annabelle looked uncertain, but when Jake and Izzie happily allowed themselves to be ushered inside, Ron saw her relax.

A short while later, with a portion of fish and chips in their hands, and a sausage for Pepe, Ron and Annabelle were sitting on a park bench, the early evening sun warming their faces, and the aroma of recently mown grass wafting over them.

'Ow! Hot!' Annabelle mumbled, around a mouthful of food, as she sucked in air to try to cool her mouth down. 'Good, though.'

Ron wasn't going to argue with that. He wolfed his supper down, faster than Pepe snaffled the sausage portions he was being fed, and very soon he began to feel pleasantly full. A can of fizzy pop washed the meal down, and he patted his stomach.

'I needed that. I was starving,' he announced, wiping his fingers on a serviette.

Annabelle bundled up the remains of her meal (which wasn't much – just a few scraps of chips) and popped the rubbish in the nearest bin.

'Do you know what I could do with now?' she asked.

'A nice cup of tea?'

'You sound like Beverley. No, not tea. Guess again.'

'Coffee? Half a lager?'

'Nope. A kiss.'

'I'm sure I can oblige,' Ron said, scooting closer, and putting his arms around her.

She tilted her head back, her lips parting, and he could see tiny grains of salt sparkling on them. Slowly, he licked them off, desire flaring inside him as she closed her eyes and uttered a soft moan of pleasure.

'You're beautiful,' he told her, then his tongue found hers and neither of them said anything for several delicious minutes.

Then Ron felt Pepe stir at his feet, and he opened one eye.

He hastily opened the other and dragged his lips away from Annabelle's.

'We've got company,' he said, and she hastened to compose herself when she realised the rest of the family had finished their suppers and had just emerged from the chip shop. Hopefully no one had noticed them canoodling.

As the family entered the park and walked over to them, Kate and Brett were smirking, so clearly they'd seen enough, and Beverley winked at him, but Helen sniffed and looked away. She's not my greatest fan, Ron thought, not feeling in the least bit bothered. As long as the kids hadn't noticed their mother being soundly kissed, that was the important thing. Ellis and Portia both had their heads down, their phones in their hands, thumbs flying over the screen, and Sam and Jack were busily chatting between themselves. Izzie's attention was on Pepe, not on her mum, so she hadn't spotted them kissing, either.

But when Jake glanced at him and caught his eye, Ron could have sworn there was a hint of disapproval on his face. He and Annabelle would have to be a little more careful, Ron decided, not wanting to upset the boy.

He appreciated how difficult it must be for him, being dragged away from everything he knew, and plonked in a foreign country to live with grandparents he'd only seen infrequently. To top it all off, he was facing having to go to a new school, make new friends, and carve out a place in this new world he suddenly found himself in. The last thing Jake needed was to see his mother smooching with another man, especially since his father was several thousand miles away.

Oh well, Ron sighed to himself, he and Annabelle would have no choice but to be discreet when they returned to Brighton. Living in two separate houses would see to that. However, he supposed there was an upside, in that by not sharing the same house and by not being in the unrealistic setting of a holiday, it would almost be as though they were starting from scratch, getting to know one another properly, and getting the children used to him being around. Despite his trepidation on the home and the job front, he found he was quite looking forward to it.

Brett had been right when he said this was a perfect day. In Ron's opinion it had also been a perfect holiday. He might not want it to end for that very reason, but he suddenly found himself looking forward to the future very much indeed.

First though, he had tonight to look forward to, and he couldn't wait for Annabelle to slip into his bed where they could make the most glorious and wonderful love.

However, Ron hadn't reckoned on the man standing on the doorstep of their holiday house when Annabelle's car pulled into the drive.

CHAPTER 18

After such a full and exciting day, and feeling pleasantly tired and quite replete, Annabelle couldn't wait to get back to the house and have a shower.

She'd change into her pyjamas, and maybe they'd crack open a bottle of wine. No doubt the younger kids would retreat to the games room, which they had claimed for themselves, and Ellis and Portia would disappear off to their bedroom to carry on texting and messaging the same people they'd been texting and messaging throughout the day. All Annabelle wanted to do was to relax in the lounge or on the terrace with a glass of something alcoholic, and she was brimming with contentment when she swung the car off the road and onto the drive.

What the—!

She barely had time to register the figure standing on the step of their house, before Jake gave a yell and was opening the car door even before the vehicle came to a halt.

Alarmed that he might hurt himself, she screamed 'Jake!' but as she did so Izzie also spotted her father.

Squealing with delight, the little girl scrambled across Sam and almost fell out of the car door in her haste to follow her brother.

Feeling sick, Annabelle yanked the handbrake up and switched off the engine, then she too was out of the car and running towards the front door.

Jake and Izzie beat her to it.

Jake already had his arms around his father's waist, his head buried in his chest, and Annabelle could hear him sobbing. Izzie, on the other hand, wasn't upset in the slightest. She was excited and happy, and was hopping from foot to foot waiting for her turn to receive a cuddle from her dad.

'Troy, what are you doing here?' Annabelle choked out the words, her heart thudding, her thoughts whirling.

Troy's eyes bored into hers and he pushed Jake away, holding his arms out to her, but Izzie took advantage and threw herself at him, and his arms came around his daughter automatically. But he didn't look at the child: his attention remained on Annabelle.

'Why do you think?' he grinned. His expression was cocky, the tone of his voice jaunty and self-confident.

She was dimly aware of the others congregating behind her, but she was frozen to the spot.

'Dear God, is that Troy?' she heard Beverley ask. 'I thought you were in Australia.'

'I've come to get my girl back,' Troy said still refusing to look anywhere else other than at Annabelle.

Izzie cried, 'Yay! Are you taking me home, Daddy?'

He finally glanced down at his daughter, and said, 'Yes, sweet pea, you're coming, too.'

'And me?' Jake sounded doubtful.

'Of course. I wouldn't be taking my two favourite girls home and not taking you as well.'

'I hate to interrupt,' Helen said, waving him out of the way, 'but are we going inside, or are we going to stand on the drive for the rest of the evening?'

With Izzie still clamped around him like a limpet, Troy shuffled to the side, and Helen fished a set of keys out of her handbag.

'I suppose you'd better come in,' she said, sounding every inch as though she was the lady of the manor.

Annabelle's instinctive cry of 'No!', was met with a scowl from her son and a pleading 'Please, Mummy,' from Izzie.

Annabelle stood frozen to the spot while Helen stalked into the hall, followed by Beverley and the rest of them. Only Ron remained outside with her, Troy and the children.

She didn't know whether that was a good thing or a bad one.

Frantically collecting her scattered wits, the question of what her ex-husband was doing here was rapidly followed by another.

'How did you know where to find us? Did my mum tell you?' Annabelle didn't think her mother would, but one never knew. May had been disgusted when Annabelle had informed her what Troy had done and she was aware there was no chance of Annabelle ever getting back with him, but on the other hand he *was* the children's father and her mother had made it very plain that Troy should step up to the mark and shoulder his responsibilities. Then there was the issue of the children missing their father dreadfully, even though he wasn't the best parent in the world and didn't seem to give two hoots about them. If Troy had contacted May, her mum might very well have told him where they were staying.

'Your mum wouldn't tell me if I was on fire,' Troy said. 'Jake gets the credit for that.'

Annabelle inhaled sharply. '*Jake?*' Her son wouldn't meet her eyes, and she glanced back at Troy. 'Is that what happened when you phoned me the other day? Jake had been playing with my phone. He must have called you and you thought it was me?'

'Yeah, I did. You weren't very pleased to hear from me.'

'That should have given you a hint,' she retorted sharply. 'You're not wanted here.'

'Yes, he is!' This was from Jake, who wore a belligerent expression. His jaw was set, his eyes brimmed with tears, and his hands were curled into fists by his side. Izzie's eyes were huge and she looked from one to the other of her parents, back and forth, like a spectator in a tennis match.

Annabelle heard Ron shuffling behind her, but she didn't have time to consider how he might be feeling right now. She had more important matters to deal with – such as how to persuade her ex-husband to bugger off and leave them alone, and how to deal with the fallout from Jake and Izzie when he inevitably did leave. Which he would; walking out on them was his trademark.

'Dad, can we go *now?*' Jake tugged at his father's arm, a pleading look in his eyes, and Annabelle's heart ached with the hurt she saw on his face. Izzie, she noticed, had plugged her thumb in her mouth again, a sure sign she was upset.

Troy shrugged him off. 'Not now, son. I've got things to sort out with your mother.'

'There's nothing left to sort out,' Annabelle said.

'Bella, Bella, can't we talk about this like civilised human beings?' Troy licked his lips. 'I've come a long way. I'm tired and thirsty. Can I at least have a drink? And a bed for the night would be nice.'

'There's nowhere for you to sleep,' Annabelle said stoutly.

'Yes, there is, Mum. He can sleep in my bed.'

Annabelle turned to Jake and said, 'I hardly think your Aunt Kate would be happy with a strange fella sleeping in the same room as Sam.'

'He's not a strange fella, he's my dad.'

'Kate doesn't know him from Adam.'

'Then Kate is stupid.'

'Don't speak about your auntie like that.' Annabelle was appalled at her son's rudeness.

'You hate him,' Jake declared. 'It's your fault we're not going back to Australia. You made us come here. I hate it here!' Jake was trembling from head to foot, his face pale, tears pouring down his cheeks.

Annabelle took a step towards him, but as soon as she moved, Jake yelled. 'I hate you! Hate you, hate you, *hate you*!' Then he whirled on his heel and fled into the house.

Izzie hiccupped a sob, and Annabelle's heart tore in two as she drew her away from her father, who'd hardly noticed her.

'He can have my bed,' Ron said from behind her.

Annabelle had forgotten he was there. 'There's no need, my ex won't be staying,' she told him.

Izzie let out a wail and buried her face in her mother's stomach.

'I miss him, Mum. Please let Dad stay.'

Annabelle turned anguished eyes to Ron. 'What do I do?'

'You do what you think is best for you and the children. Nothing else, and no one else, matters.' And with that Ron gave her a small sad smile and followed Jake into the house.

'Who's he?' Troy glowered after him.

'A friend.'

'Oh, yeah? What kind of friend?' He sounded belligerent.

'He's Beverley's lodger.'

Troy's lips twisted into a scathing grin. 'I bet that's not all he is.'

Annabelle rolled her eyes. 'When's the next flight out,' she asked, refusing to be drawn.

'No idea.'

'You *have* bought a return ticket, haven't you?'

'Of course I have. What do you think I am – stupid?'

Annabelle held her tongue. Stupid didn't cover it. 'Don't you think you'd better check?'

'There's not one today, that's for sure. Go on, Bella, you've got to let me stay here for the night, at least. I've come all this way just to see you, and you're telling me to sling my hook? Heartless, that's what you are.'

Annabelle snorted in disbelief. '*Me* heartless? I'm not the one who made our children homeless.' She bit back any further recriminations, aware that Izzie was listening to every word. As much as she despised Troy for what he did, he was still Izzie and Jake's father. They still loved him. They didn't need to hear what an asshole he was.

Annabelle straightened up, her shoulders back and her chin lifted. 'You can sleep on the couch,' she said. 'Just for tonight, and then I want you gone.'

Troy breathed a sigh of relief. 'Thanks, Bella. You won't regret it,' he said. 'I'll make it up to you, you see if I don't.'

But Annabelle stalked past him, holding Izzie tightly into her, and the only thing she could think of was that she was already regretting it. If it wasn't for her gorgeous children, she would have regretted ever setting eyes on him.

CHAPTER 19

'Jake?' Ron tapped on the door to the boys' room, hoping he was inside. He'd already checked the games room and the TV room, and there was no sign of him, although Sam was sitting on the sofa, watching something on the screen, his little mouth in a straight line. He clearly knew that something was up, but Ron hoped he had no idea what.

The situation was ugly. It was bad enough that Jake and Izzie were involved, without involving Sam as well.

'Jake?' Ron tapped again, and heard a muffled 'What?'

Relieved, he said, 'It's me, Ron. Can I come in?'

'I suppose.'

The curtains were drawn and the room was gloomy when Ron opened the door and stepped inside.

Jake was on the bottom bunk, scrunched up in the corner between the wall and the headboard, the duvet pulled up to his chin. He was trembling, and his face was streaked with dirty tears.

Ron rested his backside against a chest of drawers and folded his arms. 'Are you OK, mate?'

Jake didn't answer and Ron felt stupid. Of course he wasn't OK. He couldn't be expected to be. 'Do you want to talk about it?'

Jake's jaw jutted out and he stared at the pattern on the duvet, refusing to meet Ron's eyes.

'It might help,' Ron persisted.

Jake shrugged. 'Won't,' he grunted.

Ron tried a different tack. 'Your mum is only trying to do what she thinks is best,' he said.

'No, she isn't. She hates my dad, and she doesn't want me to see him.'

'I'm sure that's not the case. I know that she worries about you.'

'Not true. She's only worried about herself. Dad wants us to go back. She doesn't.'

Ron took a steadying breath. Should he really get involved in this? It was none of his business. Despite how he felt about Annabelle and how much he cared for her children, he was no relation and had no say in the matter.

But Jake was hurting, and Ron wanted to try to alleviate some of the boy's pain.

Ron could understand that they loved their father, and were heartbroken about being so far away from him. However, from the little that Annabelle had told him, the guy was a waste of space. But the heart wants what the heart wants, and Jake wanted his dad.

'Your mum loves you very much,' Ron said. 'More than anything else in the world.'

'What would you know about it?'

'I know your mum.'

'Yeah, I saw how well you know her. My dad will punch your lights out when he finds out you've been kissing my mum.'

Ron blinked. 'I doubt that,' he replied mildly. 'Your mum and your dad haven't been together for a long time, so your dad understands that your mum is entitled to kiss anyone she wants.'

'If it wasn't for you, she'd go back to Dad.'

Ron was astounded. 'You don't *really* think that?'

'It's true,' Jake insisted. 'She looks at you like this.' He pulled an exaggerated dreamy-eyed expression, before his face snapped back into a scowl. 'I'm not stupid, I know what's going on.'

'I never thought you were stupid,' Ron said. He unfolded his arms and stuffed his hands into the pockets of his jeans. 'Me and your mum…' He ground to a halt, not knowing how to explain it. He couldn't really explain it to himself, so how could he explain it to Jake. All he knew was that he had fallen in love with Annabelle, and that she was possibly falling in love with him, too.

'I hate her.' Jake glowered at him. 'And I hate *you*. It's your fault she told my dad to go away. I wish you were dead.'

Ron was horrified. The boy had gone from telling his mother he hated her, to saying the exact same thing to Ron, and was now blaming him for his mum and dad not getting back together. It was ridiculous and unrealistic, but Jake was just a child. He couldn't be expected to understand the intricacies of adult relationships. All Jake knew was that his mum had taken him away from his dad, and she was now playing kissy-face with Ron. And when his dad had eventually turned up wanting to take them back home, his mum had told his father to sling his hook.

'Leave me alone,' Jake added sullenly, his chin wobbling. 'I want you to go away.'

Ron hesitated for a moment wondering if he could say something, anything, to help redeem the situation. But he was lost for words. So he did the only thing he could and the only thing that Jake wanted him to do – he left.

***

'Don't you dare!' Beverley cried, when Ron offered for a second time that Troy could have his bed for the night. He was eager to make himself scarce, not wanting to spend another minute in the house where the atmosphere was so acrid.

He'd be more than happy to take a blanket and sleep amongst the dunes again. At least he wouldn't feel Annabelle's nearness, knowing that he couldn't hold her or comfort her. Quite rightly she was wrapped up in her children's misery, trying to console Izzie and trying to break down Jake's barrier, although she wasn't having much success with either.

Kate and Brett were clearly at a loss as to how to help, and the two older girls were hiding away in their room. Ron didn't blame them. Helen was sitting in one of the chairs in the living room, her lips firmly pursed. She only un-pursed them long enough to sip at her tea.

Troy, on the other hand, had made himself perfectly at home. He was sprawled on the corner sofa, his legs stretched out in front of him, his arm draped along the back of the cushions, a beer in his hand. The man didn't look in the least bit perturbed about the mayhem he was causing. In fact, he looked totally relaxed, as though whatever was happening had nothing to do with him.

Jake had come upstairs to check that his dad was still here and then he'd slunk back off again. Izzie was alternating between her mum and her dad, not knowing which one to go to.

Her father didn't seem interested in her, he just gave her an absent-minded pat on the head every now and again, as though she was a small dog. So Izzie was cuddling Pepe instead, who stared balefully at the stranger and uttered little rumbling growls deep in his throat every so often.

Kate and Brett were clearly uncomfortable with the situation. They were sitting on the terrace, nursing a drink, their heads together, whispering, and occasionally one or the other of them would shoot a glance inside.

Beverley, however, wasn't backward in coming forward.

When she'd come upstairs and found Troy on the sofa, she'd told him in no uncertain terms that he wasn't welcome. 'Not after what you did to my niece,' she said, her hands on her hips. 'Annabelle, why did you let him in?'

'He *is* Jake and Izzie's father,' Annabelle said with a sigh. She looked pale and drawn.

Ron wished he could put his arms around her and tell her everything would be all right, but he wasn't sure that it would be.

As far as he could tell, the only way to make the children happy, Jake in particular, would be for them to go back to Australia. After all, they had been ripped from their homes, their friends, and their school, to start afresh in another country.

Whether a return to Australia would make Annabelle happy, was also something to consider.

She'd suffered the same as her children, and had had to leave her home, her job, her friends, and her whole way of life behind. Admittedly she had been born and had grown up in the UK, but she hadn't lived here for years, and she must be finding it as much of a wrench as her children.

He suspected it would have been difficult enough for her to make the change, without having two miserable kids in tow. He knew she had to consider what was best for them and what would make them happy, which, at the moment, seemed to be going to Australia.

Whether she and Troy resumed their relationship was irrelevant. The point was that the children would be back with their friends in a country they knew and loved; maybe not in the same house but possibly one close by, and they'd be able to return to their old schools, and they'd still be able to see their father on a regular basis.

To Ron, Annabelle's decision was a no-brainer. She had to go back.

Even if she didn't, even if she did decide to live in her parents' house in Brighton, Ron knew there could be no future for him and her. Jake had made that perfectly clear.

He wasn't happy with his mum having a relationship, and once again Ron could understand that.

There had been so much upheaval in the little boy's life, that he wouldn't be able to cope with yet another one. And maybe he would always blame Ron for coming between his mum and his dad.

Feeling as though he had no choice, Ron made the only decision open to him, and one he should have made the minute he set eyes on Annabelle Litton – he would leave.

It was the best thing for everyone.

***

Ron was good at waiting. He'd had a lot of practise at biding his time, and patience was his middle name.

It had taken until one o'clock in the morning before the house had finally fallen silent and as far as he could tell, everyone was asleep. He'd not bothered to argue with Beverley about who was sleeping where: instead, he'd retreated to his room without a murmur, and had left the sofa to Troy.

For nearly two hours he'd sat on the edge of his bed, his trusty old Bergen at his feet, and as he waited, letting the house settle around him, he thought about where he would go.

Undoubtedly he'd make his way back to Pershore eventually – he always did – but in the meantime he'd head along the coastal path and into Cardiff, where he'd be able to buy a sleeping bag and stock up on anything else he needed. He still had some money left, safely tucked away in an old leather pouch that he'd tied next to his skin around his waist with a thin strap. He used to wear it all the time. He'd ever had much money to put in it, but when he did have some he'd liked to keep it well hidden, in a place not easily accessible to anyone other than himself. He'd forgotten it was there and had found the pouch when he was packing earlier, buried deep in one of the pockets.

Eventually, he felt the time was right, and he got to his feet, hefting his rucksack onto his shoulder.

185

There was one more thing he needed to do, something he should have thought of doing before he retired to his room, and that was to leave a note for Beverley. He couldn't simply walk out on her and not thank her for everything she'd done. Or tell her how much she meant to him.

Quietly, he slipped into the games room, hunting around for a pen and some paper, but couldn't find any. And neither was there any in the TV room, but he could remember seeing a pad that someone – Helen, he thought it might have been – had left on the kitchen counter for people to write down things that they needed the next time anyone went to a shop.

Ron frowned. There was nothing for it, he'd have to nip upstairs and retrieve it.

For a fairly big man, Ron could be exceptionally quiet when he needed to be, and he crept silently up the stairs and into the living room. He heard Troy snoring and saw the man lying flat out on the sofa, and he pulled a face in disgust.

The room was dark, but there was enough light filtering in from the occasional street lamp outside for him to see the notepad, and he was relieved to find a pen tucked into its curling tines.

Carefully, so as not to make a sound, he picked it up, but as he did so he realised the snoring had stopped.

Slowly he turned around and saw Annabelle's ex-husband staring at him from over the back of the sofa. Ron met the man's gaze silently. He had nothing to say to Troy, and there was nothing Troy could say to him that Ron wanted to hear. They locked eyes for a few moments, Troy looking away first, then Ron crept out of the room.

The note wasn't long. In it Ron said everything he wanted to say, and as he wrote it he felt the sting of tears at the back of his eyes. He was so incredibly sad to leave Beverley – she'd been like a mother to him, and that's how he regarded her, but he couldn't stay. Not now. This was the right thing to do.

He wished he could give her a hug, Pepe, too. He'd miss the little dog almost as much as he would miss the animal's mistress, and he stood there for a moment after he'd slipped the note under her door, his Bergen on his back, saying a silent farewell.

Then his thoughts turned to Annabelle, and he hoped he wouldn't hurt her too much by leaving without saying goodbye.

He knew she'd understand. It didn't make the heartache any less – he would carry it with him for some considerable time, possibly to the end of his days – but he didn't think she'd blame him for leaving as he did. Once again, he told himself it was the best for everyone, Annabelle especially.

It was the best for him too.

Smiling sadly, he opened the front door, slipped into the night, and headed for the open road, leaving his heart and his dreams behind.

CHAPTER 20

Ron had always loved being outdoors at night. Not in a city or town centre, but in the countryside or at the coast, where there were few lights and fewer people, and he could pretend he was alone in the world.

Ha! Who was he kidding?

He *was* alone, regardless of his actual whereabouts. Since his mum had passed away, his dog had died, and his marriage had fallen apart, he had been on his own and he hadn't anticipated any change in the situation, until he'd met Annabelle, and for a while he'd allowed himself to believe that he mightn't have to be alone after all.

His feet pounded the path, and he sighed as he rounded a small headland into the next bay. He'd been stupid to believe he could have a future with someone like Annabelle. He had even less to offer her than her toe-rag of an ex-husband. Actually, he *was* able to offer her something that Troy couldn't – *love*. But love didn't put a roof over her head or food on the table, and love didn't make up for the kids not seeing their father from one year to the next. He couldn't blame her for returning to Australia. It was probably for the best: for Jake's sake, if nothing else.

Ron walked down the slipway and onto the beach, toed off his well-worn hiking boots, and stuffed his socks inside. Tying the laces together, he slung the boots around his neck and set off across the sand.

He might as well make the most of these last few hours on the coast. Pretty soon he'd swing inland and head north, perhaps with a detour to the Brecon Beacons on the way. He'd climb to the top of the highest peak, lie on his back, lose himself amongst the stars, and remember Annabelle.

Above the high tide mark, the sand was warm and dry, and his toes sank into it with every step. The bay stretched ahead of him, the sea glittering darkly, the lights of the small town of Ogmore twinkling in the distance. A small river lay between him and it, which he would have to circumnavigate if he wanted to carry on along the coastal path to Cardiff.

This particular stretch of the coast, like Kenfig beach, was also backed by extensive sand dunes, and he planned on cutting through them and exploring the nature reserve as he followed the river upstream searching for a place to cross.

It was already starting to get light. In high summer the nights were short, and to the east the sky was a flat silver with a hint of coral sunrise where the land met the sky. Ron guessed it was going to be another glorious day. It was just a shame he was raining inside.

In the pre-dawn, the birds were singing. It wasn't the full rich chorus of spring but Ron appreciated it, nevertheless. The sounds of the waves, the wind sighing through the grass and the gentle burble of the river accompanied the bird song, and Ron took a moment to savour the tranquillity of the scene. He couldn't see another soul, and it was incredibly peaceful. It was just unfortunate that Ron didn't feel as peaceful inside. He'd not felt this bad since he walked out of his marriage. He actually felt worse, in fact, because the only thing he had felt when he'd left Louise had been a deep sense of guilt and regret. Guilt and regret hounded him this time too, but alongside it was heartbreak.

He'd recover from it eventually, but he knew it would be an uphill struggle, and the pain would never totally go away. After all, he still felt the loss of his mum and his dog. That kind of pain never left, it just dimmed a little with time, became less acute, tempered by the distance of the years. Annabelle was now etched in his heart, and he wouldn't have wanted it any other way. He liked having her there, despite the pain. He was glad he'd met her and glad he'd fallen in love with her, because if he hadn't known her, his life would have been all the poorer for it.

Sighing deeply, he carried on walking until he gradually moved up off the beach and onto the sandy trail. When he came to a fork he hesitated. Should he carry on until he reached the river itself and hope to cross there, or should he follow this trail? He had a vague idea where it led, up towards a small village where he hoped might be a cafe or shop where he could purchase some coffee, and maybe a doughnut or a Danish pastry. He wasn't particularly hungry, but he knew from experience that long walks meant burning up quite a lot of calories which would need replacing.

The trail through the dunes was wide and obviously well used. It led steadily upwards from the beach for a while, then all at once the gradient became considerably steeper, and Ron stopped for a moment to gaze upwards at an impressive wall of sand rising in front of him. Blimey, that was a dune and a half, he thought, and he debated whether or not to climb it.

What the heck! He had nothing to lose, and he guessed the view from the top could well be spectacular. He had plenty of water with him so he wouldn't get dehydrated, although he did discover that he'd lost some fitness since living with Beverley, as he puffed and panted his way to the top. Walking on sand wasn't easy, especially when that sand was at a fairly acute angle. Every time he took a step his foot slid backwards slightly, making him think of that old saying, one step forward, two steps back. It wasn't quite that bad, but it took him longer than he anticipated to reach the top, and as soon as he got there he flung himself down and sat facing out to sea, his chest heaving. He wryly acknowledged that it was going to take him some time to return to his pre-Beverley toughness, acquired from pounding the streets, restlessly moving from one place to the next, sleeping out in all weathers. He'd become soft, and he was going to find it hard at first.

With renewed determination he vowed to buy himself a decent sleeping bag, because he guessed he'd feel the cold for a while, even though the nights were still relatively warm. It wouldn't take long before the season turned and autumn would be upon him, then winter. And sleeping rough in winter could be a brutal affair.

The sun had risen fully now, and it warmed his back after he shrugged off his Bergen and took a long drink of water. With his breathing returning to normal and his heart rate slowing down, Ron took in the view. As he suspected, it was indeed spectacular, he thought, as he gazed out over the sea towards the Devon coast, those distant hills clearer than he'd seen them since the holiday began. In no hurry, he sat there for a while drinking it in, trying to keep his thoughts away from Rest Bay and the people he'd left behind.

It was impossible, of course. His mind kept returning to Annabelle, and he wondered if she was awake. Then he wondered whether Beverley had found the note he'd left for her yet, and his gut twisted as he imagined her reaction.

Unable to sit still any longer with such thoughts churning through his brain, Ron scrambled to his feet and hoisted the Bergen. Turning his back on the sea, he jogged down the other side of the dune, heading for a wooded area. Once under the canopy, he stopped to get his bearings and catch his breath again.

Between the trunks he could see a small clearing and he walked towards it, curious about the old crumbling stone walls he could see amongst the undergrowth. A weathered sign read Candleston Castle, although there wasn't much of the actual castle left. Still, he enjoyed poking around the tumbledown walls which alluded to a grander past. Sam and Jake would love it here, he thought, before he could stop himself.

Shaking his head ruefully, he knew he'd have to accept that it would take a while, possibly a good long while, before he stopped tripping over thoughts of Annabelle and her children and of Beverley and Pepe. His heart constricted once again as he thought of the dog. The poor little chap would be so confused. Unlike the humans, the dog wouldn't understand that

Ron had left. One minute Ron had been there, the next he was nowhere, and Pepe would have no idea what had happened to him.

When he spotted a road, he decided to follow it, hoping it might take him to the village and coffee. The lane was narrow, just room enough for one car with a few passing places along the way, but he didn't encounter any traffic, although he did hear a tractor in the distance. He passed a dog walker who nodded to him, but he didn't see anyone else, and for that he was grateful. Part of the reason for following the coastal path from Rest Bay to Cardiff was to try to avoid people as much as possible, and it looked like he was succeeding. There was the occasional house or farm along the lane, and the most gorgeous old church, but the village didn't seem to be a particularly big place. It was very picturesque though, with lush meadows on either side of the road, and lots of old big trees. However, there wasn't a cafe in sight, and neither did there appear to be a shop.

Coming to a fork in the road, he hesitated, wondering which way to go.

Almost directly in front of him was a gorgeous little house with a thatched roof, which was painted a cheerful yellow. It had an extensive lawn to the front and when he noticed a woman with a watering can in her hand, he decided to ask.

'Excuse me, sorry to bother you, but is there anywhere I could get a coffee?'

The woman stopped watering the flowerbeds, and turned to look at him. 'Not here,' she said. 'Your best bet is to go to Porthcawl.'

'I've actually just come from there,' he replied. 'I'm heading east towards Cardiff.'

'In that case, you'll need to go to Ogmore. If you go down that road—' she pointed '— and follow the path across the field, it will lead you to the river, where you'll find stepping stones from one side to the other. Beyond that is Ogmore Castle, and a bit further on is Ogmore itself. There are a couple of cafes and shops, so you should be able to get a coffee.'

Ron thanked her and followed her directions. Pepe would have had a whale of a time in the field, he thought as he traversed the lush meadow. The dog probably would have had to be carried across the stepping stones though, because the water was too fast-flowing and deep for a small poodle, and Ron wouldn't have wanted him to fall in.

Ron negotiated them with ease, and very soon he was on the other side of the river and gazing up in awe at Ogmore Castle. Now this really *was* a castle. Sam and Jake would have—

Argh! Crossly, he pushed thoughts of the boys out of his mind. If he was to find any peace at all, he had to stop thinking about those he'd left behind.

But even as he told himself that, he knew that for him, peace would be a long time coming.

CHAPTER 21

Annabelle hesitated, hovering outside her son's bedroom door. She'd woken with a start, and her first thought had been for Jake, quickly followed by the memory that his father was asleep on the sofa upstairs. Izzie was fine. Annabelle could see the hunched form of her daughter underneath the covers on the other bed, her breathing steady and even.

It was Jake who Annabelle was concerned about, and yet again she crept out of bed in the middle of the night to check on him. He, too, was sleeping soundly, which she was relieved to find, and she backed out of the room quietly, wondering whether Ron was awake.

Putting her ear to the door, her fingers brushed the handle, then she shook her head crossly before turning away. He was probably asleep; after all it was three o'clock in the morning, but even if he wasn't, what could she say? The middle of the night wasn't exactly the best time to have a hushed conversation about the sudden appearance of her ex-husband and the issues of upset children.

Yet, she continued to linger, wanting desperately to be held by him, to feel his strong arms around her, to be buoyed up and strengthened by his calm and steadfast demeanour.

It wasn't fair to wake him purely for selfish reasons. He was undoubtedly as tired as she, having been on the go all day and then having to face Troy worming his way into the family. This evening couldn't have been easy for Ron, she acknowledged; their relationship was so new and so fragile that the slightest breeze might endanger it. And Troy wasn't exactly a breeze. He was more of a hurricane.

As quietly as she could, she went back to her room, crept inside, and slipped under the bedclothes. For now, at least, the children were slumbering soundly, but that was the only bit of comfort she could glean, as her thoughts once again turned to Troy and anger bubbled to the surface. His selfishness astounded her. How dare he simply turn up and expect her to welcome him with open arms! Maybe he thought he was in with a chance because of how devastated she'd been when he'd told her he had another woman and that he was leaving. Who wouldn't feel the same if they discovered that the person who had vowed to love you and stay faithful to you had been playing hide-the-sausage with someone else?

Just because she had been distraught at the collapse of their marriage, didn't mean that she would go running back to him if he clicked his fingers. She hadn't wanted anything to do with him after that, despite her broken heart, so she sure as hell didn't want him now. Besides, the only reason he was here at all was because he and Sallie were no longer together. Troy was the sort of man who couldn't cope unless he had a woman on his arm – a woman to keep house, do the laundry, cook his meals, and keep him entertained in the bedroom. Annabelle was under no illusion that he wanted her because he loved her. All she'd be was a stopgap until someone more exciting came along.

She had to admit though, that the thought of going back to Australia was appealing. She'd spent over half her life there, she'd birthed her children there, she had friends and a social life there. She'd had a home and a job. And once upon a time she'd had a husband.

However, things change. She now had no husband, no home, no job, few friends and no social life. If she gave in to her guilt about taking her children away from everything they'd ever known, and took them back to Australia, she'd still not have any of those things and she'd actually be worse off. At least in the UK she could continue to live in her parents' house for as long as she needed.

And there was something else that, over the past few days, she'd come to think was equally important – Ron, and the opportunity to start over with someone who cared about her and her children.

All she had to do was to convince Jake that staying in Britain was in his and Izzie's best interests.

Which might be easier said than done.

***

After spending half the night awake, Annabelle finally dropped off to sleep as the morning light seeped through the curtains, and when she woke a few hours later she felt groggy and hungover despite not having drunk anything last night.

Wearily she pushed the duvet back and sat up, not wanting to face the day but knowing she had to. For one thing, she had two confused children to comfort, and for another she had an ex-husband to send packing. When she'd done that, hopefully things would settle down and she'd be able to have a talk with Ron. She could tell that he'd felt uncomfortable yesterday evening. She wouldn't have been at all surprised if he'd spent another night out on the dunes, purely to get away from the tense atmosphere in the house.

Feeling groggy and tired, she hopped into the shower, and when she emerged she saw that Izzie was awake and staring at her.

'Is Daddy still here?' her daughter asked.

Annabelle said, 'I expect so.'

She couldn't imagine Troy doing the decent thing and leaving. For one thing, he had no transport (he'd informed her that he'd caught the train from Cardiff to Porthcawl, and then had a taxi from the station to Rest Bay) and for another, he would have been too mean to shell out for a night in a hotel when he had free accommodation here. She was just glad that Beverley had insisted Ron didn't vacate his room for him, otherwise she might never get rid of the damned man.

Saying that though, today was their last day in Rest Bay, and tonight would be their last night, so unless he intended to follow her to Brighton, he'd have no other option than to go.

She felt incredibly sad to think that tomorrow evening she'd be back in her parents' home, having said goodbye to Ron, and although Beverley only lived a couple of miles away, it was going to seem much further, once reality kicked in. All she hoped was, that this wasn't just a holiday romance and that they would be able to continue to see each other when they were back in Brighton. She knew how she felt about him, and she hoped and suspected that he felt the same way about her, but she wasn't certain because he'd not told her he loved her, and she'd not said those three little words to him, either.

It was too soon, the relationship too new, to say something of such significance. Annabelle didn't fall in love lightly, and neither did she give her heart away willy-nilly. There was only one man she'd ever loved, and that was Troy, and look how that had turned out. She was all too aware that she didn't only have her own happiness to consider, she also had to consider the happiness of her children. They'd both taken to Ron, Izzie especially, and he was very good with them and he seemed to care for them, but he wasn't their father. In her children's eyes, no one could take their father's place, despite Troy being a pretty crap dad. Annabelle would love nothing better than for Ron to be in their lives. But she couldn't force it. Ron would have to earn their love, and their trust, and there was a long way to go before that happened.

Izzie watched Annabelle for a while as she brushed her hair and tied it up, then applied some makeup. She didn't normally wear a great deal of make-up, but today she felt the need of it. Similarly, she chose what she was going to wear with care. With Ron she'd been happy in faded jeans and strappy tops, but she almost felt as though today was an unpleasant business meeting. She had the same butterflies in her stomach that she'd had when she'd gone to see a lawyer about her divorce, needing to appear in control and put-together in the eyes of the world, because she had been feeling the exact opposite inside.

'You look pretty, Mum,' Izzie told her, finally getting out of bed.

Annabelle was surprised that her daughter hadn't shot out the door and gone straight upstairs to see her father, and it took a while before Annabelle realised the reason for Izzie's hesitation – she was shy. And possibly apprehensive. The children hadn't seen their father for a couple of months prior to them getting on the plane to the UK. Maybe even longer. To children of Izzie's age, four or five months was a long time. For Jake too, although he was older. Izzie might love her dad, but Jake *worshipped* him. In Jake's eyes, Troy could do no wrong, which was why Annabelle hadn't shared any details of his father's negligence with him. She didn't want to be the one to burst Jake's bubble, but unfortunately he'd heard far too much last night. He had probably heard other things too, especially in those first days after arriving at her parents' house when she'd practically fallen apart. No matter how hushed the conversation, Jake must have heard some of it. Her mum hadn't been shy about expressing her disgust at Troy's behaviour despite Annabelle urging her to keep her voice down and her opinions to herself when the children were around.

Still, she was fairly certain that Jake didn't know the worst of it – as far as she was aware, the kids only understood they didn't have a home anymore because Daddy's business wasn't doing too well, and so they couldn't afford to live there. Izzie had accepted the explanation, although she did keep asking why they weren't going back home and she was clearly upset about it. Jake had probed deeper, and it had taken

Annabelle a while to convince him that the house he'd lived in all his life no longer belonged to them. In her darkest moments, she'd actually wondered whether Jake thought she'd been making it up, because he had been so distant and withdrawn with her.

In spite of everything that Jake may, or may not, have heard, all Jake wanted was his dad.

Therefore Annabelle couldn't be cross with her son, although she wasn't happy with the way he'd gone behind her back and told his father where they were staying.

When she went out into the hall she could hear voices coming from the boys' bedroom, and she tentatively knocked on the door and asked if they were decent, before poking her head around it. Sam was still in his PJs, but Jake was fully dressed. He had a suitcase open on the bed and was busily putting things in it.

'Jake, there's no need to do that now,' Annabelle said. 'It won't take long to pack in the morning. Kate says we don't have to be out of the house until midday.'

'I'm leaving now,' Jake announced.

'Excuse me?' Annabelle blinked.

'You heard,' he replied rudely. 'I'm leaving with Dad and you can't stop me. I suppose you can come with us if you want. Izzie, too,' he added in a grudging tone.

Wow, she hadn't seen that coming.

She was about to say that Jake wasn't going anywhere without his passport, which was safely back in Brighton, but she thought it best not to shove a stick in a hornets' nest. Jake was wound up like a top already, and there was no point making it worse. She may as well let him carry on packing, because he'd have to do it in the morning anyway.

She was about to leave him to it, when she remembered what she wanted to speak to him about. 'Jake, I know you told dad where we were staying, but why didn't you just wait until we got back to Brighton?'

Jake's jaw jutted out. 'You know,' he said.

'What do I know?'

'You think I'm stupid. You think that just because I'm a kid, that I don't know what's going on. Well, I do, so there. I saw you.'

'Excuse me, Auntie Annabelle, I think I'm going to watch TV,' Sam said, slipping out of bed and squeezing past her. The poor boy; what a disagreeable end to his holiday. She'd apologise to Kate and Brett later, the others, too. But first she had her son to deal with.

Annabelle didn't want to ask, but she had to. 'Saw me?'

'You and Ron. The other night.' Jake shook his head in disgust.

Annabelle was astounded. She thought they'd been quite discreet. She'd made especially sure that Jake and Izzie were sound asleep before she slipped into Ron's room, and even then she hadn't stayed long, and she'd certainly not spent the night with him although she would dearly have loved to.

Before she could question Jake further, he said, 'You thought you were so clever, going out in the middle of the night, but I saw you.

Eh? 'Jake, when was this?'

'The day I peed on Sam.' Her son looked furtive

and she guessed the reason. That was the night she'd asked Ron to take her stargazing, the night she'd more or less thrown herself at him, the night he'd pushed her away and told her they couldn't have a relationship.

Jake's voice hardened. 'The day you wouldn't let me speak to Dad,' he reminded her.

Annabelle's blood turned to ice in her veins – the only way Jake could have seen the kiss, was if he had followed them. They'd been in the dunes, possibly a mile away from the house, although she wasn't quite sure of the distance, so that must have meant that Jake had been outside, *on his own*, in the middle of the night, when she'd thought he was safely tucked up in bed, fast asleep.

'Did you follow me?' she demanded.

He refused to look at her.

'You do know how dangerous that is, right?' Retrospective fear clawed at her. Dear God, what if something had happened to him? What if he'd fallen, or someone nefarious had seen him, or— it didn't bear thinking about. She would have gone back to bed totally oblivious that her son was hurt, or in danger, or worse.

'Jake!' The fear was suddenly overtaken by anger. 'You must promise me you'll never ever do anything like that again. *Anything* could have happened.'

'Yeah, so I saw,' was his sullen and sarcastic reply.

'It wasn't like that,' she said. 'I was upset and—'

Jake interrupted her. 'So was I! You didn't let me speak to Dad!'

'That's no excuse to sneak out in the middle of the night.'

'*You* did.'

'I'm a grown-up. And I was with Ron.'

'Yeah, I know, I *saw*.' His voice was full of scorn, and Annabelle was suddenly very glad indeed, that Ron had refused her advances.

Jake pulled a face, and she could see that tears weren't far from the surface. 'I told Dad to come and get us, because you like Ron,' he said. 'And he likes you. And I want to go home.'

'Poppet, I've explained this, we can't go back. We don't have a home there any more. Someone else owns our house now.'

'Dad's got a house. We can live with him.'

'No, we can't. The house he was living in with Sallie belonged to *her*, not your dad. He hasn't got anywhere to live now, either.'

'He can find somewhere,' Jake persisted, but she could see that he believed her, as the tears began trickling down his cheeks.

Annabelle carried on, explaining once again, 'Without somewhere to live, I'm not going to be able to get a job, and without a job, I can't find us anywhere to live, so we're stuck.'

'Dad can get a job.'

She was tempted to say "let's wait until he does, and we'll see what happens then", but she didn't want to give Jake false hope. So she said the only thing she could, which was, 'Jake, we are *not* going back to Australia.'

'*I* am. I'm going back with Dad.'

The conversation had just come full circle and Annabelle could see little point in carrying on with it. She'd be better off concentrating her efforts elsewhere. which meant kicking Troy out before he had a chance to talk to Jake.

204

This wasn't going to be pretty and it probably wouldn't be easy, but she was determined that Troy had to leave. *Now.*

CHAPTER 22

'What do you mean *Ron has gone?*'
Annabelle paused halfway up the stairs as Brett's voice drifted down to her.

'He's gone, I tell you. Gone!' Beverley cried. 'He left me a note.'

'Gone where?' Brett asked.

Annabelle hurried up the remaining steps and almost fell into the room.

Beverley was in her nightie, a dressing gown over the top and slippers on her feet, three curlers in the front of her hair. She looked distraught, and was waving a piece of paper around. Brett was in the kitchen, kettle in hand, poised ready to pour water into a mug.

Out of the corner of her eye, Annabelle noticed Troy lounging on the sofa, stretched out with his feet crossed at the ankles and one arm draped along the back, in virtually the same position he'd been in yesterday evening. He was watching with interest, a smirk playing about his mouth.

'Back on the road,' Beverley said. Her face was white and she looked close to tears, her bottom lip trembling.

Annabelle shook her head. 'He'll have spent the night in the dunes,' she said. 'He did the same thing when Pepe went missing.'

'Ya mean, I didn't have to sleep on this shitty sofa, after all?' Troy drawled.

'Shut up, Troy.' Annabelle didn't look at him. Her attention was on the piece of paper in Beverley's hand. Despite what she'd just said, Annabelle had a feeling of dread in her chest. She didn't want to believe it, but she instinctively knew her aunt was right – Ron *had* left.

'No, lovey, he's gone.' Beverley turned tear-filled eyes towards her.

Annabelle suddenly felt weak and unsteady, and she leaned against the kitchen island for support. 'Why?' she asked. 'I thought... I hoped…'

'Here. Read it.' Beverley thrust the note at her, and Annabelle hastily scanned it.

'Is that all? He thinks it's time he left? No reason, no explanation?' Annabelle read it again, looking frantically for something that wasn't there.

'What does he say?' Brett asked.

'Read it yourself.' Annabelle handed him Ron's brief letter.

Brett scanned it, then looked at Beverley, his eyes full of sympathy. 'I don't know what to say.'

'I thought he was happy living with me!' Beverley sniffled.

'He was. He says so—' Brett shook the letter '— right here.'

'But not enough.' Beverley wailed.

Annabelle let out a moan of distress. The pain was growing with each passing minute, and very soon it would overwhelm her, as the reality sank in. *Ron had left*. He'd chosen life on the streets, with all the deprivations and hardship that entailed, over having a relationship with her. She'd really thought they'd had something special. Clearly she'd been mistaken.

At least he'd told Beverley that he loved her and he was sorry.

He'd said nothing to Annabelle. Not even goodbye.

'Poor, poor Ron,' Beverley cried and burst into tears.

'What's all the racket about?' Helen entered the room, dressed in her golfing clothes, eager for a final game on the world-renowned course.

Beverley turned stricken eyes to her nemesis. 'You'll be happy,' she snapped. 'Ron has gone.'

'Gone where?'

'He's back on the streets!' Beverley exclaimed. She pointed to the piece of paper that Brett was still holding. 'He left me a note.'

Helen's mouth flattened into a thin line and she sniffed. 'I must admit, I'm not surprised. I always thought he was unreliable. Although, I must say, he did have it cushy with you – free bed and board. But then again, I don't suppose there was any future in it: you're not exactly rolling in money, so I bet he's off to find a richer victim. Or maybe a younger one.' She shot Annabelle a meaningful look out of the corner of her eye, and added, 'One with a house of her own.'

'He's not like that!' Beverley protested.

Helen made a moue. 'Believe what you want, but I think he's got an agenda of his own. No one in their right mind would choose to live on the streets when they've got a roof over their heads, three square meals a day, and a daft old bat like you to wait on them hand, foot, and finger. Mark my words, that man is up to something. You should thank your lucky stars that you're well out of it. I'm just relieved he didn't take the silver with him.'

Beverley stared at her. 'I don't have any silver.'

'No, I don't expect you do,' was Helen's sour reply.

Troy sat up. 'Hang on a sec. Did I hear you right? That this Ron-fella is a derro?'

'A what?' Helen demanded. 'For goodness sake, speak English.' She rolled her eyes and said, 'He sounds like he's on the set of Neighbours.'

'Derro,' Troy repeated. 'Derelict fella. Homeless.'

'That's right, Ron is homeless,' Helen said. 'Brett, are you going to do something with that kettle or not? I simply have to have my breakfast before we play.'

'He doesn't have to be homeless,' Beverley cried. 'He has a perfectly good home with me.'

Helen sniffed again. 'That's debatable.'

'Mum,' Brett warned and Helen subsided, closing her mouth on whatever else she was about to say.

'Holy-moly!' Troy was incredulous, as he smirked at Annabelle. 'You've been cosying up with a *derro*?'

'Yeah, well, I suppose it takes one to know one,' Annabelle shot back.

'I'm not homeless – I'm waiting for a rental to go through.'

'I was referring to myself, actually,' Annabelle retorted. 'Thanks to you and your stupidity – or should I call it selfishness – me and the kids are homeless.'

'You can stay at your mum and dad's place,' Troy said, shifting awkwardly, clearly uncomfortable with the direction the conversation was going.

'What would have happened if I hadn't already had our flights booked and the holiday planned?' Annabelle demanded. Her sudden surge of fury was a welcome relief from the anguish she was feeling. The heartache was still there – she was under no illusion that it had magically disappeared – but anger's much louder voice was temporarily drowning it out. 'Your children would have been out on the streets, that's what,' she continued. 'Unless Sallie would have taken us in, which I highly doubt.' Annabelle's tone was scathing, and Troy had the grace to look sheepish.

'The social would have sorted you out,' he said.

'Ha!' Annabelle snorted. 'That was your solution, was it? That one of the welfare agencies would have found us somewhere to live? You take the biscuit, Troy, you really do. No wonder your bloody business went under.' Disgust radiated out of her. 'I can't believe you were so reckless as to risk your children's health and happiness for the sake of a few lousy bucks.'

'It wasn't just a few,' Troy objected. 'I needed the cash to keep it afloat.'

'That didn't work out so well for you, did it?' Annabelle retaliated. 'Your business sunk without a trace anyway, taking my home with it. I would have begged stolen and borrowed to scrape enough money together to buy you out, but I trusted you to do the right thing; if not for me then for your kids. You don't give a hoot about them, do you?'

'Course I do.'

'You've got a funny way of showing it.' Annabelle was trembling violently, though whether it was from the shock of Ron's leaving or from sheer temper, she couldn't tell.

'I love you, Bella, I always have.' Troy had a winning expression on his face, an expression that had worked on her in the past, but now just left her cold.

'If you loved me that much you wouldn't have slept with Sallie. You wouldn't have walked out on me and the kids, leaving me to bring up *our* children on my own.'

'I helped,' Troy objected.

'How? You saw them now and again when it was convenient for *you*, not when they needed you. And you didn't provide for them financially whatsoever. I was the one who made sure there was enough food to eat, who kept the electricity on, who bought them new shoes for school. All you did was let me keep the house. To think I was grateful for that!' She barked out a bitter laugh.

'Come back to Stralia with me. I'll sort something out, I promise,' Troy whined.

'I hope you haven't already bought our tickets,' Annabelle snorted, 'because you'll have wasted your money.' Then when she saw the expression on his face, she realised that Troy had no intention of buying their tickets. If she was to return to Australia, she'd have to pay her own fare.

'I didn't see the point. You've already got return tickets,' he muttered.

'They expired over a month ago. They weren't open-ended,' she told him. 'So, assuming we do come back with you, are you going to fork out for the airfare?'

Troy didn't say a word.

Annabelle carried on, 'I thought not. You've not got the money for that either, have you? So just out of curiosity, where are you proposing we stay? In a tent in the hills? Borrow somebody's boat?'

'There's no need to be like that.' Troy was sullen. 'I told you, I'm in the middle of getting a rental.'

'Where? How many bedrooms does it have? Does it have a garden?' She flung the questions at him like pebbles from a catapult.

'I don't know, do I?'

Annabelle threw her hands up in the air. 'You're in the middle of getting a rental and you don't even know where it is or how many bedrooms it's got? You, Troy, are a big fat liar and I want you gone now.'

'What am I gonna do without you?' Troy asked, looking hangdog.

'You managed quite well without me before,' she pointed out. 'Oh, yes, that was when you had Sallie, wasn't it? You don't want me back at all – you just want someone to keep house for you. Even if I could live with that, I can't live with the way you treated your own children. When you took a loan out on our house, you didn't even have the decency to tell me so I could make sure they were OK. You didn't think about them at all, did you?'

'Is that true, Dad? Is it your fault?' Jake demanded, and Annabelle jumped.

She hadn't heard her son come in and she hastily turned to face him, seeing pale-faced Izzie by his side. The children had clearly heard everything, and she wished she could take the last few minutes back and spare them the knowledge that their dad was an arsehole.

'It's not all my fault.' Troy protested. 'It's as much your mother's as mine.'

'*Excuse me?*' Annabelle was astounded. How dare he!

'It's like this,' Troy said. 'Bella, you were so wrapped up in the kids that you didn't have time for—'

'Stop right there, mister, before you say something you regret. And don't think you wouldn't regret saying it, because I would *make* you regret it. Of course your children came first; they were babies. They couldn't open the fridge and help themselves to a drink; they couldn't cook their meals, or do their own washing. Hang on a sec, neither could you, if I remember rightly. You're like a kid yourself, just as helpless, expecting me to run around after you. More fool me that I did, so don't you dare accuse me of being wrapped up in the kids. You got just as much attention.'

He continued to stare at her and slowly raised his eyebrows.

Annabelle pursed her lips, knowing exactly what sort of attention he was referring to. She'd given him plenty of that too, but clearly not enough, which was why he'd sought additional attention in the willing arms of Sallie. He was no better than a tomcat. But if he mentioned that in his children's hearing, God help her she'd take his head off his shoulders.

Wisely for him, Troy didn't say anything further.

'Dad?' Jake was still waiting for an explanation, one that he could understand.

'What's your mum been telling you? What lies has she been filling your head with?' Troy was still belligerent.

Jake looked from his dad, to his mum, then back to his dad again. He licked his lips and swallowed.

'She told us that sometimes grown-ups don't love each other anymore, and sometimes it's better if they live apart.'

'She's got that right! I bet she told you I didn't love you, either,' Troy crowed.

'No, she didn't say that,' Jake said.

'No need to stick up for her, son, you can tell me the truth.'

'That *is* the truth, Dad.' Jake's eyes glittered with tears and some of them spilled over to trickle down his face.

'I don't know what *you're* crying about,' Troy growled. 'I'm the one she's telling to piss off.'

'Language!' Helen shot Troy a ferocious glare.

'Shut up, you old bat. Who are you anyway?'

Helen drew herself up to her full height and opened her mouth. However, she didn't get a chance to say anything because Brett walked around the island and over to where Troy was sitting. His eyes were hard, his face set.

'You'd better go,' he said. His voice was deceptively mild.

Troy slowly got to his feet. 'I know when I'm not wanted. Annabelle, are you coming?'

'I think you already know the answer to that.'

Troy turned his attention to his son. 'Well, that was a waste of money, wasn't it?' he said to him. 'Why did you drag me all this way for nothing?'

Jake's eyes were huge and his chin wobbled. 'I want to go back home, Dad, back to Cairns. I thought if you and Mum—' He stopped and bit his lip. Then he said in a very small voice hardly more than a whisper, 'Mum's right, you don't love us.'

'Don't listen to your mum—'

'I'm not. I'm listening to *you*.'

Eh?' Troy was flummoxed.

'I'm not stupid,' Jake said. 'I heard everything.'

'I didn't say that I don't love you.' He turned to his daughter. 'Izzie, I didn't say that, did I?'

Izzie was sucking furiously on her thumb and tears were trickling down her face.

Jake said, 'You didn't have to say it in words.'

'Get out,' Brett ordered, and Troy held up his hands.

'I'm going. There's no need to be so shitty about it.' He sidled towards the door. 'Any chance of a lift to the airport?' he asked, then hastily added, 'I thought not,' as he saw the expressions on the faces of the adults.

Just as he was about to put his foot on the first step, Jake called after him. 'Dad!'

'What, son? I hope you're not going to ask to come with me, because you can't.'

When Jake spoke, his voice was firm and unyielding. 'You've ruined my life. I never want to see you again.' And with that, he turned away from his father and buried his head in his mother's chest.

Troy hesitated, an unreadable expression on his face.

Then he was gone, and Annabelle finally allowed the tears she'd been holding to flow free.

'Don't cry, Mum. Dad's not worth it.' Jake pulled back and looked into her eyes. He was about to say something else, when Kate appeared.

'Is Ron in here?' she asked, poking her head around the living room door. 'I've got some news for him.' Her eyes widened when she heard the front door slam so violently, that it rocked the very

215

foundations. 'What was that?'

'Troy leaving,' Brett said.

Annabelle led her children to the sofa and the three of them sank onto it, Jake on one side of her, Izzie on the other. S

he wrapped her arms around them and pulled them close.

'Why, what's happened? Annabelle, are you all right?' Kate came further into the room, her attention on Annabelle.

'Didn't you hear?' Brett asked.

'Hear what?' Kate's eyes flickered around the room, briefly coming to rest on her mother and Helen, before returning to Brett.

'Troy was causing a bit of a scene, but it's OK, he's gone now,' Brett explained.

Annabelle marvelled at the way Brett had stood up to Troy. For a moment she'd thought Troy might have got aggressive, not physically, because she'd never seen him do that, but her ex was certainly an in-your-face kind of bloke, and he could have a nasty, mean mouth on him when he wanted, especially when things weren't going his way.

'Oh, I see,' Kate said. 'Are you all right?' she asked again, putting her hand on Annabelle's shoulder.

'I'm fine,' Annabelle said, her stock response reminding her acutely of Ron, and she swallowed back a sob.

'No, she's not,' Beverley said. 'None of us are. It's Ron – he's gone.'

'What do you mean gone?'

'He's gone for good,' Beverley explained, her voice hitching as she fought back yet more tears. 'He left a note.'

Brett still had it in his hand, and he held it up for Kate to see.

'When did he leave?' Kate asked.

'Sometime in the middle of the night. He could be anywhere by now,' Brett said.

'He's homeless again?' Kate asked and when Beverley let out a sob she rushed over to her mother and gathered her into her arms. 'Oh, Mum, I'm so sorry. I know how much you thought of him. Did he give a reason?'

'Not a sausage. He just snook out like a thief in the night, and there was me thinking he was happy.'

'I'm sure he was, Mum.' Kate sent a pointed look in Annabelle's direction. 'He must have had his reasons.' Over the top of her mother's head, Kate mouthed 'Troy?' at her, and Annabelle pulled a face and shrugged.

Annabelle would be surprised if it was – after all, she'd made it perfectly clear that she wanted nothing to do with her ex-husband and that she couldn't wait to get rid of him.

On the other hand, though, the timing was definitely suspect.

'It's my fault.' Jake's voice was so quiet that Annabelle thought she must have misheard.

'Say what?' she asked, cuddling him closer.

His voice was stronger this time. 'I said, it's my fault.'

'Oh, poppet, it's not. It's no one's fault.'

'It *is*,' he insisted. 'I told him I hated him and wished he was dead,'

'When was this?' On noticing that everyone was listening, she said, 'Tell you what, shall we go to my room and have a chat about it?'

Jake shook his head. 'Yesterday, after we got back from Margam Park and saw Dad waiting for us, after I told you I hated you, I went inside—' His already flushed cheeks turned a deeper shade '—and Ron followed me. I think he wanted to check I was OK, but I shouted at him that it was his fault you didn't want to go home with Dad.' He bit his lip. 'I don't really hate you, Mum, and I don't hate Ron either. I did, but I don't anymore,' he clarified.

'Is that because of what you heard this morning?'

He nodded. 'Dad's a drongo.'

'He's still your father,' Annabelle told him gently. Jake mightn't think he loved Troy right now, but he did. That Troy didn't deserve his son's love, was a matter for another day.

'Can we go find Ron? I want to tell him I'm sorry. I was a drongo, too.'

'We don't know where he is,' Annabelle pointed out.

'He can't have gone far.'

'We don't know which direction he's gone in. I'm sorry, Jake, but it'll be like looking for a needle in a haystack.'

There was silence for a few moments, only broken by Beverley blowing her nose.

'I'll have to phone Doris back and let her know,' Kate said, after a short while.

'Who's Doris?' Annabelle was confused at the sudden change in direction of the conversation.

'Oh, sorry. Doris is my manager. That's what I wanted to speak to Ron about. I've just had a call from her. Apparently, a woman has been asking after him. Doris knows that Ron is – *was* – living with you, Mum, so she asked if she could give her my number.'

'What woman, and what does she want with Ron?' Beverley demanded.

'Her name is Louise and she's his ex-wife. Doris says she needs to speak with him.'

CHAPTER 23

'What shall I say to Doris?' Kate wanted to know. 'Should I ask her to pass my number on?'

'I suppose it all depends on what she wants him for,' Helen said.

She'd been remarkably quiet for the last ten minutes, but now she was sticking her oar in again. Annabelle would have liked to have shoved that oar somewhere after the way she'd spoken about Ron, but it wasn't her place to say anything, so she held her tongue.

Helen continued, 'In my experience, ex-wives – or ex-husbands – don't go looking for their former spouses unless they want something. What could Ron possibly give her?' she wondered. 'Unless… she's heard about Ron's good fortune in falling in with an old bat who is daft enough to let a complete stranger into her house, and this woman thinks she can get in on the action.'

'Well, Miss Hoity-Toity, Ron's ex-wife is going to have another think coming when she realises he's gone walkabout again,' Beverley declared. She'd regained some of her composure and seemed somewhat back to her old self.

'There's only one way to find out,' Kate said, her thumbs flying over her mobile phone's screen. 'There, I've just sent a message to Doris telling her she can give this woman my mobile number. It can't do any harm, can it? I wonder if we'll ever see him again.' Kate caught sight of Annabelle's face and hastily added, 'No doubt we will – he'll turn up in Pershore at some point, and when he does he often kips down in the charity shop's doorway. Do you want me to message you if I see him?'

Annabelle sighed. 'There's hardly much point, although it would give me peace of mind to know he's OK. I feel so responsible for him buggering off.'

'Why?' Helen asked sharply. 'It's hardly your fault. As I said, his sort are unreliable.'

Annabelle gave the snooty woman a sour look. 'And what sort is that – the homeless sort?'

Helen was about to agree but she rapidly changed her mind when she understood what Annabelle was getting at. 'Breakfast anyone?' she asked brightly. 'Brett, you still haven't made the tea, and if we want to get a game of golf in we'd better get a move on.'

'I'm not hungry,' Jake said.

Annabelle gave her son a squeeze. 'You have to eat something. For me? Please? Izzie, you'll have some cereal, won't you? Or how about I make you a boiled egg with soldiers?'

'I haven't got time for boiled eggs,' Helen said. 'I'll have a nice cup of tea and a Danish out on the terrace, if you don't mind,' she ordered, and stalked off outside.

'I'll get it,' Brett said hurriedly, as Annabelle and Kate both began to speak at once. 'Do you want me to put some eggs on for you?'

'Yes, please, that would be great.' Annabelle gently extricated herself from her children, but before she went into the kitchen area to see to the breakfasts (she'd have to eat something herself, to set a good example to the kids), she wanted to have a word with Jake.

'I know you're blaming yourself, but don't,' she told him. 'Ron's a grown-up; he knew you were upset and that you didn't mean what you said. His leaving is nothing to do with you. He has his reasons, even if we might never know what they are, but I can assure you it won't be because of anything you said.'

God, she wished she could talk to him, to ask him why he'd taken to the road again. Didn't he love her enough to stay? Didn't he care for her at all? Or had she just been a holiday fling?

No, she refused to believe it. Ron cared for her – she knew deep down that he did. So maybe he had this ridiculous notion that if he was out of the picture the decision of whether or not to go back to Australia with Troy would be that much more clear cut.

Her heart aching so badly she thought it mightn't ever recover, Annabelle blamed herself, despite recognising that she couldn't possibly have anticipated Troy's arrival in Rest Bay.

She shouldn't have jumped in with both feet the minute a handsome man paid her any attention. But she had been lonely, goddam it! It had been a long time since a man had looked at her the way Ron had. It had been just as long since she'd been held so tenderly – Troy's embraces didn't count. They had been more like the kind of encounter an ewe had with a ram – brief and soulless. At least a ram never made any secret of the fact that he had many other ewes in his sights, so a ram actually held the higher moral ground when compared to Troy.

She was in the middle of fishing the boiled eggs out of the saucepan when she almost jumped out of her skin as Kate's phone blared out a tune.

Kate scrambled to answer it. 'Hello?' A pause. 'Oh, hi, Doris told me you wanted to speak with him. I'm afraid he's not here. He's… um… left.'

Another pause. Annabelle was listening avidly as she carried on with making the kids their breakfasts, although with Ron gone and her relationship with him at an end, it wasn't really any of her business.

Kate mouthed, 'It's Louise, Ron's ex,' at her, before saying to the woman on the other end of the phone, 'By left, I mean he's living back on the streets,' Kate said. 'No, sorry, I don't know where he might be. He'll probably show up in Pershore at some point. He usually does. If I see him, is there any message you'd like me to give him?'

Annabelle put the children's plates on the table and beckoned them over. She ignored her own, too curious about the one-sided conversation and too heartsore to think of food.

'Sorry, could you repeat that? You cut out for a second.' Kate made frantic 'keep-quiet' gestures as she put the phone on the counter next to Annabelle and pointed at it.

Annabelle's eyes grew wide, and Kate nodded frantically at her, her finger on her lips as a voice issued tinnily from the mobile.

'I said, can you tell him I need to speak to him? It's not urgent, but it is something I'd like to sort out sooner rather than later. You've got my phone number, so you can give it to him, if you'd be so

223

kind?' Ron's ex-wife had a modulated voice with no discernible accent.

'Of course. I don't know when that will be, though,' Kate said. 'It could be weeks; it could be months.'

'I know. Look, I might as well tell you, and you can pass this on to him, because if he doesn't know what it's about he might not bother calling me at all.' Ron's ex-wife took a breath, then said. 'I owe him some money. A great deal of money, actually. I don't know if you're aware, but he wasn't in a good place when we split up.'

If Annabelle's eyes grew any larger, she worried that they might pop out of her head, and her mouth dropped open into a silent scream.

Kate mouthed at her, '*What?*' before putting her finger to her lips again as Louise carried on talking.

'I admit I was rather bitter; it wasn't very nice all round. Ron's mum died and he lost that dog he loved so much.' She gave a small laugh. 'I used to say he loved that dog more than he loved me. Anyway, he insisted I kept the house, and as I didn't want to move back in with my parents, I agreed. I'm ashamed to say, that at the time I felt I deserved to have the house after everything he'd put me through, but since then I've remarried and mellowed quite a bit.' She sighed loudly. 'I'm also ashamed to say that I didn't much care about where he went or what he did with himself. He *is* all right, isn't he?'

'Er, yes,' Kate said. 'He's well.'

'That's good. Every now and again I've thought about him and hoped he was OK. Anyway, back to the story. My husband is quite well off and over the years I've been feeling more and more guilty because

I got everything and Ron got nothing, especially since technically the house was half his. We both paid the mortgage and the upkeep, so by rights he should have had half. There were no children to provide a home for, so…' She trailed off and cleared her throat before resuming her tale.

'We've been renting it out for ages – my husband and I, that is – but then we decided to sell and we feel it's only fair that Ron has half the money. It's worth considerably more than what we paid for it, I can tell you! It's taken me ages to track Ron down, though. I lost touch with him after the divorce – actually I was at a point where I never wanted to hear his name mentioned – but now…'

Louise cleared her throat again, and Annabelle felt sorry for her. It must have been hard being in love with a man who didn't love you as much as you loved him. Heck, she'd been there herself with Troy, and she knew how bitter it could make you, if you let it.

Thank God she was over him now, and it sounded like Ron's ex-wife had moved on, too.

Annabelle realised that Brett had stopped what he was doing to listen and so had Beverley. Even Helen was hanging on the woman's every word, as she'd come back into the house to see what the delay was with her breakfast.

Louise continued to speak. 'Eventually I found out through a network of his old army mates and his mum's neighbours that he'd been living on the streets.' She blew out a breath. 'I never knew that. Poor Ron. I also heard that he sometimes comes back to Pershore. The shelter at Pershore mentioned that he occasionally bedded down in the doorway of a charity shop on the main street, which led me to

Doris, and here we are.'

'Wow, that's some story,' Kate said, blowing out her cheeks. 'I can't promise anything, but if I do see him, I'll make sure to tell him. I'm sure he'll be thrilled.'

'Let's hope so. He can be a stubborn so-and-so when he wants to be.'

Kate ended the call, then turned to the others and cried, 'I know, right! Blimmin' heck! I never expected that.'

'Neither did I,' Beverley said, smiling widely. 'He can make a fresh start with the money – there's no need for him to take to the streets or to rely on charity. And before you lot say anything, that's exactly what he was getting off me – charity. I didn't look at it like that, but he did, I know he did. And I reckon that's one of the reasons he's buggered off.'

'I think I know another,' Kate said. 'It's because of the way he feels about Annabelle. He's clearly smitten, but he's not got a home of his own, or a proper job, and I bet he thought he wasn't good enough for her. Then with Troy coming back on the scene…'

'I miss Ron,' Izzie said, and Annabelle started. In the excitement of the phone call, she'd forgotten that her children had been eating their breakfast at the dining room table.

'So do I, poppet,' she said.

Izzie got down off her chair. 'Where's Pepe?' she asked, suddenly, her eyes scanning the room.

'You left it on the sofa,' Jake said.

'No, not that Pepe – the *real* one,' Izzie said.

Beverley frowned. 'He's around here somewhere. Although, come to think of it, he hasn't been out for a wee yet, so he must be bursting. I'll go and let him out.'

'But where *is* he?' Izzie asked again.

'Still asleep, I expect, the lazy little tyke.' Beverley bustled off towards the stairs, taking Ron's letter with her. 'I was so caught up in this, that I didn't give Pepe a second thought. I must have shut him in.'

'He's not in your room, Auntie Beverley. I checked when I heard Jake shouting at Mummy, because I wanted to give him a cuddle.'

'Oh.' Beverley looked surprised. 'I don't know where he is, in that case. Pepe? *Pepe!*'

It was only after the house had been thoroughly searched that it began to dawn on Annabelle, that Pepe had escaped again and must have gone to find Ron.

The problem this time was that Ron wasn't coming back, and the poodle was out there on his own. He could be miles away by now and thoroughly lost.

Dear God, what an unholy mess this holiday was turning out to be.

CHAPTER 24

He really should get a move on, but Ron was far too comfortable where he was. He had his back propped up against one of the massive stone walls and was gazing out of the river. As he'd chosen a spot around the back of Ogmore Castle on the opposite side to the car park, it was relatively quiet. He heard a few cars pull up and heard some voices, so he knew he wasn't alone, and if he turned around and craned his neck, he could see the stepping stones where he'd crossed the river, and he spotted one or two people tentatively hopping across them.

Quite content to remain there for a while, it was only the growing need for coffee that eventually sent him scrambling to his feet, and he stretched and rotated his back, feeling stiffness from sitting still for so long. God help him when he spent a night in a shop doorway – his back would be in bits. As he'd suspected, sleeping on a mattress had made him soft, and it was going to be a painful journey to get back to the toughness he'd possessed prior to moving in with Beverley.

While he waited for his back to loosen up a little, he let the remaining few minutes of peace steal over him. He'd soon be in Ogmore, where there would be people, cars, and shops. Not many admittedly, but more than he wanted.

His peace was abruptly interrupted by a dog barking. From the pitch and the timbre, it sounded like a small one, but the noise was persistent, and he wondered what was making it so upset and wished that its owner would see to it. Dogs barking didn't generally bother him, but this was insistent and somewhat shrill.

Ron picked up his Bergen and settled it on his back, adjusting the straps to evenly distribute the weight across his stomach and his chest, and all the while the little animal continued to bark.

Wondering if perhaps it might be in trouble and the owners weren't aware, or they needed some help, Ron decided to walk in the direction the noise was coming from, so he headed towards the river. The crossing point wasn't very far away, only fifty or so metres, so it wasn't exactly much of a detour and—

Dear God! Was that *Pepe*?

Ron squinted, narrowing his eyes to try to get a better look at a little black dog which was bouncing around on the opposite bank. It was casting about near the stepping stones, and every now and again it would dart forward as if to cross, before backing away again, and all the while it was barking furiously.

Ron walked a little closer, putting a hand over the top of his eyes to try to see better.

'It is,' he muttered to himself. 'It *is* Pepe.'

He'd know the animal anywhere, though he hadn't heard him bark like that before.

It was frantic and insistent, and incredibly grating, and it certainly got his attention. Ron had the feeling that was exactly what it was intended to do.

Shaking his head in disbelief, he called, 'Pepe,' and the dog froze. It ceased barking immediately and stared at him, one paw lifted.

'Good grief, this mutt is a cross between a bloodhound and a pointer,' Ron grumbled, as he trotted towards the crossing place.

As soon as he put a foot on the first stone, Pepe started to bark again, practically bouncing up and down with excitement, his tail wagging furiously. These barks were different from the ones just now: these were excited barks, happy barks. The dog was incredibly pleased to see him, and Ron hated to admit it, but was also incredibly pleased to see the dog.

As soon as Ron reached the far side, the poodle launched itself at him, and Ron had to open his arms to catch him. He staggered slightly, one of his boots going in the water as he lost his balance for a second. The poodle might be small in stature and look delicate, but he was surprisingly solid and strong for his size. He also had a huge personality and an even larger heart.

Ron's stomach clenched as he thought of the distance the dog had travelled to follow him, and all the dangers the poor little thing might have encountered.

Flipping heck, this dog must have an incredible nose on him, Ron thought, holding the little wriggling body close and listening to the excited yips as the dog tried to lick his face.

'Do you know how naughty you are?' he asked, as he put Pepe down and crouched beside him.

Pepe hadn't finished yet; he was still halfway through his greeting and nothing was going to stop him, and he subjected Ron to another round of whimpering and face licking, his tail wagging so hard that his whole backside wiggled from side to side. Eventually though, the little animal ran out of steam and he sat down, looking up at Ron and panting.

'That's one hell of a trek for a little dog,' he said. 'I don't think you're up for walking back.'

Ron didn't really want to carry him, because he'd already noticed that the dog was no lightweight, despite his size. But he didn't have any choice. Pepe wasn't a young animal, and he must have run most of the way in order to catch up with him.

Wishing once again that he had a coffee inside him, Ron scooped the poodle up and settled him in his arms. The dog lay there gazing up at him soulfully, his tongue lolling out of the side of his mouth, and Ron swore that the animal was laughing at him. He knew he was going to ache like hell tomorrow, especially his shoulders and his arms, if he walked all the way back carrying the dog, but if that's what he had to do, that's what he had to do.

There was also something else he'd have to do, and that was to steel himself for the barrage of recriminations and questions that he'd face as soon as he saw Beverley. She was going to give him merry hell. Not only had Ron walked out on her, but she was probably also going frantic at the disappearance of her beloved Pepe.

Ron wished he had a mobile so he could call her and let her know her dog was safe and sound, and would soon be returned to her. But he didn't, so he'd just have to get there as quickly as possible, hand the dog over, and make his escape again.

It wasn't going to be easy.

Beverley would beg him to stay, and he guessed she might cry, which would break his heart.

The other thing he wasn't looking forward to was seeing Troy's smug face. And neither did he want to see Annabelle again. His heart was already broken into so many pieces that he didn't think they'd ever fit back together, but seeing her once more would ground those pieces into dust.

However, Pepe's welfare came first. Ron had to take the dog back, which meant he'd have to face everyone. It was just something he had to get through, something to be endured.

In some ways, he'd been in this position before, and although the pain had been a different kind of ache, it had been just a sharp, and never a day went by without him thinking of his mum, or thinking of Dolly. He understood that grief was the price you paid for love, and he was honoured to have loved them and been loved in return.

He felt honoured to have loved Annabelle, too, even though he was unsure whether she'd felt the same way about him. How she felt about him didn't matter – the children came first, and that's how it should be. He trusted her to do what was best for them, what was best for the family, and therefore his feelings were irrelevant.

As Ron plodded along the path, his heart and his feet heavy, the dog getting heavier with every step he took, it occurred to him that it was quite fitting that he was being forced to go back and face everyone. Running away in the middle of the night had been the coward's way, and he didn't like himself for having sneaked out without saying goodbye.

He seemed to have a track record of running away. He'd run away from Louise and his marriage, and—

It suddenly occurred to him that was exactly what he had been doing ever since. For all those years on the streets, he'd been running away.

Ron saw a bench and sank down into it, the revelation stealing his breath.

How could he not have seen this before? How did he not realise that all this time he'd been trying to run away – from his mum's death, from Dolly's, and from his tragedy of a marriage. But most of all, and most significantly, Ron had been running away from *himself*.

Or at least, he been *trying* to – but no one could ever run away from themselves, could they? No matter how far they went, they still took themselves with them, and no matter how many layers they hid under, they still carried everything deep inside.

He was doing it again, but this time he was running away not *because* of love, but *from* love. Not only was he running away because of how he felt about Annabelle, he was also running away because of how he felt about Beverley. He knew she thought the world of him, and *he* thought the world of *her*, so why the hell had he left?

Did he really want to go back to living on the streets? Did he miss sleeping rough? Wondering where the next meal was coming from? Wondering if he'd still be alive in the morning?

No, he bloody well didn't.

Ron snorted to himself, having finally worked out that he'd felt the need to leave because being in one place made it less easy to run away from himself. Being in one place, safe, warm, and fed, meant that he'd had more time to beat himself up over past losses and past mistakes. Without the worry of wondering where he was going to sleep or when he was next going to eat, he'd filled his mind with something else – the very things he had been trying to avoid.

But when he looked at it logically, what was so bad about what he'd done? Marriages failed all the time. And while he'd not treated Louise brilliantly, neither had he treated her so badly. He had cared for her deeply – just not enough, and not in the way she needed to be cared for. He'd loved her, but he hadn't loved her unconditionally. He'd loved her, but he'd not been *in love* with her. Was that something he could have controlled?

He shrugged and let out a small sigh. Pepe whined in response and licked his hand.

'It's all right, boy, it's just me being silly,' he muttered to the dog, and Pepe whined again and wagged his tail uncertainly.

Ron returned to his introspection, the insights shocking him as he realised that for all this time he had been beating himself up over something he'd had absolutely no control over – how he'd felt about Louise.

He was astute enough to understand that if that had been the sole issue, it wouldn't have been a problem. He and Louise would most likely have gone ahead with the divorce, and that would have been that. Or he might even have settled down and decided that this was it, that he'd walked into the marriage willingly and it was up to him to make the best of it. They might even have made more of an attempt to have children.

But he hadn't been able to get the death of his mother or the loss of his dog out of his mind.

He'd tried, God knows how he'd tried, but nothing had worked. His grief had been like a galloping black horse bearing down on him, its hooves thundering in his heart and in his head, giving him no peace and no respite, and so he'd tried to outrun it, and he'd been running ever since.

Ron chuckled wryly. How ridiculous to expect to be able to run away from grief. He should have allowed it to flow through him and over him, and eventually the worst of it would have subsided. But instead, he'd been like King Canute, trying to hold it back, and tearing himself apart in the process.

Was he still broken?

He didn't think so, although his decision to leave Beverley in the middle of the night with just a note and run away from his feelings for Annabelle, wasn't exactly the most mature decision he'd ever made.

Getting wearily to his feet, he picked Pepe up again and resumed his steady plod. And as he walked, he thought to himself that the gods moved in mysterious ways. If Kate hadn't run away last Christmas, he never would have met Brett, he never would have met Beverley and Pepe, and he never would have gone to live in Brighton. Therefore, he never would have come on this holiday and met Annabelle.

It was also ironic to think that a very naughty little dog might now be his saviour.

Bending his head, he kissed one of Pepe's floppy ears, the animal's soft black fur tickling his face.

'I think I owe you an extra special treat,' he said to the dog, because without the little poodle coming to find him, Ron would still be lost. This little dog had found him in more ways than one, which was incredible since Ron hadn't even realised that he was lost.

CHAPTER 25

R on hesitated slightly as he rounded a corner. The house was still some distance away, but he knew the view from those large picture windows quite intimately, and if anyone was looking out through them they'd be able to see him. He didn't know whether that was a good thing if they had prior warning of his arrival, or a bad one.

His heart in his mouth, he picked up the pace, and as he did so Pepe struggled to get down.

Confident that the dog would walk to heel and not dash out into the road or run on ahead, Ron gently put him on the ground.

'Heel,' he commanded and clicked his fingers, and the dog obediently moved behind him to walk on his left-hand side, Pepe's nose almost touching Ron's calf.

Ron squared his shoulders and lifted his chin. This wasn't going to be easy but he'd get through it. Whatever their reaction (relief from Beverley? disgust from Helen?) it wouldn't last, and he'd soon be able to put it behind him.

As he'd made the return journey, various thoughts had swirled through his head, one of them being that Beverley might be absolutely delighted to have her dog back, but might not be so pleased about Ron's reappearance. He knew that she cared for him, but now that he'd made the break, she might actually be relieved to have her house back to herself.

Deciding to play it by ear, he told himself not to have any expectations. If Beverley assumed that he'd be returning to Brighton with her, he'd need to have an open and honest discussion with her to make sure that was what she really wanted. He didn't want to impose.

As he grew closer, the house looming ever larger, he focused his gaze on the living room windows and the terrace. He hadn't expected to see any movement because of the way the glass was configured, but he still wondered if anyone was in. The cars were there, but everyone might be out looking for the dog, like the last time Pepe had escaped.

If that was the case, he guessed that Helen was possibly in the house on her own, and his heart sank because he knew what would happen. He'd hand the dog over, she'd say thank you, and then she'd probably close the door in his face and he'd be on his way again.

So be it. He wouldn't argue. His attitude might be fatalistic, but the way the dice had rolled recently and in light of his newfound awareness, he'd leave it up to the gods to decide his fate.

With Pepe following closely behind, Ron crossed over the road and walked up the drive, his eyes flitting from window to window. Feeling apprehensive, he rang the bell.

From deep inside he heard the thunder of feet on the stairs and then a clatter as someone came to the door. Guessing it was one of the children, he took a surprised step back when he saw that it was Beverley. She was wearing a nightie with an anorak over the top, and had a pair of trainers on her feet, and three curlers in her hair.

Her mouth opened in shock as though she was unable to believe the person standing on the step really was him, then she threw herself into his arms and for the second time that morning Ron staggered back as he was nearly knocked off his feet.

'Steady,' he told her, regaining his balance.

Racked with sobs, Beverley clung to him, and he felt her trembling.

'There, there,' he crooned, rubbing her back, and feeling like a total heel. How could he have done this to her? After all the kindness she'd showed him, what had he done? He'd thrown it back in her face. He was just as much of a shit as Troy.

Beverley was saying something but Ron couldn't quite work out what it was, and he held her away, so her face wasn't buried in his chest and her voice not as muffled.

'He's gone, he's gone,' was all he could make out, and he felt even more of a bastard.

'Beverley,' he urged, trying to get through to her. 'I've brought Pepe back.'

She turned red swollen eyes to his, and whispered, 'Pepe?'

'He's here, look.' Ron glanced behind him and Beverley's gaze followed. Pepe was sitting obediently behind Ron's left foot, his little face expectant, his pink tongue lolling out of the side of his mouth. His tail was wagging, brushing rhythmically across the doorstep, and he was clearly very pleased with himself.

'Oh, my baby!' Beverley exclaimed, almost falling to her knees in her haste to get to the little animal.

Ron grabbed hold of her and helped lower her down, hoping to goodness that he'd be able to get her back up again.

She smothered the dog in kisses, cuddling him to her, until Pepe had enough of all the fuss and attention, and wriggled and squirmed to be set free. As soon as his mistress let go of him, he darted into the house and shot up the stairs. Immediately Ron could hear excited cries and shouts, and he guessed that the dog had been very sorely missed indeed.

It also explained Beverley's interesting choice of attire. She must have noticed the note that he had slipped under her door before she'd got dressed, and when she'd realised that Pepe was missing too, she'd thrown her anorak over the top of her nightie and had shoved her feet into some trainers, preparing to go out to look for her pet.

Ron saw Kate coming down the stairs. 'Who found him? Who brought him—?' she was saying, then she spotted Ron and cried, 'It's Ron! Are we glad to see you! Did Pepe follow you?'

'Yeah.' Ron felt unaccountably shy, and he couldn't think of anything else to say. Normally quite reticent anyway, embarrassment and guilt made him mute.

'How far did you get?' she asked.

Ron shrugged. 'Ogmore Castle.' Gently he helped Beverley to her feet, and she used him as a climbing frame until she was upright again.

Kate beamed at him. 'It's lovely there, isn't it?' she said, as though all that had happened this morning was that he'd gone for a little stroll before breakfast.

'I had a good look round it the other day, when I took Portia riding. I should have taken Sam and Jake; they would have loved it.'

'Loved what, Mum?' Sam trotted downstairs to see what all the fuss was about, closely followed by Jake and Izzie. 'Hiya, Ron.'

Izzie was taking her time coming down the stairs, as she had Pepe in her arms. But Jake didn't hold back. He took one look at Ron and hurtled towards him. With a resigned sigh, Ron held his arms open and waited for the inevitable impact.

'Oomph!' he cried as Jake cannoned into him, and it wasn't just because Jake had thrown himself into his embrace: Jake was pummelling him with both fists, and sobbing loudly.

'I hate you!' the boy yelled, and Ron took a step back.

'It's OK, Jake,' he said. 'I'm not staying. I don't want to get between your mum and your dad.' Ron had assumed his reception mightn't be enthusiastic, but he hadn't been expecting such open hostility, and it shocked and upset him. He tried to back away, but the boy grabbed hold of one of the straps of his Bergen and clung on.

Jake wailed, 'No!' and pummelled Ron even harder.

'Ow!' Ron cried, trying to catch the boy's flying fists before either he or Jake got hurt.

'If you leave again, I'll never speak to you!' Jake cried, and collapsed against Ron's rather bruised chest. Blimey, that kid could pack a punch.

His arms wrapped around the boy and he held him close. 'I thought you said you hated me,' Ron said.

'I did.'

'You don't now?' Despite himself, Ron was amused.

'I thought you were gone for good.'

'As you can see, I'm back,' Ron said, ruffling Jake's hair. 'For the moment,' he added. He mightn't be staying – it all depended on Beverley, who had an unreadable expression on her face.

Ron spied more movement from inside the house and he swallowed, his mouth suddenly dry when he saw Annabelle at the foot of the stairs. She was biting her lip and her arms were folded across her chest. From her body language, he guessed she wasn't pleased to see him.

He nodded slowly in acknowledgement, his eyes not leaving hers. At least he knew where he stood, and fresh pain tore through him even though he'd been expecting it. She'd made her choice, and it wasn't him. He hadn't honestly thought it would be.

Brett walked towards him, and when he got close enough he clapped Ron on the shoulder. 'Good to have you back, mate,' he said. 'We missed you.'

'I wasn't gone long,' Ron said, with a small smile that he knew didn't reach his eyes. Jake moved away, sniffling loudly and wiping his nose on the hem of his T-shirt, and Ron watched him go to his mum.

She put her arm around her son, and Ron was glad they seemed to have resolved their differences. Jake was clearly happy about returning to Australia. It didn't explain the lad's odd behaviour, though, but hey-ho, Ron knew nothing about kids and the way their minds worked.

Kate demanded, 'Are you going to stand out here all day, or are you coming inside? I don't know about you, but I could do with a cup of tea.' She caught hold of his elbow and Ron stumbled forward, his legs wooden, his brain turned to mush.

Not wanting to presume anything, he looked at Beverley. 'Do you want me to come in?' he asked her.

'Why on earth wouldn't I?' Beverley replied crossly. 'Get your arse in there and get the kettle on. Between you and that damn dog, I feel quite unwell. I need a cup of tea, a sit down, and a chocolate biscuit.'

That certainly told him. He still wasn't sure whether Beverley would actually want him to go back to Brighton with her, but at least she hadn't told him to bugger off.

He tried not to look at Annabelle as he was ushered inside, but he was acutely aware of her eyes boring into him, and as he drew near, he felt he should say something.

'I, just…' he stuttered as he slipped his Bergen off his back and dropped it near the front door.

'I hope you're not going to leave it there,' Helen declared, and he looked up at the top of the stairs to see her coming down them as regally as a queen, one hand on the balustrade as she gracefully glided down several steps.

'What else should I do with it?' he asked hesitantly.

'Put it in your bedroom of course,' Helen commanded, and once more he looked to Beverley for confirmation, wondering whether Troy was going to sleep on the sofa again tonight or whether there had been a further re-jigging of the sleeping arrangements.

'Go on,' Beverley said crossly, pointing down the hall. 'And don't be long. I've got something to tell you.'

Oh, God, he thought, here it comes. She's going to tell me that she doesn't want me to live with her anymore. He wouldn't blame her; after all, he had been thinking the exact same thing himself right up until about an hour or so ago.

'Oh, yes!' Kate clapped her hands. 'It's been a rather exciting morning,' she said. 'Go wash your hands and sort yourself out, then come upstairs. We'll be waiting.'

Ron wasn't sure whether he wanted to. It sounded ominous, despite the gleam in Kate's eye, but he did as he was told, and dropped his rucksack in the bedroom then went to freshen up.

After splashing water on his face and washing his hands, he gave himself a stern talking to. The eyes peering back at him out of the mirror were surprisingly steady, with no hint of the inner turmoil he was feeling. He'd faced far worse than a bunch of lovely people, who may or may not have decided they'd had enough of him. He'd have a cup of coffee then he'd leave. But this time he'd say a proper goodbye to each and every one of them (although probably not Troy) and then he'd be on his way.

With renewed courage, Ron climbed the stairs to the first floor to find out what fate had in store.

The whole family were there, he saw, as he stepped into the room. Helen was sitting in one of the armchairs, her feet crossed at the ankles. She was wearing her golfing gear, and he wondered if he'd scuppered her plans for this morning. Brett and Kate were in the kitchen sorting out drinks and snacks. Beverley was in one of the other armchairs, Pepe curled up in her lap, sound asleep. Jake, Izzie and Sam were on the sofa, and all three of them looked uncomfortable and decidedly fidgety. Ellis and Portia were sitting at the dining table, mobile phones in their hands, staring at the screens, the remains of their breakfasts in front of them.

'Coffee?' Brett asked, holding up a mug.

'Yes please, I'd love one.' Ron stood near the island uncertainly, wondering whether he should sit down,

Helen made the decision for him. 'For goodness sake, will you please sit down? Your hovering is making me nervous.'

Ron went over to the sofa and perched on it, glancing anxiously at the faces around him. The adults were looking at him expectantly, with smiles on their faces – all apart from Helen, who looked as though she'd just sucked on a lemon.

'Here you go.' Brett handed him a steaming mug of aromatic coffee and Ron took it gratefully.

'Thanks,' he said, sipping at the hot liquid and trying not to moan with delight when it hit his tastebuds, as he glanced around at everyone. There was something wrong with the picture, and it took him a moment to realise what it was. Troy was missing.

Ron craned his neck to look behind to see if the man was hiding in the kitchen, but he definitely wasn't there, and Ron wondered where he was, but didn't like to ask.

'Will you tell him?' Beverley said to Kate. 'You were the one who spoke to her.'

Ron frowned; what was going on? Who did Kate speak to?

'I suppose I better had,' Kate said, and she looked him straight in the eye. 'Ron, I don't know how to tell you this, so I'm just going to come right out and say it. You've come into some money.'

Ron blinked, wondering who could possibly have died. Apart from his mother, his relatives were few and far between. And he was pretty sure that none of them would have left him any money. They all had families of their own, who were far more deserving of an inheritance.

Kate continued, 'Louise has been in touch. She says she owes you half the proceeds from the sale of the house.'

'What house?' Ron didn't have a clue what Kate was talking about.

'The house you lived in when you two were married. Look, I've got her phone number, so it's probably best if you ring her and she explains everything herself.'

Ron was speechless. Never in his wildest imagination would he have expected those words to come out of Kate's mouth. 'I don't understand.'

Kate pushed her phone into his hands. 'Just call her, will you?'

Everyone was looking at him; even Helen had a tight smile on her lips, although he did wonder if it was indigestion. He caught Annabelle's eye and she nodded. She still didn't look particularly pleased to see him, and he hoped his return wasn't going to make things difficult between her and Troy.

'Go on,' Kate urged. 'You don't have to speak to her here, with an audience gawping at you.' She glared at the sea of faces staring at him. 'You can go to your room, if you like. Please don't be too long, though.'

'Eh?' Ron was having difficulty thinking. His brain seemed to have signed off for the day.

Kate laughed and rolled her eyes. 'Go on, shoo!' She made flapping motions with her hands and Ron got to his feet.

'Shoo,' she repeated when he continued to hesitate, and he commanded his wooden legs to start moving as he headed for the stairs.

But when he got to his room, he took a moment to compose himself. Bewildered and confused, his emotions all over the place, Ron took several deep breaths, closed his eyes, then made the call that would change his life.

CHAPTER 26

To Annabelle, as she sat on the bus taking her and the children to Brighton's city centre, it was almost as though the holiday in Rest Bay had never taken place. She'd been back not quite a week yet, but already everything about it was fading into the background. Everything except for her feelings for Ron. They were still very much in evidence, and he was the last thing she thought about before she went to sleep and the first thing she thought about when she opened her eyes.

She was delighted for him and absolutely thrilled to bits that he'd come into some money, and from the sound of it the amount was enough to buy a small property on the south coast if that was what he wanted to do. But it made her situation even more poignant.

Beverley had popped over to visit May since Annabelle's parents had come back from their own holiday, and she'd said that Ron had no immediate plans to move out. He was, however, looking, but Beverley seemed to think he was a bit half-hearted about it. Or that might have been wishful thinking on her aunt's part, because Beverley had confided to Annabel that she loved having Ron about the house, and now that he didn't feel he was a burden and living off her charity he was even more of a pleasure to have around.

Annabelle ushered her children off the bus, her head still full of Ron, and headed towards Churchill Square shopping centre. She was on the hunt for school uniforms and PE kits, and she was armed with a list of essentials that had been sent to her from the primary school that the children were due to attend in a few days' time.

It would be Jake's last year in primary and she felt a little sad to think that he would be going to secondary school the following September. He was growing up so fast. They both were. Jake, especially, seemed to have matured since their holiday in Rest Bay. He was calmer and more measured, less likely to fly off the handle and get in a strop.

Annabelle could tell that he still wasn't totally happy with the situation, but she'd had a couple of heart to hearts with him, where she'd encouraged him to express his feelings about his father and about what had happened. He was still incredibly upset, and he still hadn't forgiven Troy and possibly never would, but Annabelle was doing her best to ensure that he continued to have some contact with his dad, albeit by WhatsApp. She had finally given in and bought him a mobile phone, purely so that he could keep in contact with his friends and his dad back in Australia, because she didn't want him to feel totally cut off and isolated. She hoped that once he started school and began making new friends, they would become his priority, but for the moment she was happy to do anything to try and ease the transition for him.

Annabelle had spoken to Kate a couple of times too, to thank her for allowing them to gate crash the holiday, and also to apologise for the way it had ended. She'd already apologised profusely, numerous times, but she still felt it wasn't enough. Beverley had told Annabelle she was being daft, and that she hadn't had so much excitement in years ("well, not since last Christmas when Kate had done a bunk for a few days" Beverley had said) but Annabelle wasn't convinced. Kate had also told her not to be so silly and that she was well used to dramas, having two teenage girls and the mother-in-law from hell, but Annabelle still felt awful. That final day in Rest Bay would be forever etched on her mind.

As she led her children towards the shop that the school had recommended, Annabelle thought back to the events after Ron had been given the news about Louise and the money.

After Kate had told him to phone Louise, he'd re-joined the family in the lounge after a nail-biting half an hour, when everyone had milled around waiting for him to return. Correction: the adults had milled, the children had lost interest and wandered off to do something more exciting. Ellis and Portia went out, and the three younger children disappeared off to the basement. It was only the grown-ups who were interested in what Ron had to say after he'd finished speaking to his ex-wife.

He had walked slowly back into the living area, looking incredibly dazed and totally shellshocked, and Beverley had questioned him remorselessly, demanding to know what Louise had said to him and what Ron had said to her. Eventually Kate had taken pity on him and, as the morning was trundling steadily towards lunchtime, she'd suggested that they make some sandwiches and spend their final afternoon on the beach, which was what they had done. They had taken all the usual paraphernalia – buckets, spades, nets, a football, a frisbee and some kites that had been acquired throughout the course of the holiday, plus a cool box, some blankets, towels and two folding chairs for the oldest members of the family – and had staked a claim on a dry strip of sand near the rocks.

Annabelle and Kate had joined in with some of the games, but neither of them had been very keen on rock pooling, so they'd left it to Ron and Brett to take the children for a final dibble in the pools, while they relaxed.

After checking that Helen and Beverley weren't listening, Kate had quietly said to Annabelle, 'Ron asked me where Troy was.'

Annabelle had raised her eyebrows. 'He did? I wonder why he didn't ask me?'

'I don't know, but if I had to hazard a guess, I'd say he was worried about making waves. Apparently, one of the reasons he left last night was because he wanted to make it easier for you to decide to go back to Australia.'

'Whatever gave him the idea that I wanted to go back?' Annabelle had been shocked he'd even considered that she might.

'Troy probably,' Kate had said. 'I think Jake might have been the clincher. The poor lad. Will he be all right?' Kate had turned her worried gaze to Annabelle.

Annabelle had sighed. 'I hope so. I really wish he hadn't heard me and his dad arguing. Ever since Troy walked out, I've been the bad guy in Jake's eyes, despite the fact that his father went to live with another woman. He seemed to think it was my fault, and that I'd kicked Troy out. I hadn't, although I would have done if he hadn't had left. But not once did I bad-mouth Troy to him. He loves his dad, that's to be expected, but I must admit, I did get mighty fed up of being bad Mama, when Troy could do no wrong. I should have foreseen something like this.'

'What, Troy flying all the way from Australia to land on your doorstep? I don't see how you could have done,' Kate had pointed out.

'I suppose not.' Annabelle had sighed again, and her fingers had played with the edge of the blanket, smoothing the fringed ends, over and over. 'I just hate to see Jake so unhappy, you know? Izzie, too. I could cheerfully string Troy up for what he did. The divorce was bad enough, but they were getting over it and coming to terms with the fact that their father wasn't living in the same house as them. They weren't happy only seeing him now and again, when it suited *him* of course, and not when the kids really needed him, but there wasn't a lot I could do about that, and they were kind of coming to accept it, but then the house was repossessed…'

'It must have been awful. I don't know how you coped,' Kate had said, leaning towards her and putting her hand over Annabelle's to give it a squeeze. 'There is one thing, though… In a way, I'm kind of glad, because if you hadn't come back to the UK to live, we never would have got to know one another.'

Annabelle had smiled. 'Yes, I suppose there is that. I'm glad, too.'

She was smiling now because she felt as though she'd rediscovered her family. When she had been living on the other side of the world, her family had really only consisted of her mum and dad. More distant relations such as Aunt Beverley, Kate, and her nephew and nieces had been little more than Christmas and birthday cards, and the occasional titbit of news passed on by her mum. Annabelle didn't actually speak to any of them.

But since the holiday, she was on the phone to Kate or to Beverley every other day, or they called her. Kate tended to message more, or forward her silly memes, whereas Beverley was more old-fashioned and preferred to pick up the landline – which brought Annabelle's thoughts circling back to Ron again.

She missed him desperately and wished she could talk to him, but she didn't know what to say. Ever since she'd discovered that Ron had come into some money, and a substantial amount to boot, she felt disconnected from him. She knew he'd felt it too, because he'd gone out of his way to avoid her during that last afternoon and evening in Rest Bay. A couple of times she'd caught his eye and quickly looked away, and when she'd glanced back, he'd been looking at anywhere other than her.

She knew she was being silly, but she couldn't help how she felt.

Part of what had initially drawn them together – ignoring the fact that she fancied the pants off him and found him incredibly sexy – was that they were in the same boat, more or less. He, too, was living in someone else's house and didn't have a place of his own, and neither did he have much in the way of a job. So somehow the scales were balanced when it came to their respective situations.

But now things had changed quite dramatically for him. Ron was able to afford to buy a property if he wanted, and he could support himself, whereas her situation hadn't changed in the slightest.

Not only that, the last thing she wanted was for him to feel that she regarded him as a meal ticket. She didn't want him to think she was only interested in him because he had come into some money. She would have loved to have resumed where they'd left off before Troy had turned up and spoilt everything, but she didn't feel she could. Ron seemed to have lost interest in her, but even if he hadn't, she didn't want to restart their relationship when she didn't have anything to offer. She'd be a liability, having no job and two children to support.

Then there were her children's feelings to consider. Although Jake claimed that he didn't want anything to do with his father, neither would he want his mum to put another man in his dad's place. Annabelle felt it was too soon to jump into another relationship, especially after what had taken place in Rest Bay. Jake might be maturing, but he was still a child, and he was still having to deal with a new situation and new emotions.

She thought back to their final evening of the holiday. The whole family had gone out for a meal at the local pizzeria.

On the surface everyone had been happy and lighthearted, but she could sense waves of disquiet coming from Jake, and Izzie was unusually subdued. Annabelle and Ron had deliberately avoided eye contact with each other, which also made for a bit of an atmosphere, and Annabelle was fairly certain the rest of the family must have been aware of it.

When they returned to the house, she'd put Izzie to bed, and had stayed in their room until the little girl had fallen asleep, then she'd rounded up Jake and Sam and had persuaded them that they should retire, too. By this time most of the others had also gone to bed, although she didn't venture upstairs to check who was still up, for fear of running into Ron.

The following morning had been bittersweet, as she was sad to leave Rest Bay and all the memories that she had made with Ron. She was also glad to go because her holiday romance was well and truly over, and she needed to get away from him to lick her wounds and give her heart a chance to heal.

The drive back had been quiet, the children snoozing in the back, and she'd realised that the last day or so had been a drain on them. Annabelle had also felt wrung out, her emotions all over the place. One second she was consumed with anger at Troy, and the next she was filled with sadness at the thought of what they could have had if only he hadn't been such a prat.

After that, a much deeper heartache rose in her chest, and she thought about what she'd had with Ron, and how easily it had slipped through her fingers. In such a short space of time she'd given herself to him completely, body and heart, and now she was paying the price for her recklessness. She knew it would be a long time before she got over Ron, and she'd carry both the joy of knowing him and the sorrow of losing him with her for the rest of her life.

'There's Granny and Grandad!' Izzie cried, pulling Annabelle out of her reverie and bringing her back to the present.

School uniform, that's what she should be concentrating on, not lost loves or broken hearts. Her children could do with her full attention, otherwise she might end up buying something totally inappropriate, or had the wrong logo on or something.

'Where?' she asked, and looked in the direction Izzie was pointing. Annabelle squinted. 'Yes. I think it might be.'

Her mum and dad were standing outside an estate agent's window, peering through the glass. Her mum had her hands cupped around her eyes, and Annabelle wondered what on earth they were doing. She was even more puzzled when her dad took hold of her mum's elbow and led her inside.

That was something else that was bothering her: Annabelle's parents had returned from their cruise shortly after Annabelle and the children had arrived home from Rest Bay, and they had been acting oddly ever since.

For a start, Annabelle would have expected her mum to have spent that first morning doing all the laundry, but she hadn't. Instead, May had informed her that they were off out, and she and Terence had left the unpacking and the laundry, and had disappeared out for a few hours.

When they'd come back, they had still been acting very strangely. When the phone rang, her dad had gone outside to answer it, and Annabelle's mum had followed him, and every so often they would send furtive glances back at the house as though they were checking they weren't being overheard. Annabelle had been fascinated, wondering what could be going on, but it all became clear when she saw them going into the estate agent today – they were looking for somewhere for her to live.

She closed her eyes and opened them again slowly, feeling slightly nauseous. She knew it wasn't ideal moving back in with her parents and bringing two children with her, and it must be hard for them, having lived on their own for so many years, to suddenly have a house full. They must have had a good long talk about it during their holiday, and had arrived at the conclusion that they wanted her out.

It was all very well them trawling around estate agents to look for a suitable place for her, but there was no way she could afford to rent anywhere until she found a job. She hadn't had much luck yet, but she was trying, and she must have applied for about twenty positions in the past few days. Every time her phone rang, or vibrated with a message, she hoped it would be good news and that someone wanted to interview her.

So far, nothing. She wasn't giving up hope yet, though – she was a damn good administrator, even if she did say so herself, and sooner or later someone would recognise her qualities and give her a chance. But until that happened there was no way she could afford to pay rent, plus all the other bills, on a home of her own. Goodness knows what her parents were thinking.

Briefly she wondered whether she should follow them inside and confront them, but then she remembered she had the children with her, so it wouldn't be a very good idea.

Annabelle shifted her concerns to the back of her mind and got the list out of her bag. It was time to tackle the dreaded school uniform shop, and worry about what her parents were up to later. If she didn't sort the children out, she'd be in hot water with the school before they'd even started.

CHAPTER 27

Ron strolled into the restaurant in Tewkesbury town centre and spotted Louise sitting at a table, with her husband. She looked younger somehow and he ruefully compared her with his own careworn visage. These days rugged was the word that came to mind whenever he saw his reflection. Maybe haggard was more accurate, because all those years of living rough had taken their toll.

'My goodness!' Louise exclaimed as she leapt to her feet when she saw him. 'You haven't changed a bit.' She laughed out loud. Her husband rose too, waiting patiently while they greeted each other.

'You have,' Ron said. 'You look happy, for a start.'

Louise sobered, the arms that she had been holding out dropping to her side. 'That's because I am,' she replied sombrely.

'Were you going to give me a hug?' he asked.

'I was…'

'What's stopping you?' He held his own arms wide and she fell into them, laughing.

'You aren't an easy man to find,' she told him, sniffling back tears.

He drew back slightly and looked at her. 'Why are you crying?'

'Because I'm happy to see you. When I found out what had happened and that you were—' She stopped and made a face.

'You can say it you know – homeless.'

'Yes, that. I felt awful.'

'Why? It wasn't your fault.'

'Yes, but, if I hadn't… if we hadn't… if things had—'

'Stop right there,' he instructed. 'Could have, should have, would have, does no one any good. It is what it is, and no one is to blame.' It was his turn to pull a face, and she caught onto it quickly.

'Liar. You blame yourself, don't you?'

'Guilty as charged,' he admitted. 'I'm sorry I—'

She placed a finger on his lips, stopping his words. 'No regrets, eh? What's done is done, and yes, I didn't like you very much for a while; I didn't like myself either, but we've both moved on, haven't we?'

He gazed at her. 'You certainly have,' he said. 'You look wonderful.'

'Thank you, kind sir.' She gently extricated herself and then gestured to the man standing a few feet behind her. 'This is Gordon,' she said. 'My husband.'

As the man stepped forward holding out his hand, Ron did a quick top to toe scan, seeing a guy in his early fifties with a neatly trimmed beard and piercing blue eyes. They were wary but he was smiling, and as Gordon and he shook hands Gordon said, 'I've heard a lot about you.'

Ron chuckled. 'All bad, I expect,' he said.

'Not at all, actually. Louise doesn't have a bad thing to say about you.'

Ron looked at her in surprise, and she nodded her agreement.

'By the time Gordon and I met, I'd realised that I was as much to blame as you. I wanted what I always knew you couldn't give me, and then I berated you for it. It was selfish of me to hang onto you like I did. I should have cut my losses and walked away, but I didn't, and I made us both miserable. I knew you didn't love me as much as I loved you—' She shot a look at her husband but Gordon's expression was impassive, and Ron guessed he had probably heard this before.

She carried on, 'It's water under the bridge now. I'm happy, and I hope you can be, too.'

Ron was… content. Ish. He couldn't say he was happy, because his happiness was inextricably linked to a certain lady who'd made it clear she didn't love him. Ironic, he thought to himself – he was now in exactly the same situation with Annabelle, as Louise had been with him. Karma was a right little madam. It served him right, and it was only what he deserved.

They took their seats and Gordon beckoned the waiter over. 'Wine?' he asked.

'Orange juice, for me, please,' Ron said, settling back in his chair.

Louise and Gordon already had drinks in front of them, and Louise was playing with the stem of her glass, the deep red liquid inside swirling.

'Gordon?' she reminded her husband.

'Oh, yes.' Gordon reached inside his jacket and withdrew an envelope which he passed across the table to Ron.

'Open it,' Louise urged, and her eyes sparkled as Ron tore it open.

Withdrawing the contents, he unfolded the letter and scanned it. Hastily he took a gulp of his juice, almost spluttering as it went down too fast. Gosh, it really was a substantial amount. He looked up. 'Are you sure about this?'

'Very sure.' Louise reached for her husband's hand. 'It was Gordon who suggested it, but as soon as he did, I realised how right it was. You worked just as hard as I did to pay that mortgage. In fact, if I remember rightly, you paid the lion's share of the deposit. In the beginning, when we first split up, I felt justified keeping the house because I thought I deserved it after everything I'd been through, after all the pain and heartache. But eventually my broken heart mended, and I began dating again. When I met Gordon, when he proposed to me, it was natural that I moved in with him, considering his house is…' She paused. 'Substantial.'

Ron couldn't resist teasing her. He liked this new version of his ex-wife. 'How substantial?' He was grinning as he said it so she wouldn't take offence.

'Put it this way, we have an apartment in Chelsea, as well as the house.'

Ron whistled. 'Impressive,' he drawled. Then a thought occurred to him and he jabbed a finger at the letter. 'Are you sure this is half the market value, because I've got a feeling you might have given me more than my share?'

'It is,' she insisted. 'You'd be surprised how much property prices have risen since we first bought it. As I told you on the phone, we've been letting it out, and since the mortgage was paid off ages ago, the money we've had in rent had just been sitting there. You've got half of that as well.'

Ron opened his mouth, then closed it again sharply. He blinked. 'Really? Do you think that's fair to give me half of the rental as well? After all, I've done nothing to earn it, it wasn't as though I had to make sure the tenants were behaving themselves, or that the rent was being paid on time.'

Gordon said, 'Just take it, please, for Louise's sake.'

'Will it help?' Louise asked him. 'I mean, if I'd known you were homeless, I would have sold the house years ago, but I didn't. I'm sorry.'

'Lou, you don't have anything to be sorry for. I'm the one who's sorry.'

A waiter appeared at their table. 'Are you ready to order?'

'I think we should,' Gordon said.

Ron realised it must be a little awkward for the current husband to meet the former under such charged circumstances.

But when Louise gave Gordon a loving look, Ron felt a twinge of envy. Not because he wanted Louise back, but because he wished Annabelle loved him like that.

Once again, the irony made him chuckle, but before either of them could ask him what was so funny, Ron asked to see photographs of their children.

'I hear you've got two,' he said to Louise. 'How old are they?' Which prompted Louise to show him a phone full of photographs of two gorgeous boys who were slightly younger than Annabelle's children, and the spitting image of their father.

Once again Ron was envious, but surprisingly when he thought about children, he didn't hanker after any of his own.

What popped into his mind was Jake and Izzie, and how deeply he'd come to care for them in the short time he'd known them.

∗∗∗

Beverley had been kind enough to lend Ron her car for the journey from Brighton to Tewkesbury to meet Louise and her husband, and he'd booked himself into a modest hotel just off the main street, not wanting to face the drive back to the south coast late at night. Besides, there was something else he wanted to do, as been as he was up this way, and that was to go to Pershore to see Kate. He'd already messaged her to ask if she was at work today, and on hearing that she would be, he'd arranged to take her out to lunch.

It was a total novelty to be able to take someone out for a meal. He couldn't honestly remember the last time he'd done that. He'd bought someone a bacon buttie on occasion when he had been feeling flush, or a bag of chips when he could see that someone was in a worse state than he, but that wasn't the same as taking them out for a meal.

The only time in recent years that he'd done anything remotely similar, had been when he'd paid for the kids to go surfing, and he remembered how good it had felt to be able to treat someone to something nice. Money wasn't for saving, it was for spending, whether that was being able to afford a latte and a sandwich when you hadn't eaten in two days, or whether it was being able to buy someone a bunch of flowers. After all, you couldn't take it with you, could you?

As Ron turned off the A38 and headed east towards Pershore, he thought about last night and meeting Louise again after all this time. He was so pleased she was happy, and he was still in shock about the money she was gifting him. He was under no illusion that he deserved to receive half of the money for the sale of their former house. This was a gift, and he resolved to spend it wisely.

He wished he could do something nice for Annabelle and the children, but he hadn't heard a word from her since she'd gotten in her car and driven away from Rest Bay. She'd sped off with the two children in the back, and he'd followed, behind the wheel of Beverley's car, because she didn't like to drive so far anymore.

He'd deliberately let Annabelle get some distance ahead, not wanting to see her tail lights on the M4 as a constant reminder.

He still didn't believe the money was real, not even with a letter in his hand, not even with the bank transfer winging its way into his account. It was a wonder it was still active and hadn't been closed down, but he still had a bank card for it and every now and again he'd draw out ten pounds from the meagre amount in there, just to keep the damn thing open. It was a necessary evil, because one day he would finally be allowed to draw his army pension, and he didn't want the hassle of having to try and open a bank account with no fixed address.

Even when the money from the sale of his former house landed in his account and he could actually see it for himself, he still didn't think he'd believe it was real, and he guessed it might take some time before he accepted that it was his to spend.

He just wished he had someone to spend it on besides Beverley.

The first thing he intended to do was to take her somewhere nice. The Dorchester for afternoon tea maybe? She'd like that. Although, she might try to insist on taking Pepe which could be a bit of an issue.

Thinking about Beverley made him think about his second reason for visiting Pershore today. As per her wishes, his mum had been cremated, not buried, and he had scattered her ashes in the grounds of Pershore Abbey to drift amongst the headstones there. It had seemed more fitting than the cemetery's garden of remembrance.

It was a strange experience driving into Pershore town centre rather than walking, and it brought back poignant memories. His mother had been so full of life and love, that his heart ached with the loss of her. Cancer was a cruel, cruel disease,

What was just as cruel was that he'd been out of the country on a tour of duty when she'd taken her final breath, and he'd never forgiven himself for not being there. That she'd successfully hidden the speed and severity of the disease from him, was no consolation.

The town was different somehow and, as he walked down the high street after parking the car, it took him a moment to realise why – no one was avoiding him, or giving him the side-eye, or shooting him pitying glances, or pretending he didn't exist. Homelessness cloaked you with a very strange invisibility indeed; you were seen, but not seen. Today, no one took the slightest notice of him precisely because he blended in with the other people on the pavement. He did catch the eye of one woman as she almost bumped into him when she darted out of a shop without looking, but instead of a hasty and embarrassed look away, she smiled at him as she apologised, her glance sweeping across him in an appreciative manner. He smiled back and carried on walking towards his destination.

Ron had always found the graveyard comforting, even if he missed the lack of a headstone to focus on, and he aimed for his favourite bench and sat on it, instant tranquillity filling his soul.

Not caring who might be in earshot, he murmured, 'It's been a while, Mum. I've got lots to tell you.' Then he leaned back, closed his eyes, and silently shared his news, thinking of all the things that had happened since he'd last sat in this very spot just before Christmas.

When he'd finished, he kept his eyes closed, enjoying the last of the August sun warming his face and colouring his closed lids in sunrise shades.

As he sat there, Ron could almost feel her presence, almost hear her whispered reply in the sighing of the wind through the trees. But most of all, he sensed her love, and when he imagined the gentle boop of a canine nose on his leg, he smiled.

His mum and his dog were still with him in spirit, in his memories, and most importantly, in his heart, and he felt more at peace than he had done for years.

In some ways Beverley reminded him of his mum, but when he whispered into the air, 'You'd like her, Mum,' it wasn't Beverley he was referring to – it was Annabelle.

Ron sat on the bench for a little while longer, then realising it was time to meet Kate, he slowly got to his feet and took a last look around. It might be a while until he was here again, but he knew his mum would understand.

***

Kate was sitting at a table near the window of the cafe directly opposite the charity shop where she worked, and she waved when she saw him.

'How did it go?' she asked getting to her feet and kissing his cheek.

'Good,' he said. 'Really good.'

He'd told Kate that he had met with Louise and Gordon yesterday evening, and now she fired question after question at him before he'd even had a chance to sit down.

Over toasted sandwiches and salad, they caught up with each other's news, and even though it had only been just over a week since he'd seen her last, it felt as though it had been far longer. He'd missed her and Brett, and the children – Sam especially.

'He's fretting about going back to school,' Kate told him, around a mouthful of assorted leaves. 'He's starting at the comprehensive and it's freaking him out a bit.'

'He'll be OK, though, won't he?' Ron asked, concerned.

'Of course he will. He's done all the transition—'
She saw Ron's puzzled expression, and explained, 'That's when the primary school pupils get to visit the comp to familiarise themselves. They meet the teachers, their form tutors, and the kids from the other primaries. It's designed to make settling in easier, but you know what Sam's like, he can be a bit of a worry-wort on the quiet. Talking about new

schools, how are Jake and Izzie feeling about starting theirs? I spoke to Annabelle a couple of days ago, and she was planning on taking them shopping for their school uniform.' Kate chortled. 'Good luck with that, I told her. I always hated that. I still do! Portia is a nightmare to shop for, shoes especially.'

Ron pursed his lips. 'I don't know,' he admitted. 'I haven't spoken to her.'

'Not at all?' Kate asked, incredulously.

'No.'

'Why ever not? I thought you two...?' She raised her eyebrows.

'I thought so, too,' Ron said, pulling a face. 'Then Troy turned up and...' He trailed off.

'Yeah, but Troy was soon out of the picture,' Kate pointed out. 'So, what else is going on? Why did you really leave?'

'Because I didn't want to muddy the waters. It's complicated. '

Kate snorted. 'What are you – a Facebook status? When you say you didn't want to muddy the waters, what do you mean?'

'I thought Annabelle might find it easier to decide whether or not to go back to Australia with Troy, if I was out of the picture.' It wasn't the sole reason he'd done a runner, but it was a ruddy great big part of it.

'She never intended to go back,' Kate said, popping the last bite of her sandwich into her mouth and wiping her lips on a serviette.

'I know that now.'

'So what gives?'

'You saw how she was, that last day in Rest Bay. She practically ignored me.'

'You ignored her, too.'

'I did not!'

'Yes, you did. She told me so.'

'Only because she was busy pretending I didn't exist.'

'You love her, don't you?' Kate shot the question at him, and Ron replied before he had a chance to consider his response.

'Yes, I do.'

Kate's gaze searched his face. 'She loves you, too.'

Ron didn't believe it.

'It's true,' Kate insisted, seeing his expression. 'I'd bet my last penny on it. The way she looked at you…'

'She might have been in lust, but she wasn't in love,' Ron argued.

Kate snorted. 'Trust me, a woman doesn't look at a man with her heart in her eyes unless she means it. Do yourself a favour and call her. I bet she'll be delighted to hear from you. And if she isn't, what have you got to lose?'

What, indeed…?

CHAPTER 28

When someone says they need to have a chat with you, in Annabelle's experience it was never good news. So when her parents said those very words to her, her heart sank right down to her turquoise painted toes.

She supposed she was correct and that her mum and dad were going to tell her it was about time she moved out, and they'd found just the place.

Her mum grabbed her hand and sat her down on a kitchen chair. Her mum and dad sat opposite. They were both staring at her intently, indulgent smiles on their faces. If her heart could have sunk even further it would have done – it wasn't going to be easy bursting their happy little bubble when she explained to them that she couldn't possibly afford to live anywhere other than in this house, until she secured herself paid employment.

What if they insisted she went? If that was the case, she guessed they'd probably offer to help out with the rent, which was all well and good, but what if it took her a while to get a job? How long would they be happy to subsidise her for?

At least if she was living in their house, they weren't having to shell out a fortune in rental fees.

Annabelle had no idea where she stood when it came to claiming benefits, but she thought she'd better look into it pretty sharpish, and she made a mental note to add it to the list of the things she needed to sort out.

'Your dad and I have been thinking,' her mum started, and Annabelle raised her eyebrows. 'It's not ideal, you living here with us,' May continued, and Annabelle's eyebrows raised another notch.

You don't say, she felt like retorting. She knew she was imposing on them, but what choice did she have? It wasn't ideal for any of them.

'We've made a decision,' her mother said, and her dad nudged her.

'Go on, tell her,' he urged, and when Annabelle saw how excited he was, a wave of guilt threatened to rise up and swamp her.

'I'm sorry Dad, Mum, this can't have been easy for you,' she began, but before she could say anything further, her mother flapped her hands in a sort of pipe-down gesture.

Annabelle duly piped down. She may as well let them get on with it and say what they had to say.

'We've found a nice little flat!' her mother cried. 'You ought to see it!' Then she giggled and added, 'Silly me, of course you'll see it! Anyway, it's in one of those little streets just off the seafront. They claim it has partial sea-views, but you'd have to be a giraffe to crane your neck far enough to see anything of the sea, but never mind, it's perfect. It's on the top floor of a pretty terraced house – you know the sort of thing, Regency-looking and whitewashed, with big Georgian windows.'

Annabelle blinked at her owlishly, trying to envisage a property with so many diverse features.

Clearly, architecture wasn't her mother's forte.

'It's got a lift, so that'll be handy for when we get older and can't manage the stairs quite so well, although, I must admit, traipsing up and down them will help keep us fit, if your dad's knee doesn't play up.' She leaned forward and whispered, 'He says he hurt it playing badminton with a couple we met on the cruise, but I think it's old age.' Her voice returned to a more normal level as she continued, 'It's got two bedrooms, and a brand-new fitted kitchen, wooden floors throughout, but that could get a bit noisy, so I'm thinking lots of large rugs… and both bedrooms have en suites, plus there's a little cloakroom just off the hall. You'd be surprised how big these apartments are when you get inside them.'

May paused for breath and Annabelle took the opportunity to say something.

'*Two* bedrooms?' she asked. 'How's that going to work?' There were three people in her little family, and it would have been all right for her children to share a room if they were the same gender, but with her having one of each the kids should really have a bedroom of their own.

'Two bedrooms are plenty,' May said.

'Not in this day and age, Mum,' Annabelle replied. 'The children are going to want their own space.'

Her mum and dad looked at each other, frowning, then they looked back at Annabelle.

May said, 'But they'll have their own space. I expect Izzie will have to make do with the smaller bedroom, since she's the youngest, but I don't see that being too much of a problem, do you Terence?'

Terence shook his head. '*You're* not finding it too much of a squeeze, are you Annabelle, so Izzie should be fine.'

Annabelle scrunched her face up. Either she was being incredibly dense, or there was something she must have missed in this conversation. 'What has me sleeping in the box room got to do with anything?'

'But you won't have to, will you? You can have our room, Jake can stay in what used to be your old room, and Izzie can have the box room. Actually, calling it a box room is a bit of a misnomer, isn't it? It's not that small. One of the reasons we bought this house all those years ago, is that all of the bedrooms are a generous size. It just so happens that the third room is the smallest, but you can easily fit a single bed, a wardrobe and a chest of drawers in it, and have space to spare.'

Annabelle still wasn't getting it. 'I'm confused,' she said. 'How am I going to fit all three of us in a two-bedroomed flat, and still be able to give the children a room of their own? Am I supposed to sleep on the sofa?'

'What are you talking about?' May asked. '*You* won't be fitting in a two bedroomed flat – *we* will. Your dad and I.' She pointed to Terence and then back at herself. 'We're moving out.' Her face fell. 'I thought you'd be pleased.'

'I'm still confused,' Annabelle said. 'What do you mean *you're moving out?*'

'I told you,' her mum said. 'While we were away, we had a good long chat and decided it would be better if we gave you this house and we bought a smaller place.'

'*What?* You can't do that!'

'Why ever not? You're our only child, so when we die you'll get everything anyway. You might as well

274

have it now, when you really need it. What do we want with a three bedroomed house with just us two rattling around in it? It's more to clean for a start, and the garden is becoming a real nuisance. Your dad is forever mowing it, or weeding it, or trimming it. We were already thinking about downsizing before you moved back in with us, and when we sold the house we were going to give you a nice lump sum for you to do whatever you wanted. As I said, you might as well have it now. Besides, if we hang onto it and either one of us has to go into a home, the government would take nearly all of it to pay for our upkeep, and I'll be damned if we've worked all our lives and scrimped and saved, just so the state can take it.'

'Have you been talking to Beverley?' Annabelle asked.

'We were the ones who gave her the idea. She's already signed her house over to Kate, and we're going to do the same with you. No, we've made up our minds,' her mum said, holding up her hand when Annabelle began to object. 'We've got enough put by, what with your dad's lump sum when he retired and the redundancy payment he had a few years back. Remember? I told you about it? It was quite a nice bit of money. Anyway, we've got enough to be able to pay for this little flat outright, so don't go worrying that we can't afford it, because we *can*.'

Annabelle didn't know what to say. It was so incredibly generous of her parents that it reduced her to tears, and she began to cry, great big racking sobs that shook her to her core.

When she eventually calmed down and the news had sunk in a little, Annabelle couldn't thank her parents enough. She still wasn't sure that they should be doing this for her, but over and over again they insisted that this was what they wanted. It would make them happy to see her happy, and her mum had said, 'We won't know anything about it when we're dead and buried. At least this way we have the pleasure of seeing you enjoy it.'

Annabelle couldn't argue with that, and neither did she want to. The thought of being able to give her children the security of having a roof over their heads for however long they needed it, was incredible, and she couldn't wait to tell them.

'Of course, it's not going to happen right away,' her mum explained. 'We've got to get all the searches done, and then there's the faff with solicitors, and you know how long that takes. I'd say it will be at least three months before contracts are signed, maybe even longer. Do you think you can bear to live with us for that long?' May chuckled.

'You are the best parents anyone could ever wish for,' Annabelle declared, fresh tears threatening.

Her mum's eyes were suspiciously wet too, and May fanned her face with her hands. 'Oh, go on, it's what any parent would do,' she said.

Annabelle didn't point out that Troy had, in fact, done the exact opposite, but the less she thought about her ex-husband the better, although she couldn't help comparing the way Ron had been with the children, to the way Troy treated them.

Ron had paid Jake and Izzie more attention in two weeks than Troy had done in the previous twelve months.

Thinking about Ron made her wish she could share her news with him. He'd be delighted for her, she knew, but it wouldn't change anything. That last day in Rest Bay, he'd made it pretty clear that they were over.

She didn't blame him for that – a single mother with a belligerent ex-husband was more baggage than any potential suitor should have to deal with. Although, it was ironic that she'd initially withdrawn from him when she'd realised that he had come into a substantial amount of money, and now the same thing had happened to her. Sadness mingled with the happiness she was feeling at having a place to live, and tears trickled down her cheeks.

Blinking them away and needing to share her news with someone, she decided to give Kate a call. Annabelle had been surprised and delighted to find how close she and her cousin and grown over the course of the holiday, and one thing was certain – she didn't intend to lose touch with her. Kate was rapidly becoming her best friend, which was astonishing considering they'd had little to do with each other growing up.

Predictably, Kate was thrilled for her and the squeal she emitted over the phone made Annabelle wince.

'I'm so pleased for you! You must be so excited!' Kate cried.

'I am! I can't believe it to be honest,' Annabelle said. She was sitting on the back step, a cup of tea in one hand and her mobile phone which she was pressing up against her ear, in the other. She was looking out over the garden, ideas about what she could do with it filling her head. There was also the rest of the house to think about, but not just yet, eh? Her parents had told her that they'd be leaving quite a bit of the furniture behind because it wouldn't fit into the flat and they also wanted to buy some new pieces, so at least Annabelle wouldn't have to go out and spend a fortune on furnishing the place. However, her mum's taste was not hers, so eventually she would replace most, if not all, of the furniture. But for now, it would do. It would do very nicely, indeed.

They chatted for a while, Kate filling Annabelle in about Ellis's departure to university in a month's time, and how her daughter was getting more and more upset about the thought of leaving her boyfriend, who was going to a different university, and Annabelle shared her progress on job hunting and uniform buying.

'I had lunch with Ron yesterday,' Kate told her, after they'd shared their news. She said it almost as an afterthought, as if it was of no significance, and Annabelle's antenna immediately went on high alert. She was surprised that Kate hadn't led with this news, and she wondered why not.

'Oh? How is he?' Annabelle asked.

'He looked good. He'd gone to Tewkesbury the evening before, to meet with Louise and Gordon. It won't be long now before the money hits his bank account, he told me.'

'Has he got any plans?' Annabelle asked, attempting a mildly interested tone when she was actually consumed with curiosity.

'I don't think so,' Kate said. 'I'm fairly sure he's going to stay with Mum for the time being.'

'That'll please her.' There was silence on the other end, until Annabelle said, 'What? Is there something you're not telling me?'

'Ron loves you.'

'Excuse me?'

'He told me so,' Kate said.

Annabelle was astounded. 'I don't believe you.'

'It's true! Ask him yourself.'

'I'll do no such thing!' Annabelle retorted.

'Look, you might think it's none of my business and tell me to butt out, but I think you're being an idiot.'

'You do, do you?' Annabelle couldn't believe what Kate was saying.

Kate carried on, ignoring the warning tone in Annabelle's voice. 'You love him and he loves you, so do yourself a favour and sort it out. Life's too short to hang about.'

Annabelle opened her mouth to tell Kate that it was none of her business and that she *should* butt out, but she hesitated, realising Kate was right. Annabelle did love Ron, as surprising as it might seem considering they'd met less than a month ago.

But when you know, you know, right?

Ron was the polar opposite of Troy. He was everything her ex-husband was not, everything she'd wished Troy had been. If someone asked her to describe her perfect man, the person she'd describe would be Ron – he was considerate, thoughtful, kind, undemanding, passionate (oh, yeah, he was passionate, all right), and dependable. And he was as sexy as hell.

So what was holding her back? If what Kate said was true and he loved her, what was she waiting for?

There was one thing she could think of...

***

'How do you feel about living in this house?' Annabelle asked Jake and Izzie after dinner that evening.

She had persuaded her parents to let her be the one to break the news to them, not wanting her mum and dad to be upset if Jake went off on one. Being told that this house was to be their permanent home might relight the fuse of his anger as he understood once and for all that they weren't going back to Australia, and she wanted to try to manage his reaction. Her mum and dad were excited about their new home and what they were doing for Annabelle and the children, and she didn't want Jake to take his disappointment out on them. She guessed he might still be harbouring a faint hope that they would go back, and this news would definitely burst his bubble.

'It's OK,' Jake shrugged.

'How about if Granny and Grandad live somewhere else and we have it all to ourselves?'

Another shrug. Jake didn't appear to be very interested.

Izzie, however, was. 'Where will they live?' she asked.

'Granny wants to go and live in an apartment nearer the sea,' Annabelle explained.

'How much nearer?'

'A street away.'

Jake looked up. 'Cool.' The news regarding the location had caught his attention, and she guessed he was thinking about surfing.

Brighton wasn't renowned for its waves, but it did have a small, thriving surfing community, and although the weather was often damp and the sea was invariably colder than in Cairns, at least Jake was able to go in the water without the fear of crocodiles – so there was that. And the best time of year to catch a decent wave was in the winter, which would soon be upon them.

'I'll move into Granny and Grandad's room,' she continued, 'Jake will stay in the room you're sharing now, and Izzie can have my room. What do you think about that, Izzie?'

'Can it be pink?' she asked. 'And can we have a dog?'

Eh? What? 'No, no dog. When I find a job, I'll be out at work all day, so it won't be fair. You can borrow Pepe.'

'It's not the same,' Izzie complained. 'I want a dog of my own.'

'Can I have a surfboard? And a wetsuit?' Jake asked. 'I can keep it in the garage.'

'I expect so,' Annabelle said. His was a much easier request to grant.

'That's not fair!' Izzie was furious. 'He asks for something and you say yes, but when I ask for something you say no.'

'A surfboard is hardly the same as a dog,' Annabelle pointed out, as Jake stuck his tongue out at his sister and chanted, 'Loser, loser.'

'Jake, stop winding your sister up, or I might change my mind about that surfboard.'

It was Jake's turn to whine. 'That's not fair!'

'Kids! Give it a rest! There's something I want to ask you. You can say no, if you want, and I'll respect your wishes, because this affects you as much as it affects me. And before you ask, Jake, it has nothing to do with going back to Australia,' she added hastily.

'If I say yes, can I still have a board?' Jake attempted to bargain.

'Don't you think you'd better hear what it is first?' Annabelle suggested, then took a moment to compose herself and said, 'How do you feel about seeing Ron?'

'Yay!' Izzie cried. 'Will he have Pepe with him?'

Annabelle's reply of 'We'll see,' was said absently – her attention was on her son. It was his feelings about seeing Ron again that concerned her the most, because he would understand that what she was really asking was whether Jake felt OK about her dating.

It took ages for him to respond and when he eventually did, he didn't look at her. 'I suppose,' was all he said.

'Are you sure? I meant it when I said I'd respect your wishes.'

Jake abruptly met her gaze with a piercing stare. 'Do you like him?'

'I do.'

He nodded slowly. 'That's OK, then, 'cause I like him too.'

'I'm not promising anything,' she said. 'I haven't asked him yet, and he mightn't want to see us.'

Jake's reply was confident. 'He will. He really likes you, Mum. A lot. I could tell.' He sniggered and made kissing noises.

Annabelle shook her head, laughter playing about her lips, as she reached for her phone…

CHAPTER 29

I t seemed fitting that they met on the beach, despite the pebbles and busyness of Brighton's main beach being totally different to the sand and relative quiet of Rest Bay. People, especially families, were out enjoying the last of the summer freedom before the new term commenced, and the weather was still warm and sunny.

Annabelle arrived armed with a picnic and towels, Ron with two folding chairs and a small black dog.

As soon as Izzie saw Ron and Pepe, she tore off along the beach, shouting, 'Pepe,' at the top of her voice, and when she reached him, she flung herself down to cuddle the dog.

Jake was more reserved, holding back with his greeting until Ron plonked the chairs down.

'Hi,' Ron said, including both Annabelle and Jake.

'Hi.' Annabelle's voice was soft, and she drank him in.

She had taken great care with her appearance, ignoring the fact that Ron had already seen her at her most dishevelled, and a bolt of desire shot through her.

Jake grunted, acknowledging his presence.

Ron gave her a look. 'You OK?' he asked Jake.

'Suppose,' Jake muttered.

'We don't have to do this,' Ron said to him. 'If you're not happy with me dating your mum...?'

'I don't mind.' He was playing with a pebble, tossing it from one hand to the other, then he suddenly gave Ron an intense glare. 'You're not my dad.'

'I know. I don't want to be. But we could be friends.'

Jake thought about that for a moment. 'I guess it's OK.'

'Can I take Pepe down to the sea?' Izzie asked. 'He likes the waves.'

Ron looked at Annabelle, who nodded. 'If you like, but only if Jake goes with you,' she said.

The children trotted off, and Ron gestured to one of the chairs. 'I'm getting too old to sit on those darned pebbles,' he said, and they both sat down.

'It's good to see you,' Annabelle said. Blimmin' heck, this was awkward.

She felt as though he was a stranger, not someone who she'd shared the most intimate of moments with. How had they gone from that to this?

And how were they to return to the way they'd been with each other? This was like pulling teeth, and she was beginning to think that Kate had got it wrong, and Ron didn't—

'I love you,' he blurted. He was staring at the sea, his eyes straight ahead.

Annabelle froze. 'What did you say?' Her eyes were also on the shoreline, but her attention was on him.

'I love you. There, I've said it. We might as well get it out in the open, because if you don't feel the same way, I'll leave now. No harm done, no hard feelings.'

'Are you sure? We've only known each other a few weeks.'

'I'm sure.'

She took a deep breath. It was now or never. 'In that case, I love you, too.'

'Are *you* sure?'

Her lips twitched. 'I'm sure.'

'Good.'

Both of them were still gazing straight ahead, but as one, they slowly turned to look at each other. A grin spread across Ron's face, and Annabelle could feel an answering smile on her own.

'Where do we go from here?' she asked.

'We get to know each other properly,' he said. 'There's no rush, we've got all the time in the world.'

'Perhaps we could go out to dinner, just the two of us?'

'I'd like that.' He beamed at her. 'And afterwards I'm going to bring you down here and kiss you until you beg for mercy.'

'Just kiss?'

'Unless you've got a better idea?'

'Oh, I most definitely have,' she murmured, 'but it's not going to be easy. You live with Beverley and I live with my parents.' She sighed wistfully.

'It won't be forever,' he said. 'Both our living arrangements are in flux.'

'Have you decided what you're going to do?' she asked.

'I'll still carry on with the odd job stuff, but what I really want to do is to train dogs. Especially problem ones. What do you think?'

'I think it's a wonderful idea.'

'I hoped you'd say that. Beverley thinks it's a good idea, too, but I wanted a second opinion. Setting it up will keep me busy for a while.'

'Need any help?'

'Absolutely! I'm going to need a website, for a start, then there's the advertising, and handling bookings, and I might have to think about hiring a space where I can work with dogs and their owners away from their homes. I'm out of touch with technology and I wondered whether Jake might like to earn some pocket money? Izzie, too. Under your supervision, of course.'

'Ask him,' she said. 'I think it's a great way to keep him occupied, but he might lose interest after a while.'

'I just want him to get to know me, and to trust me,' Ron said. 'After all, one day we might be a family.'

'That reminds me,' Annabelle said, once her heart had stopped thumping quite so hard at the heady thought. 'Kate is already talking about everyone getting together at October half term for a few days – an autumn holiday. What do you think?'

'Will it be as eventful as the summer one?' Ron asked, grinning.

'According to Kate, it probably will be, because the one we've just had was a typical family holiday for them.'

'I can't wait,' Ron said. 'I want to spend all my holidays with you. In fact, I want to spend every single day with you. I realise we've only known each other for a few weeks and we've got a long way to go, but—'

'It doesn't matter,' she said, getting out of her chair and sitting on his lap. She wound her arms around his neck, her mouth close to his. 'I love you, Ron.'

'And I love you,' he replied, and as his lips met hers, Annabelle knew she would never stop wanting to hear him say the only words that truly mattered.

THE END

Want to know how it all started? Take a look at the first book in the series
A Typical Family Christmas

If you'd like to see what else Liz has written, head over to her website
chapterhttps://www.lizdaviesauthor.com
where you'll also be able to sign up for her newsletter and view her special offers.

You can also find her on
Twitter: @lizdaviesauthor
Facebook: LizDaviesAuthor1

ABOUT THE AUTHOR

Liz Davies writes feel-good, light-hearted stories with a hefty dose of romance, a smattering of humour, and a great deal of love.

She's married to her best friend, has one grown-up daughter, and when she isn't scribbling away in the notepad she carries with her everywhere (just in case inspiration strikes), you'll find her searching for that perfect pair of shoes. She loves to cook but isn't very good at it, and loves to eat - she's much better at that! Liz also enjoys walking (preferably on the flat), cycling (also on the flat), and lots of sitting around in the garden on warm, sunny days.

She currently lives with her family in Wales, but would ideally love to buy a camper van and travel the world in it.

Printed in Great Britain
by Amazon

81595023R00171